GREAT BRITAIN'S #1 BESTSELLER

"A consummate entertainer . . . Maupin has created a funny, memorable character in Cadence Roth."

—Edmund White, *Times Literary Supplement*

"An intensely enjoyable novel about friendship and prejudice: the dialogue is word perfect, the psychology laser fine, and there are some terrific jokes . . . but no synopsis can do justice to this glorious book."

—David Profumo, *Weekend Telegraph*

"*Maybe the Moon* delights, amuses, moves and angers you with the lightest of touches. It is, as might be said of Cadence herself, a small masterpiece."

—Simon Callow, *Vogue*

"What Armistead Maupin has done, with considerable poise, dash, and subversive wit, is to have created a convincing, bracing, jaunty voice for this doughty person. . . . An exhilarating and sometimes moving story."

—Anthony Thwaite, *Sunday Telegraph*

"An affecting, very persuasive attack on bigotry in its subtlest and most insidious forms."

—Jonathan Coe, *Guardian*

"The prose is airborne all right, and with Maupin at the controls you can be pretty sure that the in-flight entertainment will keep you enthralled till touchdown."

—Anthony Quinn, *Independent*

Also by Armistead Maupin

NOVELS
Tales of the City
More Tales of the City
Further Tales of the City
Babycakes
Significant Others
Sure of You

COLLECTIONS
28 Barbary Lane
Back to Barbary Lane

ARMISTEAD MAUPIN

MAYBE THE MOON

A NOVEL

HarperPerennial
A Division of HarperCollinsPublishers

This is a work of fiction.
Although it was inspired by a real person,
it is entirely a product of the author's imagination.
Any resemblance to actual persons, institutions,
or events is entirely coincidental.

Grateful acknowledgment is made for permission to reprint from the following copyrighted work: "After All These Years" by Kander & Ebb, from the musical *The Rink*. Copyright © 1983 by Fiddleback Music Publishing Co., Inc., and Kander & Ebb, Inc. All Rights Reserved. Used by permission.

A hardcover edition of this book was published in 1992 by HarperCollins Publishers.

HarperCollins books may be purchased for educational, business, or sales promotional use. For information please write: Special Markets Department, HarperCollins Publishers, Inc., 10 East 53rd Street, New York, NY 10022.

First HarperPerennial edition published 1993.

Designed by C. Linda Dingler

The Library of Congress has catalogued the hardcover edition as follows:

Maupin, Armistead.
   Maybe the moon : a novel / Armistead Maupin. — 1st ed.
      p.   cm.
   ISBN 0-06-016552-9 (cloth)
   I. Title.
PS3563.A878M38   1992
813'.54—dc20   92-52596

ISBN 0-06-092434-9 (pbk.)

95 96 97 ❖/HC 10 9 8

Mr. Woods (1981) **C-112 m.** **★★★★** D: Philip Blenheim. Mary Lafferty, Roger Winninger, Callum Duff, Maria Koslek, Ray Crawford. A shy 11-year-old boy (Duff) discovers a displaced elf living in the woods behind his family's suburban tract home. A warm, enduring fable of almost universal appeal about the nature of being different. Screenplay by Dianne Hartwig. Kevin Lauter's beguiling sets, featuring the most magical trees since THE WIZARD OF OZ, won him an Oscar. ▼

Leonard Maltin's TV Movies and Video Guide
1992 Edition

THE SPIRAL NOTEBOOK

1

THE DIARY WAS RENEE'S IDEA. SHE RAN ACROSS THIS NOTEBOOK at Walgreens last week and decided on the spot that it was time for me to start writing things down. Just so you'll know, it's a Mr. Woods notebook, the spiral kind, with a green cardboard cover and the little bastard himself gazing wistfully from his hole in the tree trunk. Renee took this as a major omen. That evening over dinner she made such a solemn ceremony out of giving it to me that I felt like Moses on Mount Sinai. Since then, so help me, she hasn't stopped peeping at me sideways, watching my every move, waiting breathlessly for the muse to strike.

I probably shouldn't start until my period is over, just to keep the pissing and moaning to a minimum, but Renee says that's exactly the time I should be writing. Some journal expert she saw on *Oprah* says all the important stuff happens while you're feeling like a piece of shit; you just don't realize it until later. I've got my doubts—serious ones—but I'm willing to risk it if you are.

At the moment, Renee is pretending to be engrossed in *America's Most Wanted*. Though she's all the way across the room, curled up on the sofa like some huge Himalayan kitten, I can almost feel her breath on my neck as I set pen to paper. The pressure is enormous, but I'll try to muddle through, since it seems to mean so much to her.

Who knows? Maybe she's right. Maybe there is a movie in my life. Maybe some brilliant young writer/director will discover these pages someday and see the perfect little film he or she has always wanted to make. And when that happens, who else but me could possibly play me? (After I've lost a few pounds, that is, and had my teeth capped.) Cadence Roth would join the ranks of Sophia Loren, Ann Jillian, Shirley MacLaine, and a handful of other actresses who've had the honor of portraying themselves on-screen. And due to the "special nature" of the material, the Academy would fall all over itself at Oscar time. I'd be a natural for talk shows too, and it's not *that* much of a stretch to imagine a sitcom spun off from the movie.

Of course, the real reason Renee is pushing this is because she knows she'll be part of the story. Yesterday, when we were sorting the laundry, she told me in all earnestness that Melanie Griffith would be her number one choice to play her in the movie. That's not as farfetched as you might think, actually. Renee's a little broader in the beam than Melanie, and her features are less delicate, but the general effect of soft, pink, babyfied sweetness is pretty much the same. (If you're reading this, Renee, that'll teach you to snoop.) At any rate, we'd have our pick of voluptuous blonde co-stars if we came up with the right script and director. That's a big if, I know, but it never hurts to have a dream or two in the pipeline.

We could sure use the cash. My last job was in November, four whole months ago, a half-hour infomercial in which I played—say it ain't so, Cady—a jar of anticellulite cream. I have yet to see this epic aired. My guess is that the FDA finally caught up with the sleazebag from Oxnard who was fronting the operation and nailed him with a cease and desist. It's just as well. Poor Renee, the last of the true believers, glopped the stuff on her thighs for three weeks and got nothing for her troubles but a nasty rash.

Renee, I should mention, brings home a modest paycheck

from her job at The Fabric Barn, and that's keeping us both in cornflakes at the moment. There's no rent or even a mortgage, thank God, since I bought this house outright ten years ago with the pittance I made from *Mr. Woods.* Still, we're feeling the pinch in this recession. While the wolf may not be at the door, he's at least casing the neighborhood. Long gone are the days when Renee and I would treat ourselves to pedicures and pore cleansings at Hair Apparent, then tool into Hollywood for a night on the town.

Frankly, I'm beginning to feel a little trapped. Since I don't drive, I'm fairly housebound while Renee's at work, unless somebody else swings by on the way to God-knows-where. That's the problem with the Valley: it isn't near anything. I moved here when I was barely twenty, largely at the insistence of my mom, who got it into her thick Jewish skull that Studio City would be much safer than, say, West Hollywood—my personal choice. We lived here for seven years, Mom and me, right up to the day she died of a heart attack in the parking lot at Pack 'n Save.

I'd met Renee when I was shopping for mock leopardskin at The Fabric Barn. (I make all my own clothes, so I've haunted most of the outlets between here and West L.A.) I took to her right away, since she was the only clerk in the store who didn't lose it completely when I walked in. She was so helpful and nice, and while she was cutting the fabric she told me a "dirty joke" that would only be dirty if you were twelve years old, maybe, and living in Salt Lake City. When I explained about the leopardskin, how Mom and me were planning to crash the premiere of *Out of Africa,* she got so excited you would've thought she was waiting on Meryl Streep herself.

"Gah," she said, "that sounds so glamorous."

I reminded her that we weren't actually invited, that the jungle getup ploy was pretty much of a long shot.

"Still," she said, "you're gonna be there. You might even meet Robert Redford!"

I resisted the urge to tell her that I had already met Mr. Redford (and found him boring), back when Mom was working as an extra on the set of *The Electric Horseman*. To be perfectly honest, I wanted Renee to like me not for who I knew but for who I was. "Actually," I told her, "it's more of a business-promo thing. I'm an actress myself."

"You are? Have I seen you in anything?"

My face betrayed nothing as I moved in for the score. "Did you see *Mr. Woods*?"

Renee's big, soft mouth went slack with wonder. "You're kidding! That's my most favorite movie of all. I saw it four times when I was thirteen years old!"

I shrugged. "That was me."

"Where? Which one?"

"C'mon." I chuckled and bugged my eyes. "How many roles did they have for somebody my size?"

The poor baby reddened like crazy. "You mean…? Well, sure, but I thought that was … wasn't that a mechanical thingamajig?"

"Not all the time. Sometimes it was a rubber suit." I shrugged. "I wore the suit."

"You swear to God?"

"Remember the scene where Mr. Woods leads the kids down to his hiding place by the creek?"

"Yeah."

"That was me in there."

Renee laid her scissors down and looked at me hard. *"Really?"*

I nodded. "Shvitzing like a pig."

She giggled.

"Also," I added, "the part at the end where they hug him goodbye."

Her eyes, which are huge and Hershey brown, grew glassy with remembrance. She leaned against the wall for a moment, heaving a contented sigh as she folded her hands across her pillowy breasts. She reminded me somehow of a figure on a medieval tomb. "I just love that part."

"I'm so glad," I said, and really meant it, though I probably came off like Joan Crawford being gracious to her garbageman.

Frankly, I've heard this sort of thing for a long time, so my responses have begun to sound canned to me.

Renee didn't notice, though; she was staring into the distance, lost in her own elfin reverie. "And the next day, when Jeremy finds that acorn in his lunch box. Gah, that was so *sad*. I just sat out in the mall and cried all afternoon." After a melancholy pause, her gaze swung back to me. "I even bought the doll. One of the life-size ones. I still have it. This is so amazing."

"Did the eyes fall out?"

"Excuse me?"

"The doll," I explained. "People tell me the eyes fall out."

She shook her head, looking stricken and slightly affronted, like a mother who'd just been asked if her child showed signs of malnutrition. "No," she said. "The eyes are fine."

"Good."

"Do you totally swear you're him?"

I held up my palm. "Totally swear."

"This is so amazing."

When I finally left the store, Renee was my escort, keeping pace a little awkwardly, but obviously thrilled to be seen in my company. I could feel the eyes of the other clerks on us as we threaded our way through the upright rolls of silk and satin. I knew Renee would tell them about me afterwards, and that made me gloat on her behalf. These gawking idiots would find that her friendliness had actually counted for something; that she'd had the last laugh, after all; that she wasn't the blonde airhead they had probably figured her for.

I became a regular at The Fabric Barn. Since none of my outfits requires more than a yard of material, Renee would save odd remnants she thought I'd like: bits of rich, dark velvet or peacock satin or pink pajama flannel imprinted with flamingos. She kept these finds in a box under the counter, and we'd skulk off to the storeroom with them as soon as I arrived, chortling like buccaneers with a fresh chest of doubloons. While I swathed myself in fabric, clowning shamelessly for my new old fan, Renee would perch on a packing crate and tell me long, convoluted stories about Ham.

Ham was the guy she lived with, a strapping, redheaded TV repairman whose likeness was captured on the baseball-sized photo button she wore on her purse. His real name was Arden Hamilton, which sounded classy, she thought, but none of his friends ever called him that. As near as I could make out, he spent most of his time on dirt bikes, but Renee was absolutely goofy over him. She fixed him box lunches every morning of the week, and—even more amazingly, I thought—didn't care who knew it.

When Mom died I was a wreck. Not only had I lost my best friend and manager, but my dreaded Aunt Edie, Mom's terminally uptight sister, swooped in from the desert "to take care of all the arrange-ments." One of the things she'd hoped to arrange was my expedi-tious removal to Baker, California—the scene of my bleakest child-hood memories. I would need someone to look after me, she said, and she had a perfectly nice Airstream trailer just going to waste behind her house. Why on earth didn't I sell this run-down little cracker box and return to my hometown, where people still remembered and cared for me?

The hell of it was, I didn't have a good answer for that. I did need someone to look after me, though God knows I never would have put it that way. Without someone to drive and manage the loftier household duties, I'd be marooned in no time amid a pile of empty Lean Cuisine boxes. What's more, none of my friends at the time had the slightest need for a housemate. My best buddy, Jeff, the most likely candidate, was no longer single in the strictest sense of the word, having fallen in love several years earlier with a nurs-eryman from Silver Lake. The others were either officially married or confirmed loners or already making payments on a mortgage.

This was very much on my mind when Aunt Edie dropped me off at The Fabric Barn two days after Mom's death. I was hardly in the mood for shopping, of course, but I needed something dark and dignified for the funeral, since a black-sequined cocktail dress was the only thing in my wardrobe that even came close. When I told Renee what I required and why, she led me with blank-faced dignity to the storeroom, where she burst into tears, fell to her knees, and flung her arms around me. I didn't want to rebuff her, certainly, but I had to maintain some degree of control. I knew that once I started blubbering I wouldn't be able to stop.

"It's OK," I said evenly, patting her shoulder.

Renee let go of me but stayed on her knees on the cold concrete floor, swiping at her mascara-smeared cheeks with the backs of her hands. I remember thinking, even in the midst of my bridled grief, that she looked like something out of Fellini, some gorgeous bad girl at a shrine, pouring out her sins to the Holy Mother.

To be honest, I was thrown by her histrionic response. I'd shopped at The Fabric Barn less than half a dozen times, and my relationship with Renee had remained on a friendly but professional level. Now, for the first time, I wondered how she really regarded me—as a valued customer whose mother had just died or as some sort of tragic curiosity, an orphaned freak? Her fandom was one thing, I felt; her pity, quite another.

"What'll you do?" she asked.

"Handle it."

This came out sounding cross, so I offered her a smile to soften it, which didn't seem to work because she looked more desolate than ever and sank back with a sigh onto her big dairymaid haunches. "I'm so sorry," she said. "I know it's really none of my business."

I told her as nicely as possible that I appreciated her concern.

She wiped her eyes again. "I didn't mean to get weepy on you."

"It's OK."

"Did you expect it?"

She meant Mom's death, I realized eventually, so I explained that my family has a history of heart problems.

"But I mean … you didn't think…?"

"No. Not then."

Renee shook her head for a moment, then said: "Is it OK if I sit down?"

"Why wouldn't it be?"

She gave me a lopsided, bleary-eyed smile. "I wasn't sure what people do."

"People do all sorts of things."

She laughed. "I'll bet."

"So," I said, trying to get us back on track, "you think there's something in a nice crepe de chine?"

"Oh … right." She was looking distracted, as if her thoughts had already wandered elsewhere.

"What's the matter?"

"Nothing."

"C'mon … spill it."

"It seems so stupid now."

"Renee, talk to me."

She gave me the most pathetic little shrug. "It's over, that's all."

"What is?"

"Me and Ham. He says I have to go."

When she drenched me with her tears all over again, sobbing so hard that she became incoherent, it dawned on me why she'd been so quick to participate in my mourning—and which one of us was really the orphan.

I won't try to build the suspense here, because you already know what happened. Renee moved in a week later, three years ago next June, complete with seventeen pairs of pumps, her Christian exercise tapes, and the aforementioned Mr. Woods doll. (As I write this, the rubbery little wretch leers down at me from his niche in the stereo cabinet.) It was Renee, by the way, who insisted we room together, though I told her from the start I had serious reservations. We hardly knew each other, after all, and I felt that the stars in her eyes might have blinded her to the practical realities of living with someone like me. For better or worse, I am not your standard-issue roommate. I just didn't think she could handle it.

I was wrong. Renee slipped into my life as deftly and unceremoniously as Mom had slipped out. To Aunt Edie, she became my reason for staying here: the "old friend" with a car who would love to room with me and was not opposed to paying rent. She even drove me to Baker for the funeral, where, predictably, she wept buckets during the eulogy, much to the bafflement of the other mourners. By the time we got back to Los Angeles we were a functioning unit. Renee had become an old hand at waiting for me to climb down from the car, or asking the waitress at Denny's for a phone book for me to sit on, or fending off the small children and large dogs I invariably attract in public places. She was natural and un-nursy about this too, as if she performed these courtesies for all her friends.

Better still, she never stopped being my fan. If anything, her fascination with my career seemed to escalate as we settled into comfy sisterhood. One day I showed her my listing in *The Guinness Book of World Records.* She was so impressed that she made a Xerox of the page and kept a copy in her purse, so that the girls at The Fabric Barn—or the post office or the checkout counter at Ralph's, for all I know—could see for themselves that she, Renee Marie Blalock, was now sharing a house with the World's Shortest Mobile Adult Human.

I feel a little fraudulent about this, since the Guinness listing I showed her was about four years out of date. In 1985 the World's Shortest title was copped by a twenty-nine-inch Yugoslavian, who appeared, so help me God, out of thin air. Mom and I went so far as to call the Guinness offices in New York to ask if this foreign pretender had legs, and we were given the most incredible runaround. One of these days, having bragged once too often, Renee will be challenged by some troublemaker with a more recent edition, and I'll have some serious explaining to do.

★ ★ ★

It's well past dark now, and a nice spring rain has begun to fall, sluicing off the awnings and shellacking the banana leaves just outside our sliding glass door. We have a pink spotlight on that part of the yard, so the general effect, if you squint your eyes just so, is of a rosy-hued aquarium. I half expect to see a school of huge red fish, or a giant crimson octopus, maybe, come shimmering past the door.

Renee has turned off the TV and is studying an old issue of *Us* as if she's expecting a pop quiz. She hasn't spied on me in a long time, so I figure she's pleased with my activity, or at least has decided that benign neglect is the best policy. I'm lying stomach-down on my favorite cushion, my "tuffet," as Renee insists on calling it, even though I explained to her years ago that a tuffet is either a small stool or a tuft of grass. The cushion is covered in a dusty-rose tapestry depicting unicorns and a maiden with a conical hat. It isn't antique or anything, but I like it because it fits my body, and because Mom gave it to me on my birthday the year before she died.

I'll tell you about the rest of the room, in case you need it for set decoration. Against one wall there's an old green corduroy sofa (where Renee is sitting), which needs reupholstering in the worst kind of way. We've covered the most gruesome splits with strategically positioned pillows, though God only knows who we're fooling. The bookshelf next to it is one of those cheapo wicker numbers, the bottom two units of which are reserved for my own library: a boxed Tolkien, half a dozen recent star bios, and a book of Mapplethorpe portraits that's so huge I peruse it only when I'm in need of serious exercise.

The walls of the living room are painted Caribbean Coral, a shade that looks subtle and warm on the little paper strip at the hardware store but is distinctly reminiscent of a whore's nail polish when actually applied. We both hate it and plan to redecorate one of these days, but the money just isn't there at the moment. I'd like to try for something stark and Japanesy, but Renee seems to have her heart set on pink-and-green chintz, a Laura Ashley nightmare. I may have to be firm with her.

There are three lights in the room—a plain brass floor lamp, a ceramic black-panther lamp with a ball-fringed shade, and a small plastic modern thing that clips onto the stereo cabinet just below the shelf where Mr. Woods lives. I bought that damned panther on an impulse five years ago at a junk shop on Melrose, mostly because my friend Jeff, who was with me at the time, said it was an extremely valuable example of fifties kitsch. Others have been less convinced. Mom wanted to toss it the moment she saw it, and Renee has seconded the motion on several occasions. I think I'm beginning to agree with them; there's something really depressing about it.

Later, in bed.

Renee is in her room now, giggling on the phone with her latest squeeze, a guy named Royal she met at The Sizzler last week. She has yet to bring him around here, but I've got a great mental image of him already: rumpled black clothes, an iodine-colored tan, and long hair slicked back to a ratty little ponytail. Renee says he's a Scientologist and makes his own beer, and she seems enormously impressed by both things. Sometimes I just don't know about her.

A little while ago she came in here and told me that I'd just bounced a check to Dr. Baughman, my dentist, for work he did three months ago. When I told her I hadn't heard the phone ring, she looked confused for a moment, then said: "Oh … no, it didn't. I knew about it earlier, but I didn't wanna spoil your concentration."

While I was writing our opus, she meant. Now it would only spoil my sleep.

"His helper, that girl with the big eyebrows …"

"Wendy," I said.

"Right. She called me at work today."

I could actually feel my face turn hot. "She didn't try here first?"

"Well, no ... I mean, she *might've,* but ..."

"She didn't. I was here all day."

"Oh."

"In the future, Renee, would you please tell her that I'm a big girl and can handle my own finances?" Maybe this sounds a little bitchy, but I get so tired of being patronized by people who think that small means dependent. Even my own mom, may she rest in peace, pulled this shit on occasion. Once, when I was about twenty-five and we were visiting Universal, a casting director, this really hip lady who seemed to like me a lot, offered to take us to lunch at the commissary. Mom put on her best Donna Reed face and said: "That's nice of you, thanks. I just fed her." I didn't say a word at the time, but I was pissed at my mother for days. How could she have made me sound so much like a hamster?

Renee looked cowed. "She didn't really call about you. She was confirming my appointment tomorrow."

"Oh."

"She was just ... you know, killing two birds with one stone."

This made me feel a little better, but not much. Wendy still should've called me personally. "How much do I owe?" I asked.

"Two hundred and seventy-four dollars."

"Shit."

Renee ducked her head, and I was pretty sure I knew what was coming next. "I could loan you some."

"No," I said firmly. "Thanks."

"Maybe I should start paying rent. It isn't really fair that ..."

"Fuck that, Renee. You do enough as it is." I smoothed the bedclothes, reviewing the options. I'd bounced three checks in a week, and there were no reinforcements in sight. Another loan from Renee would be a temporary solution at best. When all was said and done, I needed work and fast if I was to maintain my sacred independence.

"What about Aunt Edie?" Renee asked.

"What about her?"

"Couldn't she loan you some?"

I gave her a menacing look, knowing she knew better. The slightest whiff of my impoverishment would have Aunt Edie on my doorstep in three minutes. And nothing would please her more. I might be desperate, but not that desperate. There are worse fates than starvation.

"Well …" Renee fidgeted with the neck of her sweater, fresh out of solutions. "Want some cocoa, then?"

"Get outa here. Go call your studmuffin."

"But what are you gonna…?"

"It's OK," I assured her, shooing her out of the room. "I'll give Leonard a call first thing."

Leonard is my agent, the source of all hope and despair. I signed on with him after finishing *Mr. Woods.* The first job he landed for me was a role in a horror flick called *Bugaboo,* in which I played a zombie and appeared on screen for exactly four seconds toward the end. An unsuspecting housewife—Suzi Kenton, remember her?—opens the door of her refrigerator and finds yours truly crouching on the bottom shelf next to the orange juice.

This was a real advance for me, believe it or not, because you actually got to see my face (albeit gray and scabby-looking) and it filled the entire screen. According to Aunt Edie, who never tells a lie, that one brief, shining moment in the light of the Kelvinator was so recognizably mine that theatergoers in Baker actually stood and cheered. This isn't possible, since all they've got there is a drive-in, but I knew what the old bat was trying to say. In the eyes of the people she cared about, I was legitimate at last—a real movie star—no longer just a dwarf in rubber. I won't pretend it didn't feel good.

Since then everything and nothing has happened. There was a brief period in the late eighties when I worked in performance. I was more or less adopted by a space in downtown Los Angeles, where I was in great demand by artists doing pieces on alienation and absurdity. They were gentle, surprisingly naive kids, who took endless pains to guard against what they referred to as "the exploitation of the differently abled." This got to be old fast, so I pulled two of them aside one day and told them not to sweat it, that I was an actress first and foremost, that *of course* I would play an oil-slick mutant for them, that I would sit on a banana and spin if it was in the goddamned script and they paid me something for it.

This seemed to relax them, and we got along famously after that. My mom, who thought Liberace was avant-garde, came to one of the presentations and left in horror and confusion, though she pretended afterwards to find it "interesting." I have no doubt Renee would feel the same way if I were still in performance, so it's probably just as well that I'm not. Besides, the money was pretty awful (if not nonexistent), and the work was unconnected with the Industry, so I was getting nowhere fast.

Except that one night we were visited by a star: Ikey St. Jacques, the black child actor who used to play the adorable seven-year-old on *What It Is!* Little Ikey sat in the very back of the bleachers, all duded up in silver and burgundy, in the company of an extremely long-legged adult female. Word of his presence spread through the space like wildfire. The other cast members did their best to look blasé about it, of course, but they were clearly stunned that such a recognizable icon was in our midst. Frankly, I'd had my suspicions about the kid for years, so it didn't surprise me a bit when he came backstage and confessed.

It wasn't that easy for him to do, either, logistically speaking, since he was forced to wade through the refuse of the night's performance, great gooey wads of surgical gauze smeared with stage blood and about two dozen rubber baby dolls in varying states of dismemberment. His friend was waiting for him in the car, he said, but he just had to tell me that I was wonderful, a great actress, that he'd been totally inspired by my performance, since he himself was a little person and really seventeen years old, not seven. I shrugged and said, "What else is new?" and we both laughed and became buddies on the spot, exchanging phone numbers. His real friends called him Isaac, he said, so I should do the same. Before he left, he told me some great stories about other closet midgets in Hollywood, some of which, I promise you, would curl your hair.

Imagine my excitement when Isaac called a week later to say that he'd proposed a little people episode for *What It Is!* and that he wanted me to guest star. (That was just the way he put it.) I was to play a clown who meets Ikey at a Dallas mall and teaches him about the true nature of compassion. How I was to accomplish this inspiring feat of liberalism Isaac didn't say, but he assured me the role would be both touchingly hilarious and cutting-edge, a surefire candidate for the Emmy.

No sooner had I phoned half the population of Baker to spread the good news than Isaac called to say the project had been killed—by his own producers, no less. They were desperately afraid that another little person on the show might provoke a discussion of the subject in the press, thereby blowing Ikey's cover. It was just too risky, they said, given that the kid's voice had already changed drastically and he was "in grave danger of becoming a grotesque." Isaac had fought for the idea tooth and nail, or so he assured me, but the powers that be were unbending. My long-awaited showcase role never even got to the script stage.

To his credit, Isaac called out of the blue about six months ago to see how I was doing, but I didn't have much to report, career-wise. I had picked up some money doing phone solicitations for a carpet-cleaning service in Reseda, but the work had proved boring beyond belief. My boss there had said some nice things about my speaking voice, however, so it made me consider the possibility of radio work. Since Isaac seemed to think that might be a good approach, I phoned Leonard Lord, my intrepid agent, and asked him to keep an eye open. He told me his contacts in that arena were minimal, but he'd put the word out and see what he could do. I haven't heard from him since.

That's enough for tonight. It's late and I'm beginning to depress myself. The rain clouds have shifted a bit, and there's the oddest little nail paring of a moon hanging in my bedroom window. I'll concentrate on that and the nice warm breeze that's rippling my curtains. Things could be worse, after all, and I've always been able to cope. I have my friends and my talent and my commitment, and I know there's a place for me in the firmament of Hollywood.

If not, I'll get a new agent.

2

A WEEK LATER. ON MY AIR MATTRESS IN THE BACKYARD.

I've just read my first entry and can't believe how dismal it sounds. Oh, well. I could blame it on the wrong time of the month, I suppose, but I don't think you'd be fooled for long. The truth is, it's the wrong time of the century. I don't know when this happened, or how. The world simply changed when I wasn't looking—when I was out eating a cheeseburger, maybe, or buying a magazine or catching a flick in Westwood—so that when I got back it was utterly different, an alien place filled with people I'd never known and customs as inscrutable to me as the control panel on my VCR.

This morning, for example, I looked out the window and saw a huge yellow ribbon tied around my lamppost. I put aside my sewing and went outside, glaring up at this plastic monstrosity and wondering for a moment if Renee could be responsible. It was just beyond my grasp, but I managed to yank it down after a few graceless leaps. No sooner had I done so than Mrs. Bob Stoate, my next-door neighbor, came running across her perfect lawn in a neat little seersucker shirtwaist.

"Cady, what are you doing?" She looked as though she'd caught me selling dope to her kids.

I told her I was taking the tacky thing down.

"But Bob and me got them for the whole street."

I peered up and down, in both directions, and saw what she meant: there was a ribbon at every single house. "Well, that was very nice of Bob and you, but this is my front yard, and I don't want it."

She flinched a little. "It's an American tradition."

I walked back to the house, dragging the ribbon behind me. "And I thought it was just a stupid song."

She hollered after me. "We only did it because we figured you couldn't …"

"Reach," she was going to say, but she caught herself just in time.

"The war is over," I yelled. "Stop gloating."

"We're just showing the boys how we feel!"

True enough, when you think about it. Like everybody else around here, the Bob Stoates can barely contain their delight over finally having kicked some foreign butt. The shame of Vietnam is behind them at last, magically erased by that nifty little Super Bowl of a war they all just watched on television. Never mind that we flattened a country, polluted an ocean, and incinerated two hundred thousand people—the Bob Stoates are once again proud to be Americans.

When I reached the front door, I turned to see Mrs. Bob Stoate watching me in murderous silence, her darkest suspicions confirmed. I gave her a cheery wave and slammed the door. By now, no doubt, she's called her husband at his place of business—a Toyota dealership, if I remember correctly—to inform him of my traitorous behavior. By tonight the whole family will know the score, which is fine with me, since their open hostility is preferable to the sugary Christian condescension they've heaped on me for years.

If I had any sense at all, I'd sell this dump and move to

Hollywood or Santa Monica, where some of the neighbors might still think of Tony Orlando as a bad joke. I couldn't afford to buy a house, but I could rent something nice and still have a little mad money in the bank. I've always envisioned myself in a twenties hacienda with tiles on the roof and a fountain splashing in the courtyard. It wouldn't work for Renee, of course, since The Fabric Barn would be too much of a commute for her, and she'd probably be intimidated by the scary prospect of moving to that side of Mulholland Drive.

Not that we're a set that can't be broken. One of these days, I promise you, Renee will meet some slow-footed mesomorph who reminds her of Ham and be history in no time. And why not? She owes me nothing and vice versa. It's comforting, really, to know that she and I can live together and be this close and still maintain the sanctity of our personal agendas. Since she's out for True Love and I'm out for Stardom, we almost never stumble over each other on the Road to Success.

In case you're wondering, the beer-making Scientologist is no more. Renee ran afoul of him on the second date when she discovered a portrait of L. Ron Hubbard over his dresser and found out what a Scientologist is. Until then, she said, she'd thought it was "some sort of complicated scientist," which explains why she sounded so impressed earlier. Turns out the guy was only recruiting, since he spent the whole night telling Renee how L. Ron had made a new woman out of Kirstie Alley. Renee was pretty rattled by it, and seems to have sworn off men for a while. I say this because she's sleeping with her Mr. Woods doll again, a telltale sign if ever there was one.

I called Leonard the morning after my last entry and asked him if he'd had any nibbles from the radio people.

"Not really, doll."

"Where did you call?"

He waited a tad too long before saying: "Around."

He hadn't called shit, of course, having totally forgotten about me since my last call, but I decided not to force the issue. As neglectful as Leonard can be, he's a name agent, with fingers in lots of important pies. I signed on with him a decade ago, when he was still in his twenties and hanging out on the lot with *Mr. Woods.* He was representing Callum Duff, the cute ten-year-old who played the elf's human friend. We just started gabbing outside the honey wagon one day. I was half in rubber at the time, sweat pouring down my face, hardly at my cutest, and the next thing I knew I was part of Leonard's stable.

In the beginning, I think he was swept along by the novelty of knowing me. He'd call me once or twice a month to collect my latest anecdotes and to gossip about his tight little circle of friends, which, if you believed him, consisted exclusively of a handful of other gay men, Dolly Parton, and Cher. The jobs didn't exactly roll in, but I worked steadily, mostly in horror films, mugging my little heart out in this refrigerator or that.

Once, a year or so after we'd met, Leonard invited me to sing at a party he and his lover were throwing at their fancy new house in the Hollywood Hills. On the engraved invitation, the event was billed as *An Evening with Mr. Woods.* I stood on a red-lacquered baby grand in a postmodern atrium full of white plaster sculpture and did my funkiest rendition of "Stand by Your Man." The guys loved it, and I enjoyed myself thoroughly, though I'd come there largely in the hope of meeting Dolly and/or Cher. Leonard, the little slimeball, had all but promised as much when he'd asked me to perform.

Since then our contact has been strictly professional and always initiated by me. Leonard's star has risen dramatically in recent years, judging from the caliber of his clients. I see his name in the trades all the time, or in the local social columns in the company of serious power brokers like Barry Diller, Sandy Gallin, and David Geffen. I'm happy for him, I guess, but so far his success hasn't exactly rubbed off on me.

I didn't grill him about the radio stuff. Leonard just gets cranky when you force him to lie. "So," I said instead, "nothing new, huh?"

He heaved a sigh on my behalf. "'Fraid not, doll."

"I wouldn't bug you like this, but things are getting pretty tight."

"I know."

I considered several approaches, then said: "It might be a long shot, but I've been thinking about *Twin Peaks.*"

"No way."

"Hear me out, OK? I don't know what they're doing next season, but Lynch has used little people before and——"

"It's toast, Cady."

"What?"

"*Twin Peaks* is toast. It's had it. It won't make it another season."

"*Toast?*"

He chuckled.

"People say this? Where do you pick this shit up?"

"C'mon," he said with amused disbelief. "Where have you been?"

"In the Valley, Leonard." I spoke as sternly as I knew how without sounding angry. "This is what I'm trying to tell you. If you don't get me out of here soon, I won't know what *anybody's* talking about."

"That'll be the day," he said. "You never miss a trick." He was flattering me now, I realized, a very bad sign indeed, since Leonard resorts to that only when there are no other cards up his sleeve. A small rodent in my stomach warned me to prepare for the worst.

"Look," he said, "I think I know a guy who can help you."

"What do you mean?" I was holding my breath now, hoping to hell it wasn't so.

"His name is Arnie Green. He's a helluva good guy, an old-timer. He runs an agency in——"

"I know who Arnie Green is, Leonard."

"Well …"

"He books specialty acts. I'm not a specialty act. I'm an actress."

"Of course you are, but—"

"He does clowns and sword swallowers, for God's sake!"

"Cady, look, I'm trying to help you out here."

Yeah, I thought. *Out of his life. I've finally grown into a nuisance, and he's putting an end to it once and for all.*

"The thing is," he added in the gentlest voice I've ever heard from him, "you need regular employment, Cady. What's the point in being so proud? You're doing phone work, for Christ's sake. Arnie Green might not be the movies, but at least he would keep you in the public eye."

"In a dwarf-throwing contest."

Leonard sighed. "It's more than that."

"So you're dumping me?"

"Did I say that?"

"You never *say* anything, Leonard."

"I don't know why you're so angry at me. I'm just trying to help."

"I know." I tried to sound contrite.

"You've gotta appreciate ..." He cut himself off, obviously avoiding some sort of thin ice.

"What?"

No response.

"What, Leonard? What do I gotta appreciate."

"That the market just doesn't call for it. I won't lie to you, Cady. They're not writing roles for little people. I don't like it any more than you do."

"I don't want a role written for me. I just want a role. Why does my size have to be an issue? This is the real world, Leonard. Little people can turn up anywhere, just like redheads and queers."

This was a pretty speech, but a big mistake. Most of my gay friends revel in calling themselves queer now, but Leonard is obviously not among them. It took him a decade just to get to the "gay" stage. I could tell by the long, clammy silence that followed that I'd offended him.

"The thing is," I said, slogging ahead, "I'm not trying to be

Julia Roberts. They can use me wherever they use a character actress. I can play anything Bette Midler can play. Or Whoopi Goldberg. I could've been that psychic in *Ghost*."

Leonard grunted.

"Why not?"

"Too Zelda Rubinstein."

He'd brought up her name, I'm sure, just to get back at me for using the Q-word. It was his mean way of telling me that not all little people are failures, but I refused to let it get my goat. "You see the point, though," I said. "It's just a question of creative casting."

"No. It's more than that."

"Like what?"

"They'd have to insure you, Cady."

"So? They have to insure everybody."

"Well ... I'm not sure if they would now."

"Why the hell not?"

Another tortured pause and then: "How much weight have you gained?"

I couldn't believe my ears. "Excuse me?"

"I don't wanna get personal, Cady."

"Go ahead. Be my guest."

"Look ..."

"What is this, Leonard? You haven't laid eyes on me for two years. Do I *sound* fat?"

"People talk, OK?"

I had a brief, delicious fantasy in which Bruce Willis and Demi Moore, or maybe the Redgrave sisters, were gossiping over dinner at Spago: *Have you seen Cadence Roth lately? Is she a porker or what?* Coming back down to earth, I decided that one of Leonard's lovepuppies must've seen me at brunch in West Hollywood one Sunday. "And what do these people tell you?" I asked him glacially.

"It's not that I don't sympathize," he said, avoiding the question. "God knows, the weight thing is a constant struggle for me."

"Fuck you. You're practically anorexic."

"Well, it's all the same thing. You can't afford to gain a pound, doll. It's too much pressure on your system. It's just not healthy. And this is what they'll say."

"This is what who'll say?"

"The studios."

"Oh." I waited a beat. "So let me get this straight: A—I'm too short, and B—I'm too fat."

"Don't do this, Cady. You know I think you're special."

"Is that why you call me so much?"

Silence.

"Don't listen to me," I said, suddenly fearful of losing him altogether. "It's my hormones raging. I could drown kittens right now."

"Can I give you Arnie Green's number?"

"No," I said. "Thanks. I know how to reach him."

"He's a decent guy, really."

"I'm sure."

"I'll still keep my eyes open, doll."

"Thanks."

"Take care now."

"You too." I hung up, perilously close to tears and more confused than ever. I couldn't decide if "still keep my eyes open" was just one more hollow promise or Leonard's backhanded way of making the divorce final. Either way, I didn't like the sound of it. Either way, I was sure I was toast.

That night Renee and I ordered a large pepperoni pizza from Domino's and ate it on the living room floor. "This is it for me," I told her, playing cat's cradle with a loop of mozzarella. "Tomorrow it's diet time."

Renee giggled. "Sure."

"No. I mean it, Renee."

"OK." She shrugged and gave me a sheepish look. I knew she didn't believe me.

"What's that one you were telling me about last week?"

"One what?"

"That diet," I said. "The one with the protein shakes."

"Oh. The Cher Diet."

I winced. "Is it in a book or something?"

"Yeah. I've got it at work."

"Could you bring it home?"

"Sure." She picked a pepperoni off the pizza and popped it into her mouth. "What brought this on?"

"Nothing. It's just time for me to get my shit together."

Renee nodded absently.

"I've got a few ideas about work, and I wanna look my best." By this I meant Arnie Green, of course, but I couldn't bring myself to tell her yet. Renee relies on me for glamour. I dreaded worse than anything the thought of letting her down.

"Oh," she said, brightening. "Did you talk to your agent today?"

"Yeah."

"What does he have in mind?" She had that movie-mad gleam in her eye again.

"Oh, just ... various possibilities."

"Great!"

"It's nothing definite, Renee."

"Still ... if you're dieting ..." She gave me a look that said I was just being coy, concealing something truly fabulous. I felt like a total fraud. Frankly, the diet is for my own comfort more than anything. I haven't gained *that* much, really, but the extra weight has begun to leave me breathless after short walks. My self-esteem has always been pretty good, but lately, when I look in the mirror, the person who looks back reminds me of a beach ball with legs.

Renee wanted to take a drive after dinner, so we piled into her clunker convertible and cruised off down Ventura. It was a pearly pink evening, scrubbed clean by the rain, and the air seemed especially warm for April. With her streaming yellow hair and blue angora sweater, Renee played havoc with the teenage boys loitering along our route. Since the little horn-dogs couldn't see me from a distance, any more than I could see them, they just assumed that the solitary blonde with the big casabas was out looking for action. They howled with exaggerated lust whenever we stopped at a light.

"They're so awful," Renee said, the third or fourth time this happened.

I looked up at her and cackled. "You love it."

"I don't, either."

"Any of 'em cute?"

"No. They're gross. They're practically naked."

"Where?" I undid my seat belt, scooted to my knees, and peered over the top of the door. Four shirtless skateboarders sat on a wall bordering a mini-mall. They weren't my type, really. Too Matt Dillonish.

"How 'bout I moon 'em?" I said.

"Caaady." Renee rolled her eyes and giggled.

"Why not?"

"You're almost thirty, for heaven's sake."

I feigned indignation. "Are you suggesting my moon isn't what it used to be?"

"Just chill out."

"It'd be so easy. We just open the door right here ..."

She reached across and pulled my hand off the handle. "What's gotten into you?"

"You don't think I'd do it."

"Oh, I think you'd do it, all right."

We exchanged crooked smiles, understanding each other, so I abandoned the game. I wanted to tell her we couldn't be victims, that we had to take a stand and give that shit right back to them, but I kept my mouth shut. I knew she'd get whiny and accuse me of lecturing again.

I slid back down and refastened my seat belt. We just drove for a while, making rectangles. The sky became a ripe nectarine backdrop to the palm trees and Exxon signs that flickered past my line of vision. I filled my lungs with the spongy air and sank back against the seat, wallowing in the promise of summer. A tape deck in another car was playing "Kiss the Girl," a Disney tune that sounded almost pagan on this pseudotropical evening.

"Where we heading now?" I asked.

"I dunno. Mulholland? Some place pretty?"

"Go for it."

By the time we reached the hills, a purple twilight had come over them. Renee was so closemouthed on the way up that I began to wonder if something was eating her. If she had any major bombs to drop, I knew she'd save them for the very top, where long-established custom demanded that we get out of the car and watch the lights of the Valley.

Then, as we wound around a steep canyon curve, I looked up and caught her frowning into the rearview mirror. "What's the matter?" I asked.

"Just some guys."

"Guys?"

"In a car."

"Following us?"

"I can't tell."

I chuckled. "How do you do it? Is it a *musk* or something?"

Renee didn't answer, busy watching the mirror again. I could hear them hollering now, a rednecky sort of croon. The only word I could make out for certain was "dick." Why is it that some guys can't see a nice pair of boobs without bursting into a love song to their peckers? If it's boobs they like, why don't they talk about boobs?

Renee's face suddenly registered dread. "Oh, no."

"What?"

"They're pulling up next to us."

"Big deal."

"Don't egg them on, Cady, please."

"Me?"

"Oowee, would you look at that?" His voice was pure Orange County and came from just above the door next to me. I could see

the side of his hat, in fact, which had an American flag on it. *"Shit, man, she's got a kid with her."*

I restrained myself, looking straight ahead.

"Nah, it ain't a kid. What the fuck is that?"

Renee whimpered at me. "Cady?"

"What?"

"What should I do?"

"Just drive, OK? Faster."

"But ..."

"I'm not gonna moon 'em. Just keep driving."

"You won't fuckin' believe this, man. She's even got a friend for you!"

I kept my eyes ahead of me and, ever so discreetly, gave him the finger.

"Ha ha ... you see that? You see what that fuckin' midget did?"

"Cady." Renee cast me a desperate glance.

"It's all right," I said, still flipping the bird. "Stay cool."

The guys lingered a moment longer, laughing like jackals, then shot ahead of us and screeched out of sight around the bend. Checking Renee for damage, I found her cheeks shiny with tears. This kind of stuff really gets to her, poor thing. She hasn't dealt with it as long as I have.

"How can they be so ugly?"

"Practice," I said.

"If they knew who you were, they'd be so ashamed of themselves."

"We're swerving, Renee."

"Oopsy ..." She grabbed the wheel and made a quick recovery. "Sorry."

"What do you mean, if they knew who I was?"

"If they knew they were saying those ugly things to Mr. Woods."

"Oh, for God's sake!" I hooted at her. "You think they'd give a rat's ass?"

"I do ... yes ... I do."

"You are such a schmaltzbag."

"I bet they went to that movie, and I bet they cried."

"And then they went out and joined the ACLU."

Renee frowned at me in confusion.

"Just a group," I said.

Now she looked more wounded than ever. "You're making fun, and I'm serious."

"No, I'm not." Sometimes she makes me feel like I've just knocked a kid's ice cream cone into the dirt.

"I believe in Mr. Woods," she said.

"I know, honey." I found a Kleenex in the glove compartment and handed it to her. "Blow your nose."

We sat on our private hillock and watched the glowing grid of the Valley. The air was cooler but still very pleasant. A helicopter dipped and swayed on the slope below us, slashing the underbrush with garish white light. The night was so still and diamond clear that I could hear a dog barking all the way down in Sherman Oaks.

"I saw Ham today," Renee said.

"Oh, yeah?" I tried to sound as nonchalant as she had.

"He was at that baked potato place. At the mall."

"What did he have to say?"

"I didn't talk to him," she said. "I just saw him."

"Oh."

"That was the first time I've seen him in almost two years."

"Three," I said.

"He looked good."

Good God, I thought, the creep dumped her. What was there to get misty-eyed about?

She turned and looked at me. "Do you think I should call him?"

"No, I do not."

"He looks different, Cady. Sadder. Maybe he misses me. How would I know if …"

"Sweetie, he threw your stuff in the yard and changed the locks."

Playing the old tape again, Renee nodded morosely.

"I think that was a clue," I added.

"Yeah."

"Besides, you haven't missed him for years. You've told me so a million times."

Another nod.

"What's this about, anyway?"

She sighed and gazed balefully into the distance. The helicopter was rising now, heading away, growing tinier by the second. I thought she might cry again, but she didn't. She just pursed her lips and frowned a little. "I've been thinking," she said. "Maybe he was right."

"About what?"

"Maybe he *was* the only guy who'd ever want me."

"Oh, honey."

"Ya know?"

"No, I don't know. Look, Renee. Just because some men can't sustain a relationship long enough to … well, that doesn't mean …" I didn't finish, since I couldn't really say for certain where the fault lay. The truth is, I almost never see Renee around her boyfriends; when she's got something going, she tends to hang out at the guy's place. It's possible, given her insecurity, that she turns all clingy and desperate on the third date, scaring off even the nice ones.

Looking for another way out, I reached over and tucked my hand into hers—my "baby starfish," as Renee calls it, into her huge catcher's mitt—and told her it was time to lighten up. Hand holding almost always works on her, but I save it as a last resort to keep from wearing out the effect. Also, there's an unsettling sort of come-to-Mama thing that happens when the great and the small converge sentimentally. I've never been completely comfortable with it.

Renee smiled wanly. "But what else could explain it?"

"Explain what?"

She shrugged her big fuzzy blue shoulders. "Why they don't stick around."

"Because they're buttheads."

She uttered an impatient sigh. "How can they *all* be buttheads?"

"I don't know. It's one of the great wonders of the modern world. An all-butthead extravaganza." Removing my hand from hers, I wrote across the sky with my forefinger. "*The Night of a Thousand Buttheads.*"

She giggled. Finally.

"And it could be me, you know." I threw this in breezily, as if it had just crossed my mind. Cooped up in that damned house so much, with too much time to stew in my juices, I've started to fret about all sorts of things.

"What do you mean?"

I shrugged. "Maybe it's me who's scaring them away."

"Cady ..." Oh, how wounded she looked. "I brag about you all the time."

"Well, that's what I mean. Not everybody's like you, honey. Maybe you shouldn't always mention it right away."

Her hand fluttered to rest on her bosom as she stared at me in genuine horror. "That is the worst thing I've ever heard you say."

"It's just a theory."

"Well, it's a dumb one. People are *impressed* that I room with you. Especially after I tell them who you were."

Were. Get it? Sometimes she makes me sound like the Norma Desmond of elfdom.

"I just meant," I explained calmly, "that some guys might think of you as encumbered."

"What does that mean?"

"You know. That you and I are a unit."

She gave a girlish little gasp. "Lesbians?"

"No, sweetie." I chuckled.

"Then what?"

"I don't know." This was getting muddier by the minute. "I just hope people realize you're a free agent. I mean ... free to go your own way."

Now she looked utterly stricken.

"What is it?" I asked.

"You want me to move out?"

I just shook my head and smiled at her.

"Well, it sounded like it."

"You're such a mess," I said.

Renee's lower lip plumped like a pillow. "Well, you are too."

Both of us, I think, were greatly relieved.

Since that night a lot has happened. A check arrived from the cellulite people the following day, just barely enabling me to pay off the dentist and my other bad checks. Apparently they *are* going to air the infomercial—in a matter of weeks, they claim—so I'm bracing myself for the endless replay of this indignity. I can't even justify it as exposure, since all you see are two fat little legs sticking out from under a Mylar and Styrofoam jar. Renee is beside herself, of course, and is currently alerting the planet.

The money will buy me time, at least, so I've embarked on a program of self-improvement in preparation for taking a meeting with Arnie Green. Yeah, I called him, and Renee knows all about it. That's why I'm stretched out here on the air mattress, cram-tanning like crazy in the thinnest coat of baby oil, in spite of everything I've ever heard about the ozone layer and melanomas and all that. It's also the reason I'm doing the Cher Diet, if the truth be known. I said I was doing it for myself, but I'm not; I'm doing it for Arnie Green, an *alte kaker* with hair in his ears.

If you're not totally disgusted yet, try this on for size: I'm making an outfit for Arnie Green. I work on it in the morning when I'm watching Joan Rivers. I was doing just that today, in fact, when I saw that fucking yellow ribbon on my lamppost. The outfit is black-and-white satin, very *Dynasty*, like something Alexis would wear to a board meeting. That kind of eighties retro drag would be downright embarrassing in Leonard's office, but it might be right up ol' Arn's alley.

It better be. I've made a hat to go with it.

3

IT'S LATE AND I'M POOPED, BUT I'M WORKING AGAIN. THE temptation is to blow off the diary, since I'd like nothing better than to climb out of this sticky costume and into a hot bath. On the other hand, I haven't written in almost two weeks, and there's all sorts of stuff to tell you. I'm afraid I'll forget the important details if I don't get some of them down. Since Renee has just rewarded me with a cup of cocoa, I'll put the sugar rush to work and do my best to tell you about my meeting with Arnie Green.

I lost almost five pounds in the ten days I gave myself to get in shape. That's pretty dramatic for me. It didn't do much for my thighs, of course, but it gave me a lot more energy and made my cheekbones pop out again. Renee hennaed my hair the night before the interview, and I spent two hours on makeup, paying special attention to my eyes. Everyone tells me they're my strongest feature—emerald green with flecks of warm brown, sultry but reassuring. When I was a teenager in Baker, I used to study them for hours in the mirror, imagining how the rest of such a pretty girl might look.

Arnie Green's office was in North Hollywood. I made an eight-thirty appointment with him so we'd both be fresh and

Renee could take me there before she went to work. As the first client of the day, I'd also avoid the gut-wrenching chitchat of the waiting room, which was easy enough to imagine, even though I'd never been to the office. I'd be stuck there with all the others, twiddling my thumbs in quiet agony while some bleached-out accordion player bragged to me about her recent triumphal comeback at the Amway convention. Who needs that kind of stress?

We found a spot to park right in front, which I took as a bad sign. We were in a sort of ghost town, a mini-mall less than half occupied, where businesses announced themselves by painting over the flaking plywood of their predecessors. Arnie's glass-fronted office was one of a row of three facing the street. The other two were a Philippine import shop and a place with burnt-orange curtains fading along the folds to pale shrimp. The hand-stenciled sign outside said: VID-MART ENTERPRISES.

"OK," I said. "Time to lose the hat."

Renee was crushed. "Why? It looks so nice on you."

It was a rakish triangular affair, the same black-and-white satin as my dress. I'd spent a whole morning making it, gloating over the finished product, but in this shabby setting it struck me as overeager, even pathetic. I felt like some broken-down baroness flaunting her tiara at a flophouse.

"It's not right," I said.

"At least keep it on till he can see it."

"Renee ..."

She sulked a little while I undid the pins and stashed the hat in the glove compartment. I tried to check myself in the rearview mirror. "Is my hair fucked?"

"No." She adjusted a few wisps over my ears. "You look beautiful."

I grunted.

"I swear, Cady. Your skin is radiant. You're glowing."

Glowing or not, I felt like a total fool. Renee got out of the car, opened my door, and lifted me down to the pavement. I brushed out my dress, groaning at the folly of it all. How could I have listened to that evil queen Leonard? And why in the name of Jehovah had I thought black-and-white satin would be suitable for a morning meeting?

A woman in rollers and Bermudas came out of the import shop and stopped in her tracks, staring. I acknowledged her presence with a tight little smile and a vaguely royal wave. She wasn't even faintly embarrassed. "You in show business?" she asked.

"Workin' on it." I headed for Arnie's door like a bat out of hell.

"The circus?"

"She was Mr. Woods," Renee announced grandly.

"Renee, for God's sake!"

Seeing my exasperation, my housemate flushed violently, then turned back to the woman. "We have to go now. We're late for an appointment with her agent."

"He's not my agent," I muttered as Renee held the door open for me.

"Well, whatever."

We beat a retreat into a space no larger than our living room. There was a desk with a receptionist, and half a dozen plastic chairs were lined against one wall. A single row of publicity stills was the only thing in sight that kept this from being the waiting room of a veterinarian. I even spotted animals among the glossies: a cowgirl astride a palomino, a cockatoo in drag, a chorus line of poodles. The humans in Arnie's stable tended to be magicians and clowns and ice skaters and, yes, little people, all of whom seemed to tower over me. No surprises so far.

The receptionist looked up from her computer. "Cadence Roth?"

I threw up my hands and grinned at her. "Guilty, Your Honor."

She tossed off a look that said to save the cute stuff for the boss. I didn't hold it against her; the old girl must've heard a lot of shtick in her time. I wondered if she might be Mrs. Green. "He'll be back any minute," she said. "He's gone for doughnuts."

"No problem."

"Did you bring a résumé?"

I told her I'd already mailed one to Mr. Green.

"Oh." She fidgeted among the papers on her desk for a moment, then stopped and said: "Have a seat, please." Then she turned and addressed Renee, who was gawking at the wall of photographs. "You with her?"

For a moment I worried that Renee might claim to be my manager. I allow her such indulgences around shop clerks and people in movie lines, but agents are a different matter, even agents like Arnie Green. They could easily start asking things that Renee couldn't answer. In my scramble to get ready that morning, I hadn't thought to warn her about this.

Renee just said yes, though, without embellishing.

"Coffee?" asked the receptionist. "Either of you?"

"No, thanks," said Renee.

I shook my head, smiling, then hoisted myself onto the sofa, all ass and elbows. I've carried out this maneuver most of my life and still can't find a graceful way to do it.

"Ooh, look," said Renee, studying a photograph. "He does Big Bubba."

"Really?" I said this as enthusiastically as I could, since the receptionist was watching and I had no earthly idea who—or what—Big Bubba was.

"We've handled him for years," the lady said.

"How wonderful," I said, smiling like the whore I am.

"You a fan of his?"

Renee was the one she'd asked, thank God. "Oh, yes!" came the answer.

"Big," I told the receptionist. "She's a big Big Bubba fan."

That's when Arnie came in, toting his bag of doughnuts. I knew it was him right away, since he always puts an ad in the trades for Halloween and he looked just like his photo, skinny and bald and heavily tanned, with big ugly caterpillars of hair crawling out of his ears. Instead of a plaid suit, though, he was wearing pale-blue Sansabelts with a matching golf shirt.

I scooted off the sofa to give him the full impact of my height.

This usually gets the talk going when I meet people for the first time. Plus they're not as uncomfortable once they see you can walk.

Arnie bent down to shake my hand. "Miss Roth." He'd obviously done his homework.

"Mr. Green."

"I've been looking forward to this."

"Well ... good." I couldn't decide if his courtliness was phony or not, but I was grateful for it.

"Is the lady...?" He gestured toward Renee, who was still standing by the photo wall, looking useless.

"My friend," I said. "Who drove me."

"Ah, yes." He swept his blue-veined hand toward his office door, inviting Renee to join us. I could have sworn I caught a whiff of vintage testosterone. "Please," he said, "after you."

Renee pointed at her left tit. "Me?"

"Why not? We're all friends here."

I didn't like this at all. For one thing, I wanted Arnie's undivided attention. For another, I didn't want Renee to see me groveling. When she glanced at me for guidance, I made a quick slashing motion at my throat.

"I better not," she told Arnie.

"Why not?"

"Uh ... I gotta keep an eye on the car?"

Arnie looked distressed, as if my driver had just suggested that his neighborhood was less than desirable.

"The top is down," I explained. "We've got stuff in it."

"Suit yourself."

I followed him into the office, which was windowless except for a skinny slit at the top of one wall. The chair provided for clients was ominously high and on rollers, so I enlisted Arnie's help in mounting it. He was really clumsy about this, stumbling a little, and I heard something crack in his back when he set me down. So much for the Cher Diet.

Behind his desk, Arnie pecked at a doughnut while he studied my résumé. "*Mr. Woods,* eh?"

I nodded, smiling modestly.

"I took my grandkids to that."

"Mmm."

"Was that your voice, then?"

I told him no, that the elf's voice had been electronically created, that I had provided his movement only, that sometimes Mr. Woods was a robot and sometimes he was me. (I really should have a fact sheet or something. God knows I get asked this stuff often enough.)

After a while, Arnie said: "I don't think I've seen the other movies."

I gave him a sardonic smile. "I don't think you have, either."

He chuckled, showing the teeth of an old horse, impressed by my bold display of professional candor.

"They let me act," I said. "That was enough."

Arnie brushed doughnut sugar off his fingers. "You know I don't handle movie people."

I nodded. "I just want to work, Mr. Green."

"Arnie," he said.

"Arnie."

"You sing well," he said. "You have a fine voice." I had sent him a homemade demo tape of me singing "Coming Out of the Dark," Gloria Estefan's new back-from-the-brink-of-death number, thinking that it struck the right note of spunky survivorhood.

"The tape's pretty bad," I pointed out. "I mean, the sound quality."

"I can tell, though. You sound like ... what's her name? Teresa Brewer."

That's not far off, actually.

Arnie grinned. "You're too young to remember her."

I told him I knew who she was, though, and took it as a compliment.

He was looking at the résumé again. "And you do your own makeup, make your own costumes."

"Who else?"

"You didn't make those shoes." He squinted down at my black patent slippers.

"K mart," I told him. "Toddlers department."

He cracked another smile, which seemed almost grandfatherly, shook his head slowly, then returned his watery gaze to the résumé. After a long silence he said: "Don't see any wrestling work."

"No," I replied. "And you won't."

He nodded slowly, as if that sounded reasonable enough.

"And I don't want to be tossed anywhere."

The nodding continued.

"Any hope?"

He opened a drawer in his desk and pulled out a ragged-looking file. "I think maybe so."

As it turned out, he had an arrangement with a small company in the Valley called PortaParty, which provides entertainment and "color" for social functions, mostly rich children's birthday parties. One of the performers, a girl clown of average height, had just left for a job in television, and they were looking for a replacement.

Arnie assured me I didn't have to be a clown. I'd be free to create my own character, maybe even sing, as long as the boss was happy. Mostly, it involved handing out candy and putting up with the kids. If I liked the sound of this, he said, I could start work the following weekend.

I didn't *hate* the sound of it, especially the part about my predecessor leaving for a job in television.

At least it was show business. Sort of.

I thought about it overnight, at Arnie's suggestion, and called back the next morning to accept.

"This is just a start," he said.

Then why did it feel so much like the end?

My mood grew bleaker as the day wore on. I found myself brooding over the Corsos, people I hadn't thought about for years, a retired midget couple who had been in show business but had nothing to show for it when I met them except a few battered scrapbooks and an apartment full of odd mementos. Like me, they had worked in a movie that had enchanted the world, but no one ever knew that unless the Corsos took the trouble to tell them.

Mom latched onto Irene and Luther in the mid seventies at a Little People of America convention. They had presented a slide show on their long-dead career. Mom was so convinced of their wonderfulness that she drove me all the way to Phoenix so I could see them in their natural habitat. I was a moody teenager in those days, struggling more than most with my identity, so I guess she thought the experience would be inspirational.

The Corsos were both in their late fifties and lived on the seventh floor of a suburban high rise. Luther loomed over me at nearly four feet. He had a face like a dried apple and wore plaid trousers with a button-down shirt. A recent stroke had impaired his speech, so Irene, who was aggressively lilac-haired and even taller, did most of the talking. It centered on their kids, as I remember, and their bridge game, and their fleeting moment of glory almost forty years earlier as Munchkins in *The Wizard of Oz*.

Their living room was awash in Ozabilia: plastic Tin Men, stuffed Lions, Wicked Witches out the wazoo. Even the bricks on their balcony had been painted that unmistakable shade of yellow. I'd always loved the movie (still do) but couldn't for the life of me connect its legend with these hopelessly prosaic people. These were Munchkins in flip-flops, for God's sake, without benefit of Deco. Munchkins with a microwave, who ate Pop-Tarts and watched golf tournaments on TV. It just didn't scan.

Part of the problem was their size. Irene and Luther had been teenagers at MGM, and since then they'd each grown over a foot, fleshing out considerably in the process. A lot of the Munchkins were taller now, Irene told me, a shocking revelation I absorbed without comment, feeling somehow betrayed. Most of the Munchkins had been midgets, I remembered, not dwarfs, and thus proportional, so the right punch to the pituitary would have made growth possible. When you got right down to it, the Corsos weren't like me at all.

Irene brought us Cokes and Ding Dongs (get it?) and rattled off the well-worn particulars of their days in Oz. She and Luther had met on the all-midget cross-country bus chartered by Papa Singer, the full-sized procurer and "handler" of the Munchkins. When they arrived in California in early 1938, they were booked with the others into the Culver Hotel. The building's still there, by the way, though it's full of offices now. When we drive by and I imagine the old days, I can't help thinking of it as a sort of Ellis Island for my people.

Like a lot of other actors signed for *Oz*, the Corsos first worked on a turkey called *The Terror of Tiny Town,* the world's first and last all-midget musical western. Irene was in chaps and riding a Shetland pony the day Luther proposed to her. She was thrilled to death, she said, but she called her mother in Ithaca before she would tell him yes. Luther hocked his watch so he could buy her a ring, and they were married and sharing a room at the Culver by the time they got to Oz.

When I asked Irene what they were paid as Munchkins, she just smiled and said: "Not as much as Toto." This was the literal truth, it turned out, but she and Luther had been so enamored of the experience and each other, she said, that the money hadn't mattered. She'd never counted on being an actress, anyway, so the whole thing had been gravy. She and Luther were really business people at heart, she insisted, which was why they'd done so well with their mail order service. And would I like to see their citizenship award from the Kiwanis Club?

The Corsos knew only a handful of the surviving Munchkins. Three or four lived right there in Phoenix and showed up for LPA gatherings on an irregular basis. One was on their shit list: an old guy in a nursing home who'd boasted for years to anyone who'd listen that he'd been the Mayor of Munchkinland. He'd only been a soldier, Irene said, not the whiskered fellow with the big pocket watch we all remember. This seemed a tame enough fib to me, but Irene said it had caused her great embarrassment, since reporters were always calling to ask about him. The real Mayor had been a friend of hers, she said, and he'd been dead for several years.

The Corsos were even more annoyed at Judy Garland, though they still kept an autographed photo of her on their mantel. Irene said Judy had appeared on the Jack Paar show one night and made cruel remarks about the Munchkins, calling them drunks and lechers and generally getting a lot of cheap laughs at their expense. Their feelings had been hurt by that, she said, because Judy had once been so nice. The stories weren't even true, but the myth of the degenerate Munchkins became so entrenched that Hollywood eventually made an unfunny movie about it, *Under the Rainbow.* They had to hire dwarfs to play the Munchkins, though, since, due to the miracles of modern science, there were no longer enough midgets to fill the roles.

We spent about two hours in all at the Corsos'. As we were leaving, Irene gave me a ceremonial kiss and a framed poem about little people called "Small Blessings." Afterwards Mom and I bought peanut butter milk shakes and took a long drive in the desert. She didn't ask for my impression of the Corsos, so I stayed off the subject, knowing how easily her feelings were hurt. She was onto me, though, which was why she hadn't asked, presumably, and she seemed gloomy and withdrawn for the rest of the trip.

Looking back, I guess she'd expected me to bond with Irene and Luther, to exchange some secret tribal handshake and become their fairy godchild for life. At the very least she'd wanted me to feel less alone. Mom was like that. God knows I'd tried to oblige her, but the chemistry just wasn't there. I felt more real kinship with the stoned Indian hippie who sold us the milk shakes at Dairy Queen than with those sad, oversized has-beens back at the tower.

I bit the bullet and called the guy at PortaParty to make arrangements for my first gig. His name was Neil Riccarton, and he sounded friendly enough, though he had a twerpy little voice that reminded me of Kevin Costner. He told me to join the troupe (I liked the ring of that, so theatrical) in the parking lot of the shopping center at Sunset and Crescent Heights. From there we'd proceed to the party in the official PortaParty van. I couldn't miss it, he said; there were clowns and balloons painted on the side. The gig was in Bel Air, at the home of an obstetrician.

After some deliberation, I decided on a sort of Pierrette effect—black polyester with white ruffles at the neck and sleeves and big red buttons down the front. This would be eye-grabbing yet durable, good for repeat performances. I scrapped the traditional whiteface, sticking with my own makeup, since I knew it would be much more comfortable, especially when summer came. I also wanted them to see who I was.

When the big day came, Renee drove me.

"Who are the others?" she asked, her hair whipping in the wind like clean laundry. We had just reached the crooked spine of the city and begun our descent into Hollywood. It was a beautiful morning, all things considered.

"Other what?"

"In the ... party group."

I told her I wasn't sure. Clowns mostly. A few mimes.

"Gah!" she gushed.

I gave her a dangerous look.

"Don't be so negative," she said. "You can make anything work for you."

I had the creepy feeling she'd learned this pop wisdom from her Scientologist, but I didn't say so, knowing how sensitive she was about it. By unspoken mutual consent, we made conversation about the passing scenery, avoiding both her crappy love life and my crappy career, until we finally reached Sunset and she caught sight of the PortaParty van.

"Gah," she said, no longer able to contain herself. "It looks really neat."

She pulled into the parking lot and opened my door so I could see. There were several clowns in a cluster behind the van, sucking on their last preparty cigarettes. One of them, an Emmett Kelly clone in Air Jordans, did an unrehearsed double take when he saw me. Recovering, he hollered to a young black guy crouched on the asphalt in front of a box of party favors.

Neil Riccarton rose and bounded toward us with a blinding smile. He was wearing gray cotton coveralls, the kind that roustabouts wear at the circus, and the zipper was lowered to reveal an awesome expanse of silken breastbone. I caught my breath at the sight of him. It wasn't until he spoke that I actually attached this lanky dreamboat to the dorky midwestern voice I'd heard on the phone.

"You're Cadence, right?"

"Right." I gestured toward Renee, who was standing by the door. "This is my friend Renee."

"Hi," said Neil.

Renee echoed him, coloring noticeably.

He turned back to me. "Need a hand there?"

Normally, when Renee's around, I let her do the lifting, since she's accustomed to my weight and its distribution, and there are no rude surprises, but I made an exception in Neil's case. His big hands slid under my arms with gentle authority, conveying me to the ground in a single hydraulic motion. I thanked him briskly, then hid my distraction by fluffing the ruffles on my sleeves. It took all my willpower to keep from gazing across at his crotch.

Get a grip, I told myself. *Don't objectify this guy. The black man as superstud is a dehumanizing myth.* There was also the chance he was gay, of course, but I seriously doubted it, and my radar in that area is usually pretty good. Fortunately, my unclean thoughts were kept at bay by his bouncy Kevin Costner voice, which made Neil sound like the victim of a bad dubbing job. By focusing on that, I decided, I could get through the day without making an ass of myself.

Neil turned to Renee. "I'm afraid we've only got one place in the van."

Renee looked confused, so I jumped in. "She's not going with me. She's just my ride."

"Oh, I see."

Renee gave him the most fetching little smile. That girl's mind is such an easy read. "I'm going to the Beverly Center," she said. "It's my day for that."

"Right."

"We need to arrange a pickup time," I told him. "How long do you think this'll take?"

Neil's brow wrinkled. "I'm not sure I can be that exact about it. Five o'clock or so."

"I can just wait here," Renee offered, "if you're not back by then."

"Or"—Neil shrugged, looking at me—"I could drop you off myself."

I told him I lived in the Valley.

"I know," he said. "So do I."

"Really?" It was Renee who said this, and a little too eagerly, I thought.

"It's no problem," said Neil, still looking at me. "I do it for the troupe all the time."

The next thing I knew, Renee was gone and I was scrunched up in that van with Neil, three clowns, a shitload of party stuff, and a haggard-looking fairy princess named Julie. A seat would have been wasted on me, so I made a nest out of a pile of painted backdrop. As we tooled down Sunset toward Bel Air, Neil broke the ice by announcing to all and sundry that the newest member of the troupe had made her debut in the movies playing you-know-who.

"Shit," said Julie. "I could die tomorrow if I had a role like that."

I told her it hadn't exactly changed my life.

"Still," she said, "it's a *legend*."

One of the guys, a gawky red-whiskered clown named Tread, looked over his shoulder at me and said, "I really got off on that part where Mr. Woods eats the loaded brownie."

"And gets the munchies!" said someone else.

"That was way cool," said another.

"They wouldn't even make that scene now."

"Fuck no, man. No fuckin' way."

Neil gave Tread a funny sideways glance.

"Hey," said Tread. "I'm clean."

"Just not at the house," said Neil. "That's all I ask."

"Jeez," muttered Tread.

"Hey." Neil's expression was pleasant yet pained. "Do I look like Marilyn Quayle?"

"Totally!" Julie emitted a froggy laugh, then reached over the seat and slapped Neil's shoulder. "Especially when you do that little pursing thing with your mouth."

"What little pursing thing?"

"You know." Julie squinched her mouth up, prompting Tread and another clown to follow suit, to the enormous merriment of everyone but Neil.

"Guys," he said, drawing the word out in a sort of Valley whine. "Not in front of the new person."

Julie hooted, then lunged into a real get-down Janis Joplin coughing jag. Emmett Kelly regarded her in doleful silence, then thumped her on the back a few times, to no avail. Neil gazed back at me and winked. "It's not too late to back out."

"Hey," I told him. "No problem here."

The obstetrician's house was a low-slung fieldstone affair with a pristine gravel drive, crisp lawns, and a blood-red front door that seemed higher than the house itself. The caterers were erecting a tent on the lawn when we arrived. Neil received his orders from the obstetrician's wife—a nervous anorexic with one of those carefully windswept lopsided hairdos so popular in Bel Air—then parked the van, as instructed, in a space next to the tennis court.

On my feet again, I stretched and took several deep breaths. My left foot had gone to sleep during the trip, so I stamped it a few times in the gravel, like an old vaudeville horse doing arithmetic. Neil caught this action and grinned at me. "You OK?"

"Yeah."

"Whatcha wanna blow?"

"Pardon me?"

His lip flickered. "Balloons or bubbles?"

"None of the above?"

He chuckled, then dug into the back of the van and handed me a bottle of bubbles. "Give it a try. It works well with the little kids."

I asked him how little they were.

"Five or so. It's a fifth-birthday party."

"Check."

"We'll sing 'Happy Birthday,' bring out the cake."

I smiled at him. "Want me to jump out of it?"

He took that as nervous humor, I guess, because he smiled back and said, "Don't worry. You'll do great."

Anyone else who'd reassured me about this mickey-mouse gig would have caught some shit, but Neil was different. As the day wore on, I saw how much he loved his work and how much he wanted me to love it as well. He was terrific with the kids, never condescending, dealing with their minicrises like someone who remembered how it felt. Here's the image that remains with me: Neil at his keyboard, onyx eyes aglimmer, serenading the birthday girl with an up-tempo rendition of "You Must Have Been a Beautiful Baby." When I jumped in unannounced for the second verse, he was surprised I could sing so well, but he winked at me and welcomed me into the song. It was a satisfying moment.

The other guys had their functions too. Tread did magic tricks and made balloon animals, Emmett Kelly and his buddy were tumblers, and Julie shlepped around with her magic wand, telling knock-knock jokes that were incredibly lame, even for a fairy princess talking to preschoolers. I didn't fare much better with my roving bubble-blower routine, but most of the kids, bless their voyeuristic little hearts, leapt at the chance to study a grownup shorter than themselves.

We were finished by five o'clock, packed up like gypsies heading for the road. I'd already begun to think of the job in those terms, for purposes of sanity, if nothing else. It was easier somehow to tell myself that this wasn't Bel Air 1991 but Romania a century earlier (minus the pogroms), and we were all actors in a wandering troupe, plying our trade at a village fair. There was grass beneath our feet, after all, and simple music of our own making, and a blue dome of sky above our heads. So what if the villagers were all the same age and the local noblewoman had a ridiculous hairdo? Fantasy is the art of not being picky.

We dropped off the others at the parking lot, and Neil drove me home according to plan. As we climbed into the canyon, he apologized for the obstetrician's wife, who, among other things, had called me "cute as pie" to my face in the same simpering tone she used with her five-year-old.

I told him I was used to it.

"Yeah, but still …"

"Did she commend you on your natural rhythm?"

He smirked and looked over at me. "She told me how much she liked *Do the Right Thing*."

I laughed.

"They're not all that bad."

"Praise the Lord."

"The kids were fun, though."

It wasn't a question, but I made a little murmur to be a good sport. I doubt if he was fooled. I don't hate children or anything; some of them are very nice individually. I just prefer to avoid them en masse. When they hold big conventions, for instance, and get shitfaced on sugar.

Neil asked me where I'd learned to sing like that.

"At home. In Baker."

"Baker?"

"It's in the desert. No one's ever heard of it. They call it 'The Gateway to Death Valley.'" I rolled my eyes. "How's that for another way of saying Purgatory?"

He chuckled. "They don't call it that seriously?"

"Oh, very seriously. Big sign and everything. Right over the road."

"I can't picture it somehow."

"Lucky you."

"So you sang in school?"

"Sometimes. One or two assemblies. Mostly I stayed home and sang along with my Bee Gees albums."

He took this in thoughtfully. "I can see the influence, now that you mention it. Your voice has a quality that's really sort of ..."

"Gibbsian?"

"Yeah."

I told him Arnie thought I sounded like Teresa Brewer.

"No," he said, "more like the Bee Gees."

"Well, fuck you very much."

"No, really. It's a great sound. You could have something there. You should cut a record."

What's that they say about Hollywood? A town where you can die of encouragement? I didn't want to look overeager, so I reacted with a skeptical expression.

"What's the matter with the Bee Gees?" he asked.

I rolled my eyes at him. "Do I really have to explain this to a black person?"

He smiled dimly and shrugged his enormous shoulders, as if to say his tastes were catholic and he could like who he wanted. "It wasn't a bad sound. It'll be back too, you watch. They're already wearing platform shoes in the clubs."

"I can hardly wait."

"So when did you move here?"

"Nineteen eighty."

"Did you run away?"

"Well, yeah ... sort of. With my mom."

"From your dad, you mean?"

"Oh, no. He split way before that. When I was three." I smiled at him. "When he realized his little dumpling was gonna *stay* a dumpling."

"Oh."

"Mom and me were just running away from Baker. Plus I wanted to be a star." I embarrassed myself with this admission, so I widened my eyes ironically to show him I knew how silly I'd been. I didn't want him to think I take myself that seriously. Even though I do.

"You got work right away," he remarked. "*Mr. Woods* was about ... what year?"

"Eighty-one."

"Not bad for a new girl in town."

"I suppose."

"Did you audition or something?"

"No. Philip just saw me with Mom one day."

"Philip Blenheim?"

I nodded soberly, enjoying his amazement. Most people are impressed when they find out I was once on a first-name basis with a household name. "Once" being the operative word.

A smile sprawled across Neil's face. "He *discovered* you?"

"He stepped on me."

"C'mon. Where?"

"At the Farmers Market. Mom and I went there for brunch, and it was crowded, and he didn't see me. He was nice about it, though. Bought us smoothies and just kept on apologizing. I realized later he was sizing me up for the rubber suit. He took our phone number and called Mom that night, and the next afternoon I had the script."

Neil shook his head in wonder.

"I didn't catch on to what a big deal it was until he closed the set."

"I remember that. The press went into a feeding frenzy."

I told him it was the weirdest time of my life. And the biggest high.

Neil didn't talk for a while, just kept his eyes on the road in the deepening gloom of the canyon. Finally, he asked: "Have you been in a video store this week?"

"No. Why?"

"Well, there's a big promotion."

"For what?"

"*Mr. Woods.* Big cutouts with motors in 'em. Jeremy with the elf."

"Oh, yeah?"

"It's the tenth anniversary, isn't it?"

I told him it was. I'd known this was going to happen, of course, but I'd momentarily forgotten about it. I'd *tried* to forget about it.

"Maybe you'll be invited to a reunion."

"No way."

"Why not?"

"Philip likes to preserve the magic." I spoke those last three words in quotes, as I always do.

"What do you mean?"

I shrugged. "Mr. Woods is just what you see on the screen and nothing else. The movie is it. That's why the elf never makes public appearances, not even at the Oscars. Philip doesn't like to talk about how it was done and doesn't want anyone else to, either. It just reminds people that Mr. Woods isn't real. He hates that."

"But it's fascinating, I think. Especially now."

"Philip thinks it would ruin the movie, destroy the wonder, blah, blah, blah. At least he used to. I doubt if he's changed his mind since then."

"Were you credited, then?" Neil looked gratifyingly concerned on my behalf.

I told him there were a dozen "operators" for the elf listed on the crawl and that I had simply been one of them. For all the audience knew, I'd been a technician or a robotic engineer, not an actress turning in a performance. I was interviewed once about the role, I explained, by a reporter from *Drama-Logue,* and as soon as the piece appeared, Philip blew up and accused me of destroying the magic of the film. I almost lost my job over it, I told Neil, and Philip was chilly to me right up to the day we wrapped.

Neil frowned. "He's OK about it now, though?"

"Who knows? I haven't seen him for years."

He shook his head for a while, taking it all in. "What a story."

I just shrugged.

"Thanks for telling it. I'll think of you in there next time I see the movie." He turned and gave me the nicest smile. "It won't spoil the magic for me."

When we pulled up in front of the house, Renee came bounding out the door, barefoot and in jeans and wearing the embroidered yellow sweater she saves for special occasions. How long she'd been waiting there like that was anyone's guess.

"How did it go?" she asked, leaning against the van.

I told her fine.

"Did the kids have a good time?"

I told her yes, they had a fabulous time.

"Need a hand?" Neil asked this, turning to me. His face was outlined against Renee's, granite against fog. Did I need a hand? I needed two of them, thank you, big as rump roasts, one under each arm. And maybe some warm breath against my cheek, a nice gust of Juicy Fruit.

"I can do it," chirped Renee.

I shot the woman a few dozen daggers, but she missed all of them, as usual, as she galloped to my assistance, goofy with goodwill. As soon as she opened the door to the van, I slid off the seat and began the descent on my own.

"Are you sure?"

"Positive." I mugged at Neil over the edge of the seat before dropping out of sight onto the pavement.

When I straightened up, Renee was offering Neil a cup of coffee for the road.

"Thanks," he said, declining. "I've got … you know, miles to go before I sleep."

Renee took the Frost reference literally. "I thought you lived nearby."

Neil smiled pleasantly. "Not that far, I guess. There's just some stuff I have to do."

Renee nodded.

"It's been fun," he said, addressing me.

"Sure has."

We locked eyes for a moment or two, and then he pulled away from the curb. A few seconds later he hollered back at me: "I'll call you tomorrow about the next job. I've got some ideas for new songs."

"Great," I yelled.

When the van had turned out of sight, Renee walked to the door with me. "He's nice, isn't he?"

"Yeah."

"Cute, too."

"He's OK," I said.

It's almost midnight now, and I've finally had my bath. I worked on this entry for three hours, much longer than I had expected. Renee popped in several times with refills on the cocoa. I could tell she was dying to ask me about my new boss, but she resisted the urge, apparently out of respect for this strange burst of journalkeeping. It's just as well, since I can't put a name to my feelings. I would have called them carnal and left it at that, if you'd asked me earlier in the day, before the rest began. Before he sang with me and drove me home and said that sweet thing about the magic.

4

FIVE DAYS LATER. BACK ON MY AIR MATTRESS.

I should tell you a little about Jeff Kassabian, my friend of almost a decade, since we had brunch together on Sunday and he spun me the most preposterous yarn ever. This is part of what makes Jeff lovable, I suppose, but there was also something a little sad about it, given his current state of mind. It's only natural for him to be lonely sometimes, but I wish he wouldn't cope with it by weaving something rich and mysterious out of a perfectly conventional set of circumstances. Conventional for him, at any rate.

Jeff is a writer, about my age. He ekes out a living as an office temp, but his real energy goes into his work-in-progress, a rambling autobiographical novel about growing up gay and Armenian in the Central Valley. This is his second book. His first was about a Caucasian boy who falls in love with a Japanese boy at a Japanese internment camp during the Second World War. He won some sort of gay writing award for it and sold about two thousand copies. I went to his one and only book signing—at A Different Light in Silver Lake—and ended up behind the table with him, sipping white wine from a paper bag and flirting with his customers.

When I met Jeff at a video bar in West Hollywood, I knew

next to nothing about homosexuality, though my nineteen years of being myself in Baker had prepared me thoroughly for the company of fags and dykes. I could sit on a beer crate in a gay bar and amuse myself for hours, drinking and laughing and doing 'Ludes, and never once feel like a Martian. The most beautiful boy starlets in town would duck to the floor to talk to me and say the most extraordinary things. All I can remember about that first meeting with Jeff was how elated I was when he referred to a good friend of his as a "size queen" and how long it took me to realize he wasn't talking about a gay midget.

We've been buddies since then, off and on. Jeff's most recent lover died of AIDS two years ago next October. Ned was an older guy in his mid-fifties, a no-nonsense sort of person and a real source of stability for Jeff, I think. Since his death, Jeff has become increasingly prone to creative remembering. I don't mean that he lies; he just arranges the facts more artfully than anyone I've ever known. In life, as in his work, he's not so much a writer as a rewriter, endlessly shuffling the facts to give them form and function. I've learned to take his memories, as well as his projections, with a few zillion grains of salt.

He called me that morning from his house in Silver Lake.

"Is it too late for brunch at Gloria's?"

I asked him what was up.

"I've just had the strangest thing happen to me."

"Oh, yeah?" I tried not to sound too jaded.

"I need your advice about it."

"*My* advice?"

"You're gonna love it, too, if it's what I think. And if it's not, we'll have a nice lunch anyway."

"I don't suppose you'll tell me now."

"Of course not," he said.

I knew Renee was heading into Beverly Hills on a forage for shoes, so I decided to bum a ride with her. I hadn't seen Jeff for ages, and I was aching for a change of scenery, especially one that didn't involve pounding the malls. I asked him if he could drive me home.

"Whenever you want."

"Let's do it, then."

"Great. We can hang out at my house after brunch."

"You aren't gonna read to me, are you?"

He laughed at that, but a little uncomfortably, so I told him I was just kidding.

"I thought you enjoyed that," he said.

"I did. I do. I said I was kidding."

Well, mostly kidding. The last time we hung out at his house, he read to me at length from his autobiography. It was fairly interesting stuff, especially if you knew Jeff, but it went on about an hour too long. His sixth-grade seduction in the pea-sorting shed—or wherever it was—could have been trimmed by half. Plus he puts everything in the present tense, insisting that it sounds more literary. It may be, for all I know, but it can get sort of grating at times.

"Don't worry," Jeff said grumpily. "That wasn't what I had in mind."

"Now don't make it sound like that. I'm your biggest fan. Aren't I the one who called you the gay Saroyan?"

He grunted.

"I'll give you your strokes at lunch," I said breezily. "You're buying, aren't you?" There was more urgency in this question than I cared to betray. These days, every meal that isn't a Cher shake counts as a major extravagance.

"Of course," said Jeff, still a little pissed at me. "I invited you, didn't I?"

Since it was to be a laid-back Silver Lake kind of Sunday, I wore an aqua T-shirt, dolling it up with a string of pop beads and my pink rhinestone silence-equals-death pin. When I'm not in costume or evening clothes, I'm almost always in T-shirts, since they're comfortable and inexpensive and you can accessorize the hell out of them. For a while I used to belt them with various bright and spangled things, but I gave up the effort several years ago. When you're built like I am, there's not much point in pretending to have a waistline.

Renee was chirpy all the way through the canyon. She could hardly wait to buy oil paints, she said, because she'd been watching a guy on TV who showed you how to paint snowy peaks with Christmas trees on them, just by stubbing the brush against the canvas. He wasn't that cute, she said—in fact, he was kind of old—but he had this deep, velvety voice that made you feel *so calm,* even if you weren't painting. Already I have a creepy image of future nights at home: me on my pillow with this diary, and Renee at her easel, stubbing out snowy peaks in perpetuity under the weird spell of some bearded guy in a cardigan. She pumped me about Neil again too. She hasn't asked me to negotiate a date with him, but I think she's on the verge. I'd be more than happy to oblige, if Neil weren't my employer and I didn't know Renee as well as I do. Neil and I have a nice uncomplicated professional relationship, and I think it's wise to keep it that way.

When we got to Gloria's, I gave Renee directions to the nearest art supply store and sent her on her way, making my entrance on my own. The restaurant was packed, so I forged a path through a forest of legs, most of which were sheathed in the trousers du jour: those neon-print muscle pants that make gay boys look straight and vice versa. Halfway in, I made eye contact with a gap-toothed boy in peacock-green bicycle shorts. He smiled and said: "Hi, Cady," so I smiled back, though I couldn't place him. His groin hovered above me like a dirigible, iridescent as a butterfly's wing in the morning light.

"Over here." Jeff signaled me from a table. Behind him loomed a trellis of white bougainvillea, through which I could catch the angry blur of traffic on Sunset. "I brought you a pillow," he said, lifting me into a chair.

"You didn't." It was a paisley pillow, wide and flat enough and suitably firm, exactly what I needed. I settled into it and rearranged my T-shirt, then surveyed the room. "Now I suppose you expect me to tell your fortune."

Jeff chuckled.

I bounced a little on my new throne. "You brought this from home? Really?"

"Not far."

"You're sick." I gave him a quick once-over, reacquainting myself with that generous, dark-eyed face, the slate-blue shadow on his jaw, even at noon. His eyelashes have always been his best feature, and somehow they seemed lusher than ever, as if in compensation for his thinning hair. He wore green corduroy slacks and a plain white shirt, sleeves rolled up to the elbows. If memory serves, that's how he was dressed the night I met him at the Blue Parrot, so many years ago. It's his uniform for being a writer.

"I ordered us margaritas," he said.

I told him he could have mine, since I was on a diet.

"Have *one*."

"Do I have to be drunk to hear this?"

He smiled. "No."

"You look nice," I told him.

"Thanks. You too."

"So ... if you're not gonna read to me, I hope it's about sex."

He chuckled.

"Last night?"

He nodded.

"Was it bigger than a bread box?"

"Don't jump ahead."

"Tell," I said. I folded my arms across my chest and waited.

"Well, I went running in Griffith Park yesterday afternoon. I parked in my regular lot and saw this kid leaning against a car."

"Description, please."

"Oh ... about twenty, twenty-one. Sandy hair, dressed like he'd just come from a class at UCLA."

"Cute?"

"Very."

"Go on."

"So I just headed up the path on my run, since that's what I ̣e there for ..."

"Of course."

"... and I ran for half an hour, nearly killed myself, and came back to the lot, and there was the kid, still leaning against his car."

"Uh oh."

"What?"

"He wasn't a cop, was he?"

"No. Just be quiet and let me finish."

"Sorry."

"So I started to get in my car, and he sort of ... you know, headed over toward me, and made this really clumsy effort at conversation. Sort of hesitant and scared, but completely charged with lust. It was the oddest thing, like stepping back in time somehow. He reminded me of me back when I was first trying to be a homo. It was touching, almost."

I nodded. I wasn't about to get smart with him while he was waxing rhapsodic.

"So I kind of took charge—like I wish somebody had done with me. I told him I had a place we could go to, and he knew what I meant, so he followed me back to my house in his car, and we had the most amazing sex. It wasn't that exotic or anything, your basic vanilla, really, but he was so young and appreciative, and he kissed like an angel."

I fanned myself with my napkin.

He laughed. "He had the prettiest dick, too."

"Big?"

"Pretty, I said."

"Did he stay for the night?"

"Oh, yeah."

"Did you read to him?"

"No," he said flatly, "and fuck you."

"Yes you did. You made that poor child listen to the next chapter." I could see the whole thing: Jeff propped against the headboard, yellow legal pad in hand; the tangle-haired kid snuggled cozily, postcoitally, against his side. I could even hear Jeff laughing at his own jokes, sighing extravagantly at his own poignant prose.

He doled out his words slowly, ominously. "So help me ... I am ... never ... ever ..."

"Oh, lighten up. Are you gonna see him again?"

"I doubt it."

"Why not?"

He shrugged. "I gave him my number, but he wouldn't give me his."

"Where does he live, then?"

"I don't know."

"What was his name?"

"Bob, he said. But who knows?"

"Is that the whole story?"

"Not exactly. He took off this morning, early, while I was still asleep. He left a note on my dresser that said 'Thanks, take care' and just slipped out. I haven't tricked like that for about a hundred years, and I felt so ... I dunno ... abandoned suddenly, dumb as that sounds. I thought we might go to a movie today or something. At least have breakfast."

"Sure."

"But ... he was gone, so I made some coffee and worked on the book for a while and then walked down here to return a few videos that were overdue, and when I walked into the store, they had this big display for *Mr. Woods*. Have you seen that thing yet, by the way?"

I told him I'd heard about it.

"Well, it moves, you know, and it's got a big picture of Mr. Woods and ... the little boy. I couldn't remember his name."

"Callum Duff."

"In the movie, I mean."

"Oh ... Jeremy."

"Right. Of course."

He seemed lost in thought for a moment, so I said: "And?"

"And ... I just stood there, glued to the spot, having the weirdest feeling all of a sudden, because I realized it was him."

"Realized who was him?"

"Bob, the guy I slept with last night."

"Was who?"

"Was Callum Duff."

I squinched up my face at him. I could grasp the concept, wiggly as it was; I just couldn't pin it to the cardboard. "You mean he looked like him?"

"I think it *was* him, Cadence. He was just what the grownup would look like."

"C'mon."

"Well ..."

"Callum lives in Maine," I said.

"He does?"

"Yeah. For years."

"Oh." He looked terribly deflated.

"His parents took him home after we wrapped. *Mr. Woods* was the only movie he ever made. He came back for the Oscars, and that was it."

I remembered that long-ago night of nights. Callum onstage with Sigourney Weaver, copresenting some boring technical award, the childish "damn" that tumbled from his lips when he flubbed a big word on the TelePrompTer. The whole world was captivated by the only moment of true spontaneity to arise from an otherwise packaged event. Callum left the stage to thunderous applause, those freckles converging in a blush you could see even on black-and-white TV. The town was his on a platter, but all he wanted was to go back home to Rockport, to see his friends again, to study hard and be a lawyer like his dad. Or so he told the press at the time.

Jeff just wouldn't let it go. "Maybe he came back."

"I think I would've heard," I said gently.

"You still know him, you mean?"

"Well, no. Not anymore. But Leonard would've told me if he were back."

"Who's Leonard?"

"My agent. Leonard Lord."

"Oh, yeah."

"He's Callum's agent too. Or was. That's how I got him. During *Mr. Woods*. I know I must've told you this."

Jeff nodded listlessly, drained of his dream.

"The likeness was that strong, huh?"

"Maybe not," he said.

"He sounds nice, though. The note was really sweet."

"Yeah."

I couldn't help feeling sorry for him. This was the first guy he'd even told me about since Ned's death. "It makes a great story," I said feebly. "You should do something with it."

Our margaritas arrived, so we ordered lunch—grilled chicken sandwich for him, fruit plate for me. To pull him out of his funk, I told him about my new job, leaning heavily on my cute boss to keep it interesting.

"Is this guy married?" Jeff asked.

I shook my head. "Divorced. With a seven-year-old kid. The kid lives in Tarzana with the ex-wife."

"Mmm."

"What does that mean?"

"Sounds like he's ready, that's all."

I rolled my eyes at him. "He's my *boss*, Jeff." I could see how much he wanted to build a case for me and Neil, but I wasn't about to let him. He's already mythologized my sex life to the point of absurdity. It delights him no end to paint me as some rabid little horndog, humping her way around Tinseltown. I told him once that many little people are offended, much in the way that gay and black people are, by the commonly held notion that they're over-sexed. He wasn't fazed a bit. He said he'd never considered that an insult and that I shouldn't, either.

The fact remains: I'm no Jezebel. The last time I had sex with anybody was over five years ago. The guy's name was Henry some-thing, and he was an old friend of Jeff's, someone he'd known at UC-Davis, visiting from Kentucky. He was sort of a hippie, skinny and goofy-looking, but nice enough. One afternoon at Jeff's house, while Jeff was out shopping for dinner, Henry gave me a massage, using cedar oil he carried in an embossed leather case. When his fingers strayed accidentally—and how could they not, on this body?—I responded with a not-so-subtle moan of appreciation. After that we were off and running.

And, yes, penetration was achieved. I know that's your first question, so let's just get it out of the way. I'm a dwarf, remember, not a midget, which means that certain parts of me are closer to average size than others. That may be a little hard to picture, but trust me; I wouldn't lie to you about this. At any rate, poor Henry seemed even more surprised than I was, fretting a lot afterwards about whether he'd taken advantage of me. I assured him he hadn't, but he was a wreck for the rest of his visit.

The following December he wrote me a long, earnest Christmas card from Bowling Green, apparently to determine whether I'd been permanently traumatized by the experience. He hadn't told Jeff about it, he said, and swore he never would, as if that would somehow protect my honor. Jeff already knew everything, of course, since I'd spilled the beans as soon as we dropped Henry off at the airport. Ever since then, Jeff has tended to exaggerate my sexual potential the way he exaggerates everything else.

While we're on the subject: I haven't had much luck with men my own size. There aren't a lot of them, in the first place, and the ones I've met just haven't turned me on. Mom tried on several occasions to fix me up with men she met at LPA meetings, but I found them ridiculously macho and unappealing. Some people would say that this apparent inability to eroticize my own kind reflects serious self-loathing on my part. Maybe they're right. Or maybe I just like big guys. God knows, other women aren't required to apologize for their taste in men.

For a while in the early eighties I did all right in the sex department. Nice men propositioned me in the weirdest places, and I became a sort of serial slut, though not without occasional misgivings. Sometimes, in my darkest moments, I wondered if they really

wanted *me,* Cadence Roth, or were just being kinky. Then I realized how thoroughly I'd been victimized by the semantics of the
larger world. If sex with a little person was kinky by its very defini-
tion, I had no choice but to embrace kink when it found me and
be damned grateful for its existence. When long legs and big tits
worked for other women, why shouldn't my body work for me?
And if the guy laughed with his buddies about it later and never
called me again, I would cope with that too, like any other modern
woman. It was a question of perception, I decided, and taking control of my own destiny.

These days, the pickings are pretty slim. My sex life revolves
largely around Big Ed, an industrial-strength marital aid I bought at
The Pleasure Chest last year. This marvelous device and a good
Keanu Reeves movie have been known to make my evening while
Renee is out on a date. Which, frankly, is one of the reasons I'm
worried about her landscape-painting scheme, since it would mean
a significant loss of privacy. I could always put a TV in my room, I
guess, but Big Ed is about as quiet as a Stealth bomber.

After lunch Jeff insisted we stop by the video store so I could see
the new *Mr. Woods* display, complete with moving arm on the
beloved elf. He stared at the figure of Callum for a long time but
made no attempt to resurrect his theory. He was still harboring it,
though, I could tell.

"Why don't we rent it?" he said.

I made a face.

"C'mon, why not?"

"Well, for starters, it doesn't work on me."

"When was the last time you watched it?"

"Three years ago," I told him, "when Renee moved in."

"Well, I haven't seen it since it came out, and I'd love to see it
with you. You can annotate."

I groaned softly.

"It's not about ... that guy," he said. "I'm over that."

I told him it was the movie that bothered me.

"C'mon, then," he said. "I'll get you stoned."

"Jeff."

"Please ..."

Note to the set designer:

Jeff is not overly concerned about his surroundings. The bungalow he rents up the hill from Gloria's is painted a puky mustard color and is flaking badly. There's a balding palm in the front yard and a row of ratty hollyhocks along the driveway. On this particular day an abandoned toilet greeted us rudely from the sidewalk, left there for pickup by one of the neighbors. (Angelenos, I figure, must renovate their bathrooms more often than anyone else in the world; you can't turn a corner in this city without seeing somebody's no-longer-stylish crapper sitting on the curb.)

Jeff justifies the house by seeing it as something out of Nathanael West, but that won't cut it for the rest of us. If it weren't for the wind chimes on the front porch and the rainbow flag serving as a curtain at the bedroom window, you'd think an ax murderer lived there. The inside is even worse: stacks of unread newspapers, dirty clothes everywhere, dozens of anemic houseplants pleading to be released from their misery.

Jeff rolled a joint and made a big pitcher of iced tea before we watched the movie. I hadn't been high for months, so I got silly fast, giggling uncontrollably as soon as the credits rolled. Jeff shushed me like a librarian, totally consumed by the mission at hand. When Callum made his first appearance on the screen, pedaling his bike home from school, Jeff's eyes narrowed in rapt concentration.

"What's the verdict?" I asked.

"Who knows?" he said. "It doesn't matter."

After that we talked only about my performance or the technical wizardry involved. As expected, I found it utterly impossible to surrender to the film. All it evoked for me was heat and boredom, the pulse of my own dead breath against wet rubber, the needling pinball sounds of the circuitry encasing my head. That heartrending sound track didn't work on me, either, since I had lived in the core of the fantasy, the emotionless eye of the hurricane. I may be the only person in the world with a good reason not to feel something from that movie.

Toward the end, during the scene when Jeremy and Mr. Woods say goodbye, Jeff knelt before the VCR and froze the frame on a close-up of the boy's face. I wondered what he was looking for. The color of the eyes? A particular expression? A telltale constellation of freckles? He just sat there, though, saying nothing, bathed in the pearly blue light of the box, his face in dramatic silhouette against Callum's. I felt almost as if I were intruding.

"Maybe not," he said finally.

I mourned his loss with a murmur.

"Sorry," he said.

"Hey."

"I could've sworn."

"I'm just glad you got laid," I said.

To do my bit, though, I called Leonard's office first thing Monday morning. His secretary said he was in a meeting, so I asked her to have him call me "regarding Callum Duff," knowing damn well he wouldn't phone back if he thought it was just about me. He didn't return the call until yesterday, and even then he sounded peeved that I'd managed to command his attention twice in the same month. I said I hated to bother him, but a friend of mine thought he'd seen Callum in town, and I'd appreciate his phone number if it was available.

Leonard said he had no such number. He hadn't represented Callum for years, and as far as he knew, Callum was still attending "some college back East."

I haven't had the heart to tell Jeff.

5

IT'S LATE, BUT I OWE YOU AN ENTRY.

I've been working like a madwoman for PortaParty, sometimes with as many as two gigs a day. Word of mouth has done wonders for us in Bel Air and Beverly Hills, where we've been passed around like a favorite recipe from one rich doctor's family to another. Some of the kids are so used to us now that they know me by name and have begun to get adventurous when I call for requests during the singing portion of the show. Last week at a dermatologist's house, an eight-year-old girl made such an eloquent plea for "Like a Virgin" that I finally gave in and sang it sotto voce while the grownups were out at the cabana drinking decaf. I don't need to tell you I brought down the garage.

The attention is nice, I admit, but I'm a little disturbed by the vaguely captive feeling this specialized audience gives me. Every time I perform, I feel less like a gypsy trouper and more like a court jester. I haven't said this to Neil, of course, since he's ecstatic about the new surge in business and attributes it largely to me, which—let's be honest—is probably true. If nothing else, I'm a novelty, so it's easy enough to imagine the scenario: "Can I, Mommy, please, please? Zachary had the midget lady for *his* birthday."

My secret fantasy is that one day we'll do a party for the children of, say, the Spellings or the Spielbergs, in the process of which Aaron or Steven, or their wives, or at least someone who works for them, will discover the huge talent I'm hiding under this walking bushel and offer me a contract on the spot.

Farfetched? Maybe. But a girl can dream. We're working the right neighborhoods, certainly, and we're bound to run out of doctors sooner or later.

Renee and I drove into Hollywood today to see *The Rocketeer* at the El Capitan. I was less curious about the movie than about the movie house, a huge Deco extravaganza that Disney just renovated as its flagship theater, whatever that means. They had a live show before the film, with tap-dancing ushers and usherettes in snappy uniforms singing a hopelessly hokey song about the El Capitan and those fabulous stars of yesteryear. Renee adored it. To me, the kids looked like animatronics figures, robots from a ride at Disneyland, with smiles so grim and waxen that they might have been greeting you at the gates of hell.

The Rocketeer hasn't got much for grownups, but the audience today seemed to enjoy itself thoroughly, stomping and hooting like goons. The biggest cheer came when a gangster took a stand against the Nazis and said, "I may run a crooked business, but I'm a loyal American."

Yellow ribbon fever is rampant. You can't make it a block along the Walk of Fame without running into some asshole in a General Schwartzcoff T-shirt. (No, I don't know how to spell it, and I don't plan to learn. As far as I'm concerned, he's just one more Mattel action doll we've been sold for the summer.) Even the hookers—I swear to you—are wearing Desert Storm camouflage tube tops. Whores for Oil. Bimbos Against Baghdad. It's too surreal for words.

A billboard has just gone up in West Hollywood depicting a sleek and sinister-looking car (I forget which make), headlined by one word: STEALTH. How's that for subtle? The people who buy this car should be issued license plate holders that say MY OTHER CAR IS A BOMBER. Look at what has happened to us: warfare has become so attractive again we can actually sell cars with it—to guzzle the gas we killed all those people for.

After the movie we went to Book City, this huge old Hollywood bookstore with floor-to-ceiling shelves. I like it because there's always lots of stuff at eye level and because I can lose myself so thoroughly in its maze. Renee gets bored easily with this routine, so she usually runs out for a milk shake while I'm there. At least that's what she tells me. I think she's really checking out the panties at Frederick's of Hollywood. She has a terrible weakness for them. All I want out of Frederick's is a spot on the sidewalk in front, the perfect location for my star.

I found a copy of *Rumpelstiltskin* at Book City. I've been looking for a good one for ages, since it would make a fabulous movie and I'd be just right to play him. I wouldn't mind cross-dressing one more time, as long as my face remained visible. In this new version of the fable, which I read tonight while I drank my Cher shake, Rumpelstiltskin is delicately described as "a little man" rather than an evil dwarf. Such liberal revisionism is progress only if one prefers complete invisibility to outright scorn. I'm not sure I do.

The legend was pretty much as I'd remembered it, with the poor dude getting his usual bum rap. When he's banished at the end, having stomped himself completely into the ground, his only crime has been to establish an adoption contract and attempt to abide by its terms. The real villain of the piece, if you ask me, is that venal bitch of a miller's daughter. Following the dwarf's instructions, she spun whole rooms full of gold for the king, eventually luring him into marriage, knowing from the start that the fee for Rumpelstiltskin's services was her firstborn child. *Then* she has the gall to act wronged when he comes around to collect. No wonder he sends her out to learn his name; she's treated him like a complete cipher, someone whose feelings count for nothing. The book doesn't say that, of course, but it does let you know that little guy couldn't be bought off for all the gold in the kingdom. He valued human life above all else, which was why he wanted a child of his own so badly.

Call me a nut, but I think there's a real story inside the fairy tale, which would make for a fascinating movie: a crusty, cantankerous but entirely human old dwarf, living on his own in the woods and longing for single parenthood.

When I explained all this to Renee, she said: "Yeah, but most people are used to the old story."

I told her this *was* the old story, just another way of looking at it.

"Yeah, but, you know … it's no fun if he isn't …"

"A turd."

She giggled.

"It's not funny," I told her sternly. "Dwarfs are always the bad guys in these things—vicious, vindictive little bastards who live under a bridge and eat children for lunch."

"Really?" she asked meekly, trying to look serious but making a total mess of it.

"I know you've noticed it, Renee. Name me one nice dwarf in a fairy tale."

After a moment of serious pondering, she screwed up her face and said: "Dopey?"

If there had been beer in my mouth, I would have spewed it at her. *"Dopey?"*

"Well, I don't …"

"Good, Renee. Dopey. Good answer."

She stared at me, slack-mouthed, apparently wondering how badly she'd fucked up.

"That'll look fabulous on the poster," I said, retaining my acid tone. "CADENCE ROTH IS DOPEY." I knelt on my pillow and imagined a review for her. "'Not since Linda Hunt's Grumpy has there been such an Oscar-caliber performance.'"

When Renee finally realized I wasn't mad, she giggled in relief and bounced once or twice on the sofa. "I didn't know we were talking about a role for *you*."

"Since when are we *not* talking about a role for me?"

"Well, I don't see why Dopey is any sillier than Rumpelstilt-skin."

"It is. Trust me. It's myth versus kitsch."

I'd lost her completely.

"It doesn't matter," I added hastily. "It's all just speculation."

"Did you talk to Leonard about it?"

"About what?"

"Rumpelstiltskin."

"There's nothing to talk about," I said. "There isn't even a script. It's just a concept."

"Oh." She rose and headed for the kitchen, stopping in the doorway. "Want some popcorn?"

"Sure. Thanks."

"Is it on your diet?"

"If I don't have butter."

"Oh."

"Butter it," I said.

She giggled and ducked into the kitchen.

"I need my animal fats," I yelled after her. "I've been working too hard."

After we finished the popcorn, Renee offered me a foot rub, which I accepted without protest. I lay on my pillow on the living room floor, stomach down and feet toward the ceiling, while she sat next to me with a squeeze bottle full of pink lotion. It was sheer heaven. (If you'd like some inkling of this experience yourself, start by imagining a massage from someone whose hands can engulf your entire foot.)

During the rub, Renee kept up a running commentary on Lorrie Hasselmeyer, a new employee at The Fabric Barn. As near as I can make out, Ms. Hasselmeyer is the only woman at the store who outdoes Renee in the doormat department—romantically speaking—which, presumably, is why Renee can't stop talking about her.

"She's just so desperate," she told me.

"Mmm." I was a little more involved in the massage than in the anecdote.

"When the guy didn't call, she went over to his house and left a note on his Harley."

"No."

"She did. I swear."

"God."

"She was bragging about it, Cady. She thought she was being really cool." Renee let go of my foot for a moment to replenish the lotion on her hands. When she squeezed the bottle, it made a noise like a baby with the runs. My foot felt unexplainably deserted and naked, awaiting her there in midair. When her hands finally returned, all sweet-smelling and slippery, they fit me like a glass slipper. "Too cold?" she asked.

"No. 'S great."

"You'd tell me if I got like that, wouldn't you?"

"Like what?"

"Like Lorrie Hasselmeyer."

"Oh, God, yes."

"I don't think any guy's worth begging for."

"Fuckin' A."

Renee turned her attention to my other foot and was quiet for a while. Her thoughts hung heavy in the air, endearingly obvious, like the scent of the lotion. I swear to you I knew exactly, almost to the word, what she would say next:

"Has Neil ever … said anything about me?"

"What do you mean?"

"You know," she said.

I hesitated, considering several routes, then said: "He's only seen you twice, Renee."

"Three times."

"Whatever."

"So what did he say?"

"He said you seemed nice."

Her fingers stopped. "Is that all?"

"Well … he said you had great tits."

"You're kidding!"

I chuckled. "Yes, I'm kidding."

"Gah, Cady, that's not very nice."

"Sorry."

She began to work my toes again. "I just thought he might've said something."

"No," I said evenly. "Not really." This sounded too hard, so I added: "Mostly we just talk about work."

She seemed to drift away for a moment. "He's real smart, isn't he?"

"I suppose." Let's put it this way: Neil is a genius by Renee's standards. I soft-pedaled it, though, because I know she's in the process of fixating on him, and I'm not sure he's ever given a moment's thought to her. It seems like one more quick way for Renee to get her feelings hurt.

6

RENEE WAS A NAVY BRAT, BORN AND RAISED IN SAN DIEGO.
Brat status is something we share, in fact, since my dad was a drill
sergeant at Fort Irwin, down the road from Barstow. This was half
the reason I was named Cadence; the other half had to do with
Mom teaching piano. Cadence, apparently, was the only thing my
parents had in common. Plus the Cady Mountains were right there,
flanking the bleakest stretch of the interstate, so my nickname came
ready-made. Mom had a long, boring rap about this, which she
rattled off at every audition, come hell or high water.

Renee's mom was the military parent—a Wave, I guess you call
it. Her dad had some sort of civilian job on the naval base. They
were always entering her in beautiful-child contests; she had baby
lipsticks and her own batons by the time she was five. When she
was a teenager, she ran for Miss San Diego but didn't get into the
finals. Her parents divorced the same year, and Renee, who was a
guilt-bearer even then, felt chiefly to blame. One more beauty
crown, especially that one, would have saved their marriage, she
claims. She moved to L.A. after high school with a guy she met
while working at Arby's. He walked out on her only days after they

found an apartment in Reseda. I have no idea what the problem was. Renee almost never talks about him.

Things Renee likes
Water slides
The color pink
The gum that squirts when you bite into it
Extra mayonnaise
Stories about Michael Landon's cancer
Angora
Me

Things I like about Renee
Her loyalty
Her flawless skin
Her sense of color (except in regard to pink)
Her rice pudding
The way she has a name for her car without knowing where her battery is
Her smell after she's come out of the shower

Renee talks in her sleep, though she won't admit it. You can hear her all the way through the door—a sort of ladylike drone, completely unintelligible, that seems somehow intended for an audience. There's something so formal and melancholy about it, so redolent of loss, that I think of it privately as her Miss San Diego acceptance speech.

I can't help wondering if the guys in her life hear the same monologue, and if they're freaked by it. Or does she have different dreams when she's sleeping in other bedrooms?

I'm afraid I'm making her sound tragic, like Delta Dawn or something, and that's not the way it is at all. She's a great person, really. I'm lucky to have her.

7

TODAY, ACCORDING TO THE PAPERS, L.A. HAD ITS LAST TOTAL solar eclipse of the millennium. About three thousand people mobbed the Griffith Observatory for the occasion, but I watched it from a house in Pasadena, where we were working a bat mitzvah. Just before it happened, while I still had the attention of my audience, I sang "Lucky Old Sun" and "Moon River." Our clients, the Morrises, provided their guests with welders' masks, cleverly upgraded with gold glitter, so they could watch that eerie ebony fingernail as it slid across the surface of the sun.

Since they weren't watching us, Neil and I slipped off for a breather to a quiet corner of the garden. I sat on a patch of grass under the trees. Plopping down next to me, Neil dug a pack of cigarettes from the pocket of his coveralls. "Did you get a good look at it?"

I told him I had, that one of the old ladies had lent me her welder's mask and that, frankly, I wasn't sure it had warranted all the fuss. The traffic was living hell this morning, and there were serious madmen everywhere.

Neil wanted to know which old lady.

"With red hair and wobbly teeth."

"Oh, yeah."

I told him that when I gave the mask back to her, she said: "Isn't it amazing? It makes you feel so small."

Neil chuckled, then shook a cigarette out of the pack, lighting it with his Bic. "What did you say?"

"I agreed."

That made him laugh. "I thought it would get a lot darker. You know, this great shadow across the land." He swept the air with the hand holding the cigarette.

"Oh, well. It was better than the Harmonic Convergence."

"Shit. I forgot about that."

"Well, there you go."

"What was supposed to happen then?"

"Who knows? The harmonies converged. The harmonicas. Something."

Another chuckle.

"At least there was something to look at this time."

"True," he said as he stretched out his legs. Then he leaned back on his elbows and tilted his head toward the sun, which you couldn't really see for the branches. A lacy, dappled light fell across his face. He was like a beautiful mountain range, I thought. "How long is it supposed to last?"

I told him another fifteen minutes or so.

He was quiet for a moment, then said: "You were incredible out there."

"Thanks."

"Especially on 'Moon River.'"

"Good."

"I liked your patter too."

I'd done a bit for the crowd about how the sun and moon were siblings, and how rare it was for Sister Moon to have any chance at all to upstage her loudmouthed big brother. I know it looks dumb on paper, but it worked swell for a bat mitzvah in Pasadena during an eclipse.

"You know what?" said Neil.

"What?"

"I think you should make a video."

My heart leapt at the thought, even as I archly discounted it. "That ought not to cost much."

"Well," he said, "I know somebody."

"With money?"

"No, but she wants to make a video."

I gave him a jaded look. "A girlfriend or something?"

"Hell, no." He smiled at some private vision of this woman. "Just this person I know. She's a student at the American Film Institute. She has to make a short film for one of her classes."

"Oh."

"If you're not interested …"

"No … I could be."

He sat up energetically and crossed his legs, Indian style. "She'd give it style, Cady, I know that. She's got good taste. Some of her ideas about it are pretty interesting."

"You've already talked to her about it?"

He looked a little sheepish. "Some."

I assured him I wasn't offended.

"She wants to do it in black and white, with long shadows and a simple set, a sort of Lotte Lenya thing. Haunting and beautiful. She's got access to a studio, and I could play the synthesizer. We could do it for almost nothing."

I thought about it for a moment, gazing up at the trees. "What would I sing?"

"I was thinking of 'If.'"

"The old Bread song?"

"Yeah. I think it would work with your voice."

"Really?" I couldn't quite take in the idea that he'd spent time thinking about me and my potential. No one's really done that since Mom died. I could feel an awful weight lifting that I didn't even know had been there.

"It's a poignant song," Neil said, "and nobody's heard it for ages."

"Except in elevators."

"But you'd give it a new dignity."

"I suppose."

"It would work, Cady, I know. And with you singing it … it would rip their hearts out."

I felt a tiny alarm go off. "Is that what we wanna do?"

He shrugged.

"I'm not a poster child, Neil."

"I know that."

"If your friend wants that …"

"She doesn't. I told her all about you—what a great person you were, what a strong and beautiful spirit. She gets it, Cady, she really does."

Neil had never said anything like this to me directly, so I felt myself reddening on the spot.

"Maybe I'm out of line," he added.

"No. I see what you're after."

"You do?"

I nodded.

"You could sing something more upbeat, I guess."

"Fuck that. I want hearts ripped out."

He laughed; we both laughed.

"We'd have a good time doing it," he said. "We've got nothing to lose."

"I hear you."

"You'll do it, then?"

"Why the fuck not?"

"Great."

"OK."

His gorgeous brown eyes settled on me for a moment, then seemed to turn nervous, darting away distractedly. "Think we've played hooky too long?"

I smiled at him. "You're the boss. Who's gonna rap your knuckles?"

"Yeah, but …"

"What's the matter? You leave Tread in charge?"

"You got it."

"He can handle it," I said.

"Yeah, but we don't know what happens to him during an eclipse."

We both thought this was hilarious. We were laughing our asses off, in fact, when the object of our amusement came loping around the corner, big red whiskers akimbo. "Oh, hi, guys. Been lookin' for you."

We greeted him in unison, looking guilty as hell.

"Mrs. Morris wants you. There's a big toast or somethin' coming up."

"Oh ... well." Neil gave me a wry, conspiratorial look, then hopped to his feet and brushed dead grass off his butt. A round of muted applause—more solar worship, no doubt—rolled toward us from the house. I rose and shook the wrinkles out of my Pierrette outfit, feeling somehow that an idyll had passed.

Tread was predictably stoked about the eclipse—what a mystical, primal, humanizing thing it was—and proceeded to tell us about how he'd taken special care to align his crystals for this morning of mornings. Neil was sweet and kept a straight face throughout, though his smile seemed just on the verge of bolting for freedom like a herd of white horses. I didn't dare catch his eye. Tread's a real bran flake sometimes, but there's no point in hurting his feelings. The fact that Neil understands this—and knows that I know he does—makes me like him even more.

"Look at the ground," Tread said, as the three of us headed back to the festivities. "The best show is down there."

I looked and saw nothing.

"What do you mean?" asked Neil.

"I think you have to smoke something," I said.

"Now wait a minute," said Tread. "Just look."

"I'm looking."

"See all the little crescents?"

I did see them. What I'd accepted as the usual variegation of light and shadow was, in fact, thousands of tiny half-moons—half-suns, if you prefer—scattered across the ground like the hairpins of an untidy goddess.

"They're photographs," Tread explained. "Under the trees here the leaves filter the light, so it actually takes a picture of the eclipse."

"Amazing," murmured Neil.

"Yeah," I said, genuinely impressed. "Good one."

Tread gave me a big, crooked, metaphysical grin—about as close as he ever comes to saying I told you so. "You should look down more often."

"Oh, yeah?"

"Sure. There's good stuff everywhere."

"I'll try to remember that," I said.

It's dark now and I'm in my bedroom, looking out at the same moon that caused all that commotion this morning. Renee is in the living room, painting snowy peaks with her secret television lover. The world is back to normal again, they tell us, but I can't help feeling expectant, on the brink of something truly significant. Neil says his video friend, whose name is Janet Glidden, will want to get started right away. That's fine with me, though I'm not nearly as thin as I'd like to be. Oh, well. I'll wrap myself in something dark and get the makeup right and do it all under a three-watt blue bulb. The voice is what counts, anyway.

Jeff called earlier this evening to say he'd recognized my legs in that cellulite infomercial. We had a good laugh about it. I asked him, proceeding carefully, if he'd heard from his friend in the park. He said no, without elaborating, so I let the subject drop. I think his pride's a little hurt. As near as I can make out, guys usually call Jeff back.

A moment ago Aunt Edie called from Baker to inquire about my well-being and express her belated dismay over Merv Griffin. She had just seen an old *Globe* at the beauty parlor. "Did you know he was that way?" she asked.

I told her pretty much everybody did.

"Poor Eva Gabor," she said.

8

THERE'S SOME BIG STUFF TO TELL YOU, BUT I'LL START WITH THE morning and how I got my butt sniffed on Rodeo Drive.

Since Renee is off work for a week, we dolled ourselves up and drove into Beverly Hills for what Renee is fond of calling "an elegant day." We were standing outside Bijan, window-shopping and looking as tastefully blasé as we knew how, when this big, ugly dog appeared out of nowhere and, without so much as a howdy-ma'am, stuck his big, wet nose up my dress. Renee shooed him off several times, to no avail. He'd caught his first whiff of condensed woman and could not be contained.

"Oh, gah," groaned Renee. "I hate it when this happens."

"*You* do?"

She giggled, then shooed him some more and told me: "Don't. We can't laugh."

"Why not?"

"He'll think you're friendly."

"Maybe I am," I said.

"I mean it, Cady. Look mean."

"Oh, for God's sake."

"Back up against the wall, then."

"He'll just go for the front." I reached up with both hands and pushed the dog's muzzle away. "How 'bout it, Renee? This elegant enough for you?"

"Shut up."

"He doesn't have a boner, does he?"

We were both crippled with laughter when a snippy-looking woman in red leather came out of the store and gave us the evil eye. "Is there something I can help you with?"

I don't know why that was funny, but it was. I lost it so completely that Renee had to explain things for me. "This dog has been ... harassing her."

"Is it your dog?"

"No." Renee sounded terribly accused. "We've never seen it before."

I was holding my waist now, gasping for breath. The dog had backed off a little, observing my madness, his head tilted in genuine puzzlement.

"Are you all right?" asked the woman.

I nodded.

The woman studied us a moment longer, then went back into the store. I leaned against the building, trying to compose myself, while Renee proffered a sickly, mortified smile to a pair of matrons who'd stopped to gawk. Almost as if he'd realized the fun was over, the dog lost interest and sauntered off down the street.

"Thanks a lot," Renee said sullenly.

"Who? Me or him?"

"You."

I wiped my eyes, then waved at the gawkers, who eyed each other nervously, then skulked away. "It was funny," I said, trying to explain myself.

"You could've said *something*."

"No way." I held up my palm to show her how much I meant this. "I could barely breathe."

"She thought you were having a fit."

"I know." I tried to look contrite. "I'm sorry."

"And you messed up your mascara." Renee knelt in front of me, pulled a Kleenex from her purse, and began repairing my face. "I always forget about dogs."

"It's OK," I said.

She just kept on dabbing away. "Where do you think he came from?"

I thought for a moment, then said: "Got me licked."

She laughed really hard at this, so much so that her face began to squinch up and her big, friendly knees squared off in a disquietingly familiar way.

"Renee …?"

She squealed incoherently, like some old-time movie damsel trying to shake off a gag.

"You're peeing your pants, aren't you?"

All she could manage was a nod and another squeal. She was doing a full jackknife now, impressively enough, yet somehow remained standing.

"They're gone," I said. "Go for it."

The morning was not a total washout, I am happy to report, because Renee keeps an extra pair of panties in her purse for just such emergencies. She picked up this helpful hint, she explained, during her kiddie pageant days, when unnasty undies were apparently a point of real pride in the dressing rooms. After skulking off to a rest room in a nearby coffee shop, she joined me for pie in one of the booths.

"Why do you suppose they do that?" she asked.

"Who?"

"Dogs."

I shrugged. "Because they can."

"It must be so weird for you."

I told her it was like living in a world with dragons.

She frowned for a moment, then gave me a wan smile and

gazed out at the street. "I hate Beverly Hills, anyway. People are so stuck up."

"Mmm." I didn't care where I was, really. I was mostly just glad to be off my feet, to be back in air-conditioning again and buzzing merrily along on caffeine and sugar.

"Let's go home and change."

"You just did."

"Into something casual, I mean."

"I thought this was our elegant day."

"Well …" She looked down at her pale-peach blouse and white linen skirt. "I guess we could wear this there."

"Where?"

Her eyes were avoiding me.

"Where, Renee?"

"Icon?"

"Why would we go there?"

"You know…"

It took me a while to get it, maybe because I'd blocked it out: the brand-new Mr. Woods ride was being launched to great fanfare and heavy press at Icon Studios this week. Renee and I had seen a big story about it on *Entertainment Tonight*—with Charlton Heston and Nancy Reagan climbing out of the fucking thing. The mythology that required yours truly to remain invisible at all costs had found a lucrative new life in the Valley as a high-class midway attraction. Try to imagine my excitement.

"I know you think it's dumb," said Renee.

"It'll be hideously crowded."

"Maybe not."

"What does the ride do, anyway?"

"I dunno," she said. "I think they fly you over the woods."

"I hate theme parks, Renee. I really do. I loathe and despise them. Couldn't you go with Lorrie or somebody?" (That's her friend from work.)

"Please, Cady. It wouldn't be any fun without you."

I knew I was doomed to lose, so I told her I would go, with two provisions: that we go straight to the ride and leave as soon as the ride was over and that she not reveal my identity to a living soul while we were there. The last thing I needed was for her to trot out my tired elfin credentials for some flat-butted Lutheran family on vacation.

Icon Studios, I should tell you, is within spitting distance of my house in Studio City. It's built on the side of the mountain, on two levels, with a connecting escalator that looks like a giant Lucite rodent run. The lower level is really two operations, a working studio and a theme park, with almost no connection to each other. The hordes of tourists who troop through the park each year to cluck over the family photos in "Fleet Parker's Dressing Room" have no more chance of meeting the star himself than they do of meeting the real Mickey Mouse at Disneyland. The place is plastic on plastic, an illusion about an illusion.

I hadn't been to the park in almost seven years. Mom and I took Aunt Edie there, at her request, on her first visit to L.A.—it's that sort of place. It was much as I'd remembered it, just as soul-deadening, certainly. The plodding, Necco-colored people on the rodent run were what I tend to think of when I hear the term New World Order. Renee ran interference when the crowd got too thick, but it was slow going most of the time. The air was stale and muggy under the blurred white sky, and there were way too many children off leashes for my taste. We headed straight for a soda stand as soon as we reached the lower level. I'd already had quite enough.

Renee stooped to hand me my Diet Coke float. "Are you doin' OK?"

"I preferred the dog," I said.

"Cady."

"I'm kidding." I licked the foam on the edge of the float.

"I want you to like this," she said.

"I love this."

"I mean the Mr. Woods Adventure."

I grinned into the foam. "How long is the line?"

"Not long."

"I bet there's a lot more you can't see."

I was right, but I didn't rub it in. For almost half an hour all I saw was poles and legs, poles and legs, as several hundred of the faithful were led through an elaborate cattle chute for humans. To keep us docile there were a dozen video monitors suspended from the ceiling, offering not only clips from *Mr. Woods* but a gooey tribute to "the little guy himself" by Philip Blenheim himself. Renee adored this, of course, swooning and giggling at all her favorite moments. Me, I was grateful for the air-conditioning.

There was a sign, just before we boarded the ride, that said: CHILDREN UNDER 35 INCHES MUST BE ACCOMPANIED BY AN ADULT.

"Uh oh," I said ominously, teasing Renee. "Look at that."

"So?"

"They'll never take me. I'm four inches under."

"Well, I'm an adult."

I told her they might want proof.

"I have an ID," she said, missing the joke.

"Why do you think they say that?" I said, beginning to worry for real.

"I'm sure it's nothing," said Renee.

"It won't be nothing if my ass is flung into Kingdom Come."

Renee must have suspected a last-minute change of heart, because she frowned and poked out her lower lip. "It's not that fast, Cady. Nancy Reagan's hair wasn't even messed up."

The woman in front of us, a plump, white-haired lady in pink sweats, turned around and smiled down at me. "It's really mild," she said. I wondered how long she'd been waiting to leap into the conversation. "I was the same as you, but it's a piece o' cake."

"Thank God."

The woman nodded. "I was exactly the same as you."

"You've done this before, then?"

"Brought my sister's kids last week."

Renee jumped in: "Is it fun?"

"Well ... if you love Mr. Woods as much as I do."

"Oh, I do!"

The woman laughed.

"I mean, I probably do." Renee tittered, then cast a guilty glance in my direction. I could tell how much she was dying to blab, so I admonished her with a stony look. The pink-sweats lady seemed nice enough, but I was tired and cranky, and too preoccupied with ideas for the new video. I just didn't have the stamina, or the time, for the draining little ritual of explaining myself.

The ride turned out to be a sort of glorified fun house: a chilly, dark space the size of an airplane hangar, through which we lurched and glided in "bark"-covered trains. The scene of our Adventure, according to Philip in the preride video, was not the suburban forest we knew from the movie but the "faraway, mystical realm of Mr. Woods' origin." Translation: I may be cheesy enough to exploit this character, but I'm not going to fuck around with a classic.

What this change of locale afforded, of course, was the perfect setup for cloning Mr. Woods, for creating a whole race of lovable robots in his image. That familiar wizened face, once so charmingly singular, popped up behind every bush and tree stump as we sailed along, as a teenage girl, say, or a romping baby, or a campful of lumberjacks marching home from work. There were Mr. Woods farmers and their wives, Mr. Woods soldiers going off to war. There was even a wedding ceremony in which everyone in church looked like Him. In the pyrotechnical finale, at least a hundred of the little fuckers (evil ones, I presume; the plot was too much for me) were hurled through the forest by a giant catapult.

I was profoundly unmoved. When we lurched out into the daylight again, Renee and the pink-sweats lady swapped notes. Renee was pleased, but thought Mr. Woods looked weird as a bride. I bit my tongue and said something vague about the old-fashioned thrill of being led by the hand through a darkened room. Renee looked at me funny, unconvinced, then resumed gabbing with the lady.

When we were alone again, Renee announced stiffly that she had to pee.

"Then pee."

"Look," she said. "I didn't tell her."

I told her I knew that.

"Why are you mad, then?"

I told her I wasn't, that I was just tired, that I thought *she* was mad.

"You wanna go with me?" She meant to the ladies' room.

I shook my head, gave her a weak smile, and asked her to help me find a place away from the traffic.

This turned out to be a small but highly groomed patch of grass around the corner from Fleet Parker's Dressing Room. I was sprawled there amid the birds of paradise, like some live-action garden gnome, when I heard a youthful male voice call my name.

"Cady?"

The guy knelt on the lawn to address me, completely natural about it. He was cute and in his early twenties, snub-nosed and sandy-haired. He wore a blue checked shirt with chinos and bore a marked resemblance to half the cutie-pies in West Hollywood, but I honestly couldn't place the face.

"Yeah?"

"It's Callum."

All I can tell you is that the name just stayed there in the air for a while, everywhere at once, like the hum after a bell has been tolled.

"You're shitting me," I said.

Without showing teeth, he gave me the prettiest smile. "No."

I hit the ground with my hand. "What in the world are you doing here?"

"Same thing you're doing, I guess."

My thoughts were galloping way ahead of me, of course, so it was a real chore just to function in the moment. "Have you done the Adventure yet?" I asked Callum.

"A few hours ago."

"Pretty tacky, huh?"

He just shrugged and smiled, remaining sweetly noncommittal. I wondered how much loyalty he still felt for Philip, whether he still kept up with him, whether he had come here as Philip's guest, maybe, as an official part of the tenth-anniversary hoo-ha.

"It's not *terrible*," I said, backing down a little, "but it's not an improvement on Pirates of the Caribbean."

"Can I join you?" he asked.

"Of course. Sit."

He eased onto the lawn next to me.

"I'm waiting for a friend," I explained, taking in this new grown-up version of him. "She's in the john."

He nodded.

"What are the fucking chances of this?" I asked.

"Got me."

"Can I say that around you now?"

He laughed. "You always did."

I laid a hand on my chest to convey my horror.

"I survived," he said, grinning.

"Are you here on vacation or something?"

"Sort of. Not exactly. Well, it's a combination."

I chuckled at this familiar indecision, a mature variation on the little gavotte he used to do around the candy bar rack at the roach coach.

"I may be working," he said brightly. "In a movie."

I felt the little stab in the gut I always feel when I hear of anyone else's movie. It's awful, I know, really petty of me, but I just can't help it. "Hey," I said as gamely as possible. "Good for you."

To receive congratulations, Callum ducked his head like a bashful prince: a quirk—or perhaps a device—I remembered from a decade earlier.

"Who with?" I asked.

"It's not definite yet."

"Ah." *It's with Philip,* I was thinking. *Some big-bucks project they've sworn him to secrecy about.* Then I realized how silly it was to get paranoid about a kid who'd been cooling his heels in a fishing village for half his life; he was probably just too nervous to talk about it. "I thought you'd retired," I said blithely.

He picked at the grass while he decided what to say. "How well did *you* know yourself when you were eleven?"

Pretty damn well, actually, but I thought it unfair to say so. Our circumstances were different, after all. Mine, looking back on it, had compelled me to get my shit together fast. "So it got in your blood, huh?"

He nodded.

"Well," I said, "welcome back, then."

"Thanks."

"Who's your agent?"

He shrugged. "Still Leonard."

"Oh," I said colorlessly, "that's good." So that little weasel *had* known that Callum was back in town and had willfully lied to me about it. But why? To keep me out of his hair? To insure that I didn't pressure Callum about a role in this new movie, whatever it was? Probably. What was brutally clear, if nothing else, was that Leonard wanted me out of his hair for good.

"He's as tough a cookie as ever," said Callum amiably. "You know Leonard."

"Oh, yeah."

"It's what's required, I guess."

"Absolutely."

"Are you still in the business?"

I tried to be as pleasant and offhanded as I knew how. "Oh, yeah."

Right away Callum looked so mortified that I felt a little sorry for him. "That came out wrong," he said.

"Hey. You've got no reason to know."

"What are you up to?"

I told him I was making a video and left it at that. I didn't tell him about PortaParty, since he would only make an effort to be positive and encouraging about it, and that would depress me more than anything.

"Singing, huh?"

"Some."

"I remember how well you sang."

"Thanks."

"I saw you in that horror movie," he said.

"Which one?"

He widened his eyes and mugged, unable to remember the name.

"Did I have gray shit hanging off me?"

"That's it," he said.

"Bugaboo."

"Right. *Bugaboo.*" He laughed.

"That came to Maine?"

He shook his head. "Cable."

"Oh, yeah."

He picked at the grass some more. "I got your Christmas cards. Thanks."

"Sure."

"I'm sorry I never sent you one back."

"Hey," I told him, shrugging it off. "You had pubic hair to grow."

He laughed. "Just the same."

"My Christmas card list is enormous," I said, letting him know it was much less a give-and-take ritual with me than a sort of therapeutic hobby. "Lots of people don't write back. I send cards to Phil Donahue and Tracey Ullman. Sometimes I send cards to people who aren't even alive."

This got a laugh, because it sounded like a joke, which I guess it was, but it was also the truth. I lose track of friends sometimes, and they get sick and die, and I don't find out until months later, often in the most casual way, at a party, say, or standing in line for *Truth or Dare.* And I say "How awful" and pass the word on to whoever else might've known the guy and cross him out of my address book. I've done it so often now, it's become shockingly routine, just another domestic ritual. I didn't spell this out for Callum, but I wondered if he knew what I meant. I wanted him to know that I knew what the world was like now, that he could talk to me about anything.

"How are your folks?" I asked.

"Fine. Pretty much the same."

"Any other ... people in your life?"

He grinned like an errant schoolboy. "Am I married, you mean?"

"Whatever."

He held up a ringless hand. "See."

I smiled at him. "It doesn't have to be official."

He shrugged. "A few girlfriends."

"A *few?*"

He laughed.

"Here?"

"What?"

"The girlfriends."

"No. Back there."

"Maine?"

"Yeah."

"That can't be any fun."

He shrugged again. "I haven't been here that long. How is your mother?"

I took note of this abrupt change of subject, then told him my mother died three years ago.

"I'm sorry."

"Thanks."

For the life of me, I couldn't think of a graceful way to bring a Griffith Park pickup into this conversation, so I asked him what he'd done since he'd been here.

"Not much," he said ruefully. "A lot of lunches."

I nodded knowingly, as if I, too, had borne—and borne recently—the terrible burden of being overlunched. I could see

Callum making the rounds again: at the Hollywood Canteen, say, springing that fresh, yet oddly familiar, young face on some aging baby mogul who hasn't seen it for a decade. What a potent impression it would make! And what a hook for the media: this kid who conquered Hollywood at ten and gave it up for the simple joys of teendom in New England returns to the big screen as a grown-up heartthrob. If the movie's any good at all, he could be a huge star again before the year is out.

"Are you reachable?" I asked.

"Sure. I'm at the Chateau Marmont."

"Oh. OK."

"The switchboard will put you through."

"Great."

He smiled like a cat in the sun. "Remember when Ray used to live there?" He meant Ray Crawford, the cranky old geezer who played Callum's grandfather in *Mr. Woods.*

"Sure do," I said. I had never been invited by, but I knew that Ray had a suite at the Marmont. If you remember him in the movie, he looked pretty much the same as that, except that he wore ascots under short-sleeved shirts, instead of cardigans. He died about five years ago without much fanfare. There was a brief mention of it on *Entertainment Tonight.*

"I have the balcony next to his," Callum said.

"Is this progress?" I joked, since nobody much liked old Ray.

He laughed. "I like it there, though."

I could see Renee heading toward us, so I made a quick excavation in my purse and handed him one of my cards. "This is me," I said.

He studied it for a moment. It says *Cadence Roth Acts for a Living* and gives both my number and Leonard's office number. "That's clever," he said, and stuck it in his shirt pocket. "I forgot Leonard is your agent too."

"So does he."

He chuckled, but sort of uncomfortably.

"When you see him, say hi for me," I said.

"I will."

Then Renee came up and Callum made a move to introduce himself. I stopped him with a yank at his sleeve. "Promise me you won't scream," I said to Renee.

"Huh?"

Callum looked at me and grinned.

"Promise me, Renee."

She shrugged. "I promise."

"This is Callum Duff."

As Renee homed in on him, her mouth slackened noticeably and her eyes began to narrow. It's the look she gets when she's trying to think of a phone number, or painting snowy peaks with that guy on TV.

"Thank you," I said, when a scream failed to materialize. "Callum, this is Renee Blalock, my housemate."

Callum sprang to his feet and stuck out his hand. "Hi."

Renee echoed him meekly.

"Renee is a big fan of yours."

"Do you totally swear?" Renee asked Callum.

Since he looked completely baffled, I said: "She doesn't think it's you."

"Oh ... well ..."

"Don't make him swear, Renee. It's him." I got up and brushed off the seat of my T-shirt, making signs of leaving. Callum had begun to look restless, and I'd seen quite enough of humanity's march for one day. I was ready to go home and veg out completely, sit under the sprinkler, maybe, with nothing but a Walkman on. Renee was just getting warmed up, of course.

"You were so great as Jeremy," she told him. "I wanted to be you so bad."

"Thanks."

"I really, truly, mean it."

"I can tell," said Callum. "Thanks."

Renee bounced a little in her excitement, never taking her eyes off the poor kid.

"OK," I said. "Time to move on."

"Oh. OK." Renee got all sheepish in front of Callum. "I hope I wasn't …"

"You were very nice," said Callum. "I like the movie too."

Renee shot me an excited glance. "You know what would be neat?"

I gave her a wary look on Callum's behalf. "What?"

"If I could get a picture of you two."

I reminded her nicely that no one here had a camera.

"Back there they do." She pointed down the chaste postmodern midway to an exhibit sponsored by Fuji Film, a sort of high-tech playroom for grownups. "They take your picture in front of any backdrop you want."

Callum didn't hesitate. "You could be in it too, then."

"Oh, could I?"

"Why not?"

"Oh, gah, that's so great."

"Don't you have to be somewhere?" I asked Callum.

"Not for a while." He gave me an earnest, just-between-us-grownups look. "I really don't mind. I'd like a souvenir myself."

"There's no line," Renee said.

"Well … whatever."

It had dawned on me finally that we'd each get a picture, and that mine would come in very handy indeed. I was already imagining the way I would tease Jeff with it.

We ended up choosing a rear projection of plain blue sky and clouds. Renee argued pitiably for the *Mr. Woods* backdrop, but Callum seemed a little uncomfortable about it, so I stood firm with her. Callum sat in a chair, while I posed in his lap, and Renee stood behind, one hand resting delicately on Callum's shoulder. We attracted a small but fascinated crowd with this curiously Victorian tableau.

"You're a good sport," I told Callum as he set me down again.

"Hey."

"Where's your appointment?"

"Over there," he answered, gesturing with his eyes. "The other side." He meant the real side—the working side—of Icon Studios, the place where we'd once made a movie together, so many years ago.

I nodded knowingly and left it at that, not wanting to come off as nosy.

Callum insisted on paying for the photos, and told Renee, who was already in seventh heaven, to order a poster-sized one for herself. The shot turned out much better than I'd expected. Renee looked placidly lovely, her hair a sort of three-strip yellow against the phony blue sky. I had cheekbones for once, and my eyes, or so Renee assured me, were at their sultry best. Callum looked far more like the child I had once known than he did in real life. Something sweetly uncomplicated and true had surfaced in his eyes in time to meet the camera halfway. It was downright eerie.

"Do people recognize you?" I asked.

"No," he said. "Not usually. Almost never."

"Me either."

He laughed. "We're even, then."

Sensing his restlessness, I told him how glad I was we'd bumped into each other, and to call me whenever he felt like it. He thanked me nicely but didn't commit himself, which came as no surprise, since we had never been all that close. Renee thanked him profusely for posing with us and, pushing the limits even further, gave him an awkward peck on the cheek.

We left him roughly where he had found me, then headed up the giant escalator toward the parking lot.

When we got home, I called Jeff first thing. After six rings and the usual annoying musical interlude from k.d. lang, I was informed that the gay Saroyan was at a motel in Palm Springs and would not be back until Monday morning. I felt hideously let down, so I left him a cruelly cryptic message to call me anytime for information regarding "the latest Jeremy sighting." I wasn't about to waste this one on a tape, and I knew from experience that Jeff would appreciate the story more if I wrapped it festively in a little intrigue.

I haven't heard a peep out of him all evening. This is puzzling, frankly, since he's usually good about checking his machine, no matter where he is. The phone hasn't rung at all, in fact, since Renee and I sat down—or stood up, in her case—to our respective creative endeavors.

Renee's painting is coming along nicely. She's doing a waterfall now, the next step after snowy peaks. She says "Oh, poo!" out loud so often that I want to throttle her, but she shows a real knack for this technique. And I see what she means about the instructor; he does have a way about him. As I lie here on my pillow, his low, reassuring voice floods over me like warm honey, or some kindly old uncle murmuring nursery tales over a crib. I wonder if he has a cult or something, if other people tune in just for his voice.

I'm almost to the end of this notebook. Another twenty pages or so and I'll have to find a new one, something a little classier this time, that doesn't have Mr. Woods' ugly face on the cover. That was it for me today, I've decided, my last sayonara to the little dickhead. Every time I relent and reimmerse myself in that bankrupt mythology, I come away feeling drained and discarded, a relic before my time.

Life is too short for looking back.

Especially mine.

It's past midnight, and Jeff still hasn't called. Renee turned in half an hour ago, after donning a new nightie and slicking her face drastically with Vaseline.

I picture Jeff in a room by a pool, with a sleazy desert moon hanging low in the palm trees. He has just had spectacular sex (sorry, I can't quite see the face) and is on the verge of springing the next chapter on his unsuspecting victim. In which case, he could well be planning to check his machine before he calls it a day.

The hell with it. I need my beauty sleep.

9

I woke up this morning and found a mouse in a trap Renee had laid in the kitchen. This might have been manageable had it been a regular trap, but it wasn't; it was a rectangle of white plastic, covered in a sort of yellow goo, to which the poor thing was stuck, very much alive, twitching horrifically. Even the side of her face was caught in the nasty stuff. In her frantic struggle to escape, she was straining every muscle under her command, but so far all she'd managed to do was shit. I hate to think how long she might have been there.

Renee is the official exterminator at our house, just as Mom once was, but she was out on a morning mall crawl and unlikely to return for hours. I opened the cabinet under the sink and made a frantic search for the mousetrap box, in the dim hope it would tell me what to do next. When I couldn't find it there, I flung open the cupboard and spotted a likely candidate on the top shelf: a red-and-yellow box with the name E-Z Catch printed on the end. I swatted at it with a broom handle until it tumbled toward me in a pungent avalanche of cleaning rags.

There were instructions, all right, printed in Spanish and English: *Eche raton con trampa. Discard mouse with trap.* There was also

a charming illustration of a mouse caught in the sinister goo, rendered so playfully as to be almost a cartoon, complete with vivid
little beads of mouse sweat (or were they tears?) popping from her
head. *No Springs, No Snaps, No Hurt Fingers, Disposable, Sanitary,
Ready to Use.*

What to do? If I hurled this living creature, ever so conveniently,
into the garbage can, as advised, it would lie there for hours in the
dark, panic-stricken and exhausted, until its life ebbed away and the
ants came to eat it alive. There was no way I could be a party to
that, so I filled my low-level kitchen sink with several inches of
lukewarm water (thinking that might make it more pleasant) and
drowned the little bandit.

It took her the longest time to stop moving; I held her down
for a while after that, just to make sure. When I finally raised the
tiny, dripping corpse, checking anxiously for signs of life, I flashed
perversely on Glenn Close bursting out of the bathwater in *Fatal
Attraction*. The mouse was perfectly still, though, so I took the trap
outside and dumped it into the sunken garbage can by the street.
Then I hurried back to the house, shuddering a little, and took a
long, hot shower with a loofah.

I am not, as they say, a born killer. I was wasted for the rest of
the morning. You'd think Renee would be the prissy one in this
respect, but she's not at all; she's held her own mousy My Lai's
before, racking up deaths by the dozen, and it doesn't faze her one
bit. She can be downright cheery about it, in fact, when she's
checking her traps in the morning.

I'm writing this on the beach at Santa Monica. Renee has three
more days of vacation left and plans to make the most of them.
We're encamped under a new floral-pattern beach umbrella she
bought at K mart yesterday. I'm wearing my latest creation: a pink
gingham bathing suit, heavily ruffled, that makes me look like a
huge Victorian baby. Renee is in a royal-blue bikini, poring over
the latest *People* for the juicy details of Annette Bening's pregnancy
by Warren Beatty. There's a soft, lulling breeze off the water, and
the sky is remarkably clear and blue. Though my housemate doesn't

seem to have noticed, a Chicano guy two blankets over has been giving her the eye for ages, with a nice boner in his Speedos to prove it. I guess I should tell her—sooner or later.

To catch up:

Jeff called the morning after I left that message on his machine. "OK, Cadence, what is it?"

Since he sounded edgy, I decided not to be coy. "Callum Duff is in town," I said. "He's been here for several months."

He was silent for so long that I wondered if he was mad at me, though I couldn't think of a reason he should be.

"You're entitled to gloat," I added.

"How do you know this?"

"I saw him. We talked."

"But you don't know it's the same person."

"No, but I've got a great way to find out."

Another pause, and then, furtively: "He's not there, is he?"

I chuckled. "No, Jeff. I've got a photograph. Taken yesterday."

"Oh."

"What's the matter?" I said. "I thought you'd be overjoyed."

"You didn't tell him that I ...?"

"I didn't tell him a thing. Your name never came up."

"Good."

"The next move is strictly yours."

"No, it isn't."

"Well ... whatever." I let my tinder-dry tone convey the message that it was no big deal to me, since I was beginning to feel vaguely pimpish about the whole affair. He could find his own boyfriends, for all I cared.

"He had my number, you know, and he never called back."

"So?"

"Well, I can't just call *him* now, out of the blue like that. He never even told me where he lived."

"Oh, I see."

"There's such a thing as pride."

"Mmm."

"Where *does* he live?"

"Does it matter?"

"Cadence ..."

"The Chateau Marmont."

He made a little murmur, or maybe a grunt, of recognition.

"That's where you pictured him, wasn't it? In a castle?"

"Very funny."

"He's a dreamboat, Jeff. I see what you mean."

"Yeah, well, a fucked-up dreamboat."

"Why? Because he didn't call you back?"

No answer.

"Do you wanna see the picture or not?"

He emitted a protracted groan that meant yes, so I told him he knew where he could find me. He said he'd be on his way as soon as he finished his sit-ups. I hung up and went into the living room to fluff the pillows, feeling the glow I always feel when I lure someone I really like into the soul-sucking reaches of Yellow Ribbon Land.

He showed up an hour later, bearing wilted carnations he'd bought from "a Hispanic person at a stoplight." He tried to stay cool about it, but his muffin-round, sandpapery face wore expectation like rouge. After kneeling briefly to bestow a ritual peck on my cheek, he went straight for the photograph.

"Where was this taken?"

I told him.

"I thought you hated it there."

"I do. Renee made me go. Is it him, Jeff?"

He nodded.

"Are you surprised?"

"No. Are you?"

I shook my head and gave him a crooked, apologetic smile.

"Did he say anything that made you think he was gay?"

I told him about the girlfriends back in Maine.

"Oh, great."

"Maybe he was just covering," I suggested.

"That's what I mean. He sounds fucked up. And if there really *is* a girlfriend, forget it."

"I think he's just young, Jeff."

He sighed and dropped into the armchair. "Too young. I don't feel like being a tutor. If he's still in the closet, I haven't got time to wait for him."

His jaded world-weariness was beginning to annoy me. I settled into my pillow and pointed out that Callum was only ten years his junior.

"Well, yeah," he said, "but look what happened in those ten years."

I couldn't argue with that. A decade of living with death and dying can certainly change the way you look at things. Given Callum's cloistered New England upbringing and Jeff's growing militancy, it was entirely possible that the two men weren't on the same wavelength at all. I just thought they'd look cute together. Jeff thought so too, I know damn well, though he'd done his best to convince me otherwise.

"You know," I said, after a pause, "people do lose phone numbers."

He brooded a moment longer. "So if I called him, what would I say?"

I shrugged. "That you'd bumped into me, and that I'd told you about seeing him at Icon, and that had made you realize who he was."

"At which point he hangs up on me."

"Maybe not."

"You don't mind if I mention you?"

"Of course not."

"That would at least be a conversation point. What a coincidence it was, and all that."

"Sure." I thought about this for a while. "If he told you his name was Bob, will he be freaked out that you know his real name?"

"Probably," he said.

"Oh, well. Can't hurt to say hello. You wanna borrow the phone? There's one in Renee's room, if you want privacy."

"She's not here?"

"Nope."

He heaved another sigh. "This is going to be irretrievably humiliating."

"Then don't do it," I said. "Or do it, anyway, and write a chapter about it."

He gave me a sardonic, brotherly smile, then went into Renee's room and closed the door.

I was making tea for us when Jeff returned to announce that Callum wasn't in his room at the Chateau Marmont. He said he hadn't left a message, since as far as Callum was concerned, he, Jeff, was just a one-night stand of several weeks back. How he'd come to discover Callum's whereabouts, not to mention his true identity, wasn't the sort of thing to be entrusted to a desk clerk. Even a desk clerk at the Chateau Marmont.

Jeff waved toward the teapot in my hand. "That isn't for me, is it?"

"Both of us. Yeah."

"I have to run, Cadence."

"You dick."

"I know. I'll make it up to you."

I set the teapot down. "Go on. Desert me. Leave me out here with all the wives."

He laughed. "I'm meeting with an editor. Otherwise …"

"That's OK. You'll be sorry. When my video is all the rage on MTV, I'll remember this."

"What video?"

"Never mind. You're in a hurry."

"You've got a video?"

"I'll tell you about it later. You want the picture of Callum?"

He hesitated for a moment. "To keep, you mean?"

"I've got two of 'em."

"Oh … thanks, then." He went into the living room and picked up the photo, giving it a once-over. "It'll be nice to have. Mostly because you're in it."

"Right. Kiss my butt, now that you're leaving."

He smiled. "How's Renee, by the way?"

I told him Renee was fine, that she was on vacation this week, that she was just out for a few hours. I didn't put much into it, because I knew he didn't really care. Jeff has always thought of Renee as a hopeless mess; especially since Easter, I think, when he caught a glimpse of her here in high Protestant drag, complete with handbag and corsage, on her way to church. They're not enemies or anything; they're just not exactly two peas in a pod. Most of my friends are that way; I'm all they have in common.

"Do me a favor," I said.

"Sure."

"Find out about his movie."

"What movie?"

"The one he's making. What he's come here for."

"Oh."

"Don't say I asked or anything. Just let it come up. I'm sure it will."

"OK." He thought for a moment before giving me a snaky look. "So that's your stake in this."

"I have no 'stake in this,'" I said firmly. "This is just a favor you can do for me." For a moment it sounded like something Rumpelstiltskin might say, a wicked dwarf's decree, so I laughed self-mockingly to convince him of my innocence and offered my cheek to be kissed.

"I'll call you soon," he said, scrambling to his feet. "About a movie."

"Oh." He meant seeing one, I realized. "OK."

"Did you read about Pee-wee, by the way?" (For a while, Jeff and I used to watch *Pee-wee's Playhouse* together on Saturday mornings. We're also serious fans of the movie—the first one, not that embarrassing sequel where they tried so hard to make him look straight.)

"What about him?" I asked.

"He was arrested in Florida for wagging wienie in a porn theater."

"Oh, no," I said. "With another man?"

"No. Alone."

"Can they arrest you for that?"

Jeff was already out the door, heading for his car. "In Florida they can."

I waved goodbye from the front door, watching until his rusty Civic had rounded the corner, out of sight. Back in the kitchen, as I searched for a vase for his carnations, I wondered if he really had a lunch date with an editor or was on his way to the Chateau Marmont for an all-day stakeout of the lobby. He wasn't above that sort of thing, and I had noticed a certain gleam in his eye.

The following day, in an empty greenhouse on La Brea, we began shooting the video. It was the second time Neil and I had met with Janet Glidden, his American Film Institute friend. She was a tall, skinny white girl with enormous teeth and a slab of straight black hair, shimmering like spun acrylic, that she continually swatted from her eyes. Her manic, fidgety manner, which hindered her work at every turn, might easily have been mistaken by some for cocaine abuse or plain old tenderfoot jitters, but I knew better.

The greenhouse belonged to a friend of Janet's, who had lent us the place for two days only. That would be pushing it, to say the least, even for a simple lip-syncing job, so I did my best to keep things moving along. This meant standing still, for the most part, resplendent in pink sequins on a tiny, thrown-together stage, while Janet from Another Planet skittered around the room in a terminal tizzy, endlessly apologizing. Her fingers were long and ivory-colored and trembled visibly as she adjusted and readjusted the various sources of light.

The lighting was all natural, she said, and she was very proud of it. She had a drop cloth on one slope of the roof, arranged in such a way as to send melodramatic little God-rays streaming down across the stage. From time to time, she would scurry up a ladder outside the greenhouse and poke at the cloth with a bamboo pole. She was building a set with light, she told me, just as Orson Welles had done in *Citizen Kane;* it was the only way to achieve "grandeur" on a limited budget.

Neil watched the grandeur from a distance, leaning against a potting table at the far end of the greenhouse. He was in slacks that day, dark-brown gabardine, and a white cotton sweater that hugged him like skin. While he didn't talk much, he would catch my eye and wink from time to time, as if in acknowledgment of Janet's loopy, befuddled nature. I think he'd realized, as early as I had, that she just didn't have it in her to deliver the goods.

When she excused herself and flapped out of the building in search of a missing lens, Neil ambled down to the stage and took a seat next to me on the wobbly plywood.

"Is this safe?" he asked.

It took me a while to realize he meant the stage. "Is anything?" I replied.

He laughed. "You got that right."

I asked him how it had looked.

"Well ... it's hard to tell, of course, without the music behind it."

I grunted. "Yeah, well ... I'm not holding my breath for MTV." He smiled.

"Or public access, for that matter."

"You wanna bail out?"

I told him I was OK about it. There was only one more day, I said, and Janet's poignant little film, whatever its quality, would work as a résumé I could show to producers. I was a good sport about it for Neil's sake, since he'd had such high hopes for the project and seemed even more let down by Janet than I was. I also wanted him to see me as a nice person, someone far too magnanimous to pull a prima donna number, however justified, on some ditzy film student. I cared what he thought about me, I guess. Care. Present tense.

"She's not usually this way," he said.

I asked him where he'd met her.

"She was a friend of my ex-wife's."

I nodded soberly. "And you got her in the divorce."

He smiled. "Not exactly. I ran into her on the street, and she told me what she was doing at AFI. She sounded so together about it."

"Oh, well," I said.

"Yeah."

"Maybe we should fix her up with Tread."

He laughed. "He could use some of her energy."

I told him not to mistake panic for energy.

"Panic?" Hieroglyphics formed on his forehead. "About the shoot, you mean?"

"About me."

This seemed to rattle him. "I dunno, Cady. She's pretty cool."

"She may be," I told him pleasantly. "But she's also in the throes of dwarf panic."

"But she was fine when we saw her before."

"Sure," I said. "And then she had a week to think about it. I've seen the pattern, Neil. I've known too many women like her."

"You really think so?"

"Yeah, I do."

He asked if it was always women.

"Women empathize," I said. "Some of them do it too much. 'There, but for the grace of God ...' and all that. Janet looks at me and sees herself and can't take it. She has to get away from it as fast as she can." I smiled at him. "You must've noticed. She's been running her little buns off all morning."

Neil didn't respond, just nodded blankly for a moment, then

smiled at something in the distance. Turning, I saw that Janet had returned.

"Find what you need?" Neil asked.

"Oh, yes. I'm sorry, people. I was sure I'd brought it."

"No problem." Neil and I actually said this together, like a couple of cats who'd just shared a canary. I hoped Janet hadn't heard my quickie analysis of her behavior, since it would only heighten her guilt, and she had way too much already. I found her exasperating, of course, but I knew she was doing her best, so there was no point in getting mean about it.

When you're my size and not being tormented by elevator buttons, water fountains, and ATMs, you spend your life accommodating the sensibilities of "normal" people. You learn to bury your own feelings and honor theirs in the hope that they'll meet you halfway. It becomes your job, and yours alone, to explain, to ignore, to forgive—over and over again. There's no way you can get around this. You do it if you want to have a life and not spend it being corroded by your own anger. You do it if you want to belong to the human race.

"How are you?" Janet's voice was just a tad too loud to be natural. "You must be tired."

I told her I was fine.

"I can run out for coffee or something …"

"I think we should just finish up," I said.

"Oh … OK."

Neil bounded to his feet, making the little stage wobble a bit. "I'll get out of the way."

"I like what you did there," I said. "Those slanting beams."

"Oh … me?" Janet was so cranked up that the compliment had flown right past her. She wheeled around like a confused crane and examined the delicate play of light and shadow on the wall behind us. "Really? You think so?"

I told her it reminded me of those long shadows on the buildings in *The Third Man.*

"Well …" She allowed herself a quick shutter-flash of a smile and blushed violently. "That's really nice, but I'm not sure it's … Did you notice the latticework up at the top?"

I told her that I had, and that it must look wonderful in black and white.

"Oh, it does," she said. "I mean, I hope. Would you like to see?" I'm sure she hadn't considered the logistics of this exercise before making the offer, because she suddenly looked flustered again. "Unless …"

"Neil can give me a boost," I assured her.

"Oh, well, then … if you'd really like …"

So Neil helped me down off the stage and held me in his arms long enough for me to look through the lens at Janet's handiwork. Janet served as my stand-in, sitting cross-legged where I had stood, so I could see how the light would fall on my face. It was quite an effect, all right—starkly dramatic and spare—yet not nearly as memorable as the warm mahogany of Neil's flesh through the nubby roughness of that white cotton sweater.

"Do they teach you that at AFI?" I asked Janet, after Neil had set me down.

"What?"

"Lighting. You seem to have a knack for it."

"Oh … no. Well, yeah … some."

"It's amazing that you can do that with natural light."

Janet looked at it again for a while, then back at me, a little calmer now that I had shifted the focus onto her work. In some ways, I think she was seeing me for the first time. "I'm so glad you like it," she said.

Neil and I held a postmortem on the way back to the Valley.

"She might surprise us," he said.

I agreed that she might and left it at that.

"I hope you aren't pissed," he said.

"About what?"

"That I roped you into this."

I gave him a stern, half-lidded look and told him I was never roped into anything.

"Still," he said.

I asked if his ex-wife was like Janet.

"No." He turned and looked at me. "Why?"

"Well, you said they were friends, so I just wondered how much they have in common."

"Not much," he said. "Linda was organized. Is organized. That must be why Janet appealed to her. Another messy life to tidy up."

"Did she tidy up yours?"

"As much as she could."

"Is that why you broke up?"

"Not entirely."

"What else?"

He seemed to resist for a moment, then said: "Are you scouting for Oprah or something?"

"No, but pretend I am."

"She wasn't much on romance," he offered.

"Didn't bring you roses?"

He shook his head. "Or expect them to be brought."

"Ooh," I said. "That *is* a problem."

"It got to be."

My teasing had begun to unsettle him, so I veered away from the tender spot. "Was she in show business?"

He shook his head. "Hospital administration."

Immediately I pictured this chilly bitch with a clipboard; make that chilly *stupid* bitch with a clipboard, since she'd let Neil get away. I asked him how he'd met her.

"At Tahoe. When I played piano in a show lounge."

"And she was a tourist?"

"Yeah."

"Were you in love with her?"

"Yeah. I guess so."

"You guess so?"

"For a while, yeah, I was."

"You don't sound that much alike."

"We aren't."

I would have felt much better if he'd said "We weren't," but I didn't remark on it. It was getting clearer all the time that Linda still weighed heavily on Neil's mind, for whatever reason. "What did you love about her?" I asked.

He thought about that for a moment and then shrugged. "She made me feel talented."

"You are talented."

He smiled sleepily. "Not that talented."

"She liked the way you played piano?"

"Yeah."

"Nothing wrong with that."

"No," he said. "Unless it's all there is."

"Well … yeah."

"There was more to it than that," he said. "I'm making it simpler than it is. I was young then. I needed somebody to believe in me. My family wasn't great at it."

I asked him how long he'd been divorced.

"Almost two years."

"Why don't you see other women, then?"

Boy, did *that* rattle him. "Why are you so sure I don't?"

"Do you?"

"Some. When I can. The job doesn't make it very easy. And I spend a lot of time with my little boy."

"Oh, right."

"I will. I mean, I will more."

"Will more what?"

"Date more."

I nodded.

"Do you always pump people this way?"

"Yes."

"Why?"

"Because people always answer me."

He laughed. "They do?"

"Oh, yes."

"Wanna see where I live?"

For a moment, I thought he was just being snide, underscoring my nosiness. "Look, I didn't mean to ..."

"No," he said, "I mean it. Come by for a while."

"Well ... OK. Sometime."

"What's wrong with now?"

I couldn't think of a thing.

He lived on the second floor of a motel-style apartment house in North Hollywood. It was a clean, serviceable place built of rough white bricks and ornamental iron, with a plastic NOW RENTING banner flapping noisily in the breeze. The front doors were painted either orange or cobalt blue. On the patch of lawn out front, a small child with red braids sat perfectly still on a yellow plastic trike. As we approached, I noticed the eerie fish-scale sheen of the lawn and realized it was plastic too.

There was an elevator, thank God, so I arrived at his apartment in a state of manageable breathlessness. He lifted me into an arm-chair in the living room, a pleasant, sunny space that had almost certainly been furnished on a single Saturday morning at Pier One Imports. There was lots of wicker stuff in plums and greens, match-stick shades, a preposterous trio of giant Italian wine jugs. The beige carpet smelled marvelously new. Beyond the sliding glass doors, the railed ledges overlooking the parking lot had been converted into twin ecosystems, rife with jungly potted things. Neil's seven-year-old son, Danny, who was staying with his mom for the summer, was more than amply commemorated by a photo shrine on top of the TV set. Neil handed me one of the larger pictures to examine: the fruit of his loins seated at an upright piano, grinning infectiously.

"In Daddy's footsteps, eh?"

He shrugged. "Maybe. If he wants to. I don't push it."

"Right."

"I don't. My old man did that to me."

I asked what his father had done for a living.

"Does," he corrected me. "He's a pharmacist. In Indianapolis."

I nodded.

"Puts you right to sleep, doesn't it? We lived above the pharmacy. It was all he ever talked about. There was no way to get away from it."

I pictured this wide-eyed, twerpy-voiced little kid sitting glumly among the towering shelves of pills, while a gray-templed patriarch à la James Earl Jones drones on endlessly about the glories of filling prescriptions. "What did he think of you and the piano?" I asked.

"Not much. He got better about it later." He shrugged. "He came to Tahoe, anyway. Heard me play."

"Well, that was something."

"Yeah," he said. "Something."

"At least you know what your father looks like," I said.

He hesitated for a moment, apparently confused, then said: "You don't remember anything?"

"Well, I remember he existed, but the rest is a blur."

"You never even saw a picture of him?"

"Nope. Mom just erased him after he left."

"I see."

"And believe me, I looked. I used to dig through Mom's stuff when she was out of the house. She had this special drawer in her dresser—way up high where I couldn't reach—with all her letters and snapshots and shit. When she went out shopping, I'd drag the step stool out of the kitchen and play detective."

"But no pictures, huh?"

I shook my head. "The most I ever found was a gift card that said 'To my darling Teddy.'"

"That was his name?"

I smiled. "Her name. Short for Theodora."

"Oh."

"I used to imagine it was from him. I'm sure it wasn't."

"Do you know his name?"

"Oh, sure. Chapman. Sergeant Howard Chapman. At the time, anyway. He left the service just before he left us."

"Do you know where he went?"

"No. But I used to think Mom did and just wasn't telling me. One summer when I was about ten, we drove to New York and visited cousins. It was my first trip out of Baker, so Mom made a big fuss about it. Somehow, along the way, I convinced myself that she'd finally found my father and was bringing me to New York for a reunion. There was no evidence for that whatsoever, but that didn't stop me. When we got to my cousins' house in Queens, I even checked the phone books and found an H. Chapman in Manhattan. I was sure it was him."

Neil smiled. "Did you call?"

"Oh, God, no. I wouldn't have dared. I just thought of it as evidence. In case I worked up the nerve to ask Mom about it."

"Did you?"

"Yeah, but not for a long time. I kept thinking she might spring it on me one night, as a special surprise, when we went out for ice cream or something. We'd get off a bus somewhere and ride an elevator, and there would be the Sergeant. He'd be tall and redheaded and smell like pipe tobacco and be much nicer than we thought he'd be."

"What made you think he'd be in New York?"

"Go figure. It just seemed like the place fathers would hide. Mom was great about it when I finally asked her. She took me to a deli and bought us big gooey desserts and let me drink coffee for the first time. She said she'd brought me there—to New York, I mean—because she wanted me to see where her family came from. She said she had no idea where my father was and that she wouldn't take him back even if he did turn up. She said he was a bastard and a coward and she was deeply, truly sorry she hadn't made that perfectly clear to me earlier."

"How'd you take it?"

"OK, actually. It was kind of a relief."

"It must have been."

"It was the way she did it, I guess—from one grownup to another. She made a rite of passage out of it." I smiled at him while an old reel played in my head. "You know what else I remember about that night?"

"What?"

"Well, Mom went out to flag a cab and left me cash to pay the waitress—one more thing I'd never done before. There was still coffee in my cup, which was Styrofoam, so I took it with me and finished it on the sidewalk while I waited for Mom. I was standing there holding the empty cup and feeling like the coolest person in the world, when this guy in a suit walks by and sees me and stops and stuffs a five-dollar bill into the cup."

"Oh, no."

"I had *no* idea what had happened. Not the slightest. I tried to give it back to him, but he just waved me off. I told Mom about it when she got back, and she was furious. I think she would've hit the guy if he'd still been around."

Neil shook his head slowly. "Did that really happen?"

"That really happened," I said.

I hadn't told that story for years.

We polished off a few beers, and then a few more. We got pretty jolly, in fact, escaping in tandem from the debacle of our day. When it started to get dark, Neil offered to make supper, and I accepted without protest. It was scrambled eggs and toast and peanut butter and apple sauce with cinnamon—all we could scrounge from the kitchen. Neil spread a tablecloth on the floor, so we could dine at the same level. Afterwards we just sat there, propped up by one end of the sofa, while cicadas played for us in the bushes below.

"I should call Renee," I said.

"Why?"

"Just to tell her where I am. Sometimes she holds dinners for me."

He smiled. "I could use a roommate like that."

"Don't be too sure."

He laughed. "How long has she been with you?"

This made Renee sound like an attendant or something, but I let it pass. "Three years," I told him.

"Seems to work well."

"Yeah."

"You're not much alike, though."

I smirked at him. "Can't get anything past you."

He chuckled.

I told him that Renee and I had learned to "respect each other's differences." My way of letting him know that I knew she wasn't the brightest gal around but that we still managed to communicate. It was an awful thing to say, but there you go. I do weird things around Neil sometimes.

"You want me to get it for you?" he asked.

I had no idea what he meant.

"The phone. So you can call her."

"Oh … sure."

Neil retrieved a cordless unit from the bedroom, or what I guessed to be the bedroom, and laid it in my lap. Renee answered right away, as if she'd been waiting by the phone. All I said was that things had taken longer than we'd expected, so not to worry about dinner. I knew she would've giggled or something if I'd said I was at Neil's house. She asked if anybody interesting had shown up at the shoot. I told her nobody much, just Princess Di and Marky Mark. She believed me for about a nanosecond, then said: "Oh, you!"

I hung up, then excused myself to pee. To my relief, the toilet was modern and low-slung, easily navigable, a graceful dove-gray oval that bore me in imperial splendor as I studied Danny's artwork on the bathroom door. The walls held postcards from Hawaii and more snaps of the kid, plus an assortment of PortaParty shots, one of which featured yours truly onstage during the eclipse bat mitzvah. There was a sweet shot of Neil and Tread at the beach, and another one with a dignified older woman whom I guessed to be his mother.

I felt so cozy there in that small, personal space, so thoroughly embraced by my surroundings, by *his* surroundings, that I fell into a kind of reverie. My eyes slid from picture to picture, absorbing the march of his life, wanting to know it all. Outside, above the whir of cicadas, I could hear the comforting clatter of dishes as Neil cleaned up. I was a little drunk, I'll admit, but something rather different was happening too. I felt such a part of him suddenly, such a perfectly natural adjunct to his life. I wouldn't make a big deal out of that, I promised myself; it was enough just to know it was there.

When he drove me home, we talked about the scary new coup in Russia, about Pee-wee, about the white man's black man Bush wants on the Supreme Court. Then, as if by some prearranged signal, we both fell silent. In the absence of our voices, the languorous night seemed to expand and spill into the van, a heady blend of diesel fumes and over-the-hill jasmine. From where I sat, there wasn't much to see, of course, but I could hear sirens and boom boxes and Valley kids howling at the moon as if they owned the night. I knew just what they meant.

THE LEATHERETTE JOURNAL

10

A NEW JOURNAL, PLEASE NOTE—SMALLER THIS TIME BUT MUCH fancier, with maroon leatherette and pretty marbled endpapers. Neil bought it for me in a mall in Westwood after we finished a particularly obnoxious gig there. I'd fully intended to pay for it myself, but Neil was insistent, saying I could buy him a beer one night. The journal cost a lot more than that, of course, so it was a nice thing for him to do. I almost never write in Neil's presence, but he's heard me talk about the diary from time to time, and I think he senses how much it's become central to my life.

The video went surprisingly well on our second day of shooting. Janet seemed looser and less fidgety, much surer of her objectives. I've even begun to get excited about it. Janet knows somebody with a chain of arty-type repertory movie theaters (if three is a chain), who might be interested in showing the film as a short subject between trailers. That's such a quirky idea that it might just attract attention, generate a little press, at least. And the audiences would certainly be more savvy and receptive than your typical MTV viewer. This could be just the right venue for me, the more I think about it.

I'm on the balcony of Callum's suite at the Chateau Marmont, six stories above Sunset. I'm in terry cloth after a noontime swim, cool-skinned and wet-haired, my nipples still pleasantly taut. A lovely, warm breeze is blowing. Callum and Jeff are down at Greenblatt's, buying sandwiches, since there's never been room service here. They've promised to bring me back a turkey on rye. Our view is toward the south: an unbroken sweep across the palmy, saffron-hazed plains of West Hollywood, with a four-story Marlboro Man looming preposterously in the foreground. The hotel itself is a funky jumble of towers and terraces, with a sixty-something-year history that's almost inseparable from legend.

Most people think of the Chateau as the place where Belushi bit the big one, but it's got a lot more going for it than that. There's all sorts of gossip in a book Callum bought at the front desk. For starters, an extremely young and horny Grace Kelly used to cruise the halls here, looking for guys who'd left their doors open. Howard Hughes and Bea Lillie and James Dean all hid out at the Chateau at one time or another, in varying states of emotional disrepair.

What's more, when Garbo was in residence, she always floated facedown in the pool, they claim, to keep from being recognized. ("Look, there's a corpse in the pool!" "That's no corpse, silly, that's You-know-who!") The very canvas awning above my head was the one that broke Pearl Bailey's fall—well, caught her, actually—when she toppled from the ledge of her balcony after a festive lunch. She was feeling no pain, according to the book, and was in no particular hurry to leave when a hook-and-ladder came to her rescue.

As you must've guessed, Jeff and Callum are an item now. Having spent the better part of last week shacked up in this suite, they finally surfaced and invited me over for a morning of sun by the pool. Jeff is trying his damnedest not to look dramatically altered, but any fool can see he's dorky with happiness. Callum, on the other hand, appears pretty much the way he did at our first meeting: just as sunny and steady and obliging, just as unreadable. Even in the midst of laughter he seems to be holding something back, as if observing himself—and everyone else—from a safe distance.

Callum did lose Jeff's phone number. Or says he did, anyway. I guess it's possible he never intended to call Jeff back and was merely shamed into a second date by the fact that they had me in common, but I seriously doubt it. Not the way they're acting now. Earlier, down by the pool, I caught them swapping a look of such pie-eyed lovey-doveyness that I find it hard to believe anyone was pressured into anything.

Not that we've discussed such matters—*or* the question of those girlfriends back home. I'm assuming that was Callum's way of getting me off his case. We've mostly just talked about *Mr. Woods* and my video and Callum's new movie, which is a big-budget thriller that has no connection whatsoever with Philip Blenheim. Callum plays a rookie cop whose little brother is kidnapped by a psychopath. I hinted around coyly about any "small roles" that might be available, envisioning myself as a crime lab researcher, say, or an observant street person who provides the missing clue, but Callum just smiled sweetly and said the script was already set. They'll be shooting in two weeks at Icon. Marcia Yorke is the other lead, playing Callum's girlfriend. He told me the name of the director, but I can't remember it.

I must admit it's a novel sensation to see Jeff paired off with someone younger than himself. Ned Lockwood, after all, had a couple of decades on Jeff, so I guess I've come to think of the younger man's role as Jeff's natural, perennial state. Ned was a nurseryman, for the record, a big, hulking sweetheart of a guy whose bald head stayed nut brown throughout the year. He was a lot less serious than Jeff, a real joker sometimes, and I was just crazy about him. He was somewhat of a legend in his youth, Jeff tells me: a generous soul generously endowed. Ned was Rock Hudson's lover for a brief period during the *Pillow Talk* era, when Hudson, in his mid-thirties, was clearly the older man.

Ned was no fading twinkie, though, when I knew him; he wore his age with an easy, shambling grace that was completely out of sync with the desperate pretenses of most people in this town. He and Jeff never lived together—Ned had a tiny cubbyhole next to his nursery in Los Feliz—but they borrowed each other's lives with the offhanded efficiency of brothers who could wear the same clothes.

Maybe there's a pattern here, after all, some unwritten law of gay genealogy that compelled Jeff to pass the torch to a younger man, just as his lover had done, and his lover's lover before that. Whatever the reason, I'm glad he finally got laid. Jeff suffered for a long time after Ned died and deserves to be happy again. I'm not at all sure this is true love, but it's a start, at least. I was beginning to think it wasn't possible, that Jeff would bury himself so completely in the navel-gazing of his writing that he'd lose the knack for intimacy with another person.

After lunch. The guys have come and gone again. They invited me to join them on a drive, but I decided to stay here with my journal, basking in my solitude and the delicious oddness of this place. Just before they took off, Callum realized he'd left his sunglasses by the pool and raced down to retrieve them, giving me and Jeff the moment I'd been waiting for.

"I'm so fucking proud of myself," I said.

"Yeah … well …" He gave me an embarrassed smirk.

"You look good together. I knew you would."

He stood at the mirror and ran a comb through his remaining strands of hair. There was something so tentative and teenagery about this gesture that I couldn't help but be moved.

"So what's the deal?" I asked.

"What do you mean?"

"With Callum. He knows I know, doesn't he?"

"Know what?"

"That he's a homo, Jeff."

He looked vaguely annoyed. "Of course."

"He doesn't act like it."

"Well …"

"He knows I'm cool, doesn't he?"

"Sure."

"Well, tell him to lighten up. Tell him I'm the biggest fag hag this side of Susan Sarandon."

"Tell him yourself."

"Well, I would, but ... he seems like he'd take that as an invasion or something."

"You think so?"

"Yeah. I do."

"I hadn't really noticed it."

"You hadn't?"

"He's just young," he said, laying down the comb.

If I'm not mistaken, it was I who first suggested this to Jeff, and not that long ago, either. That he'd loosened his moral requirements for a bed partner so drastically in such a short time could only mean one thing: Jeff's poor little overworked politics had been no match at all for a great piece of ass. I gave him a long, hard look with a Mona Lisa smile.

"What is it?" he asked.

"I just figured something out."

"What?"

"Why you weren't wearing your nipple ring at the pool."

"What?" He frowned and looked away, picking up the comb again.

"He asked you to take it off, didn't he? It was too gay for him."

"Oh, yeah, right."

"This is getting serious."

"Cadence ..."

"Is this a permanent arrangement, or did you put it back on?"

"In the first place, nipple rings aren't just a gay thing anymore."

"Oh, yeah?"

"Yeah. Axl Rose has one, and he's a homophobic pig."

"Oh, well, in that case ..."

"In the second place ..."

He didn't get to finish the thought, because Callum came bursting through the door, looking sleek and cryptic behind his shades. Seeing Jeff turn scarlet on the spot, I showed mercy and shooed them both out the door without further ado. I knew too much about what was driving Jeff to rag him any further.

Like I've always said, love wouldn't be blind if the braille weren't so damned much fun.

11

I HAVEN'T WRITTEN FOR WEEKS. I'VE BEEN STRICKEN WITH WHAT
Mom used to call "the mauves"—something vaguer than the blues
but just as debilitating. If I knew what the problem was, I could fix
it, or at least bitch about it, but I can't nail down my emotions long
enough to give them names. I feel empty and adrift, I guess, devoid
of purpose. The simplest rituals of existence, like shaving my legs
or replacing the trash can liner, leave me racked with the futility of
it all. I long for serendipity, but there is simply none to be had. And
that hateful, familiar voice in the back of my head reminds me that
I've probably already done all I was meant to do—and ten years
ago, at that. I am a husk of a person, nothing more, a burned-out
organism tumbling toward oblivion.

When I get like this, Renee turns hideously chirpy, trying to
snap me out of it. It never works, but I usually end up faking at
least a partial recovery, just to get her off my case. Last night, in an
effort to cheer, she made my favorite meal (pot roast) and regaled
me with half a dozen Jeffrey Dahmer jokes she'd heard at work. I
groaned and laughed as much as I could, pretended to be my old
self again, and went to bed early, crying myself to sleep. I had
another long, vivid dream about Mom.

In this one we were attending a sort of premiere party for my new video. Renee was there too, and Neil and Jeff and Tread and Philip Blenheim and even Aunt Edie, fresh off the bus from Baker. Mom had her hair in the sort of beehive she stopped wearing about the time I was born. She looked really modern like that—so out she was in—and I told her so, which thrilled her no end. The video was on an endless loop projected onto a huge cube above the buffet table. Philip Blenheim was impressed by my voice and how thin I looked. When I introduced him to Aunt Edie, she got way too gushy about *Mr. Woods,* but Philip took it all in stride and winked at me secretly, one professional to another. He offered me a role in his next film, but I played hard to get and said something vague about an obligation to Marty Scorsese.

Then the scene shifted abruptly, and Mom and I were on a bluff above the Pacific. It was sunset, and Mom's skin was all golden and smooth, like a nymph in a Maxfield Parrish painting. She sat next to me, brushing my hair and singing softly. When I told her I thought she was dead, she laughed and said she'd just been in Palm Springs, developing a miniseries about Lya Graf—a real person I'll tell you about later. Mom said an executive at Fox, somebody just under Barry Diller and extremely excited about the project, thought I'd be perfect for the role. I squealed and hugged her and felt a warming rush of relief. I thought she'd left me for good, and here she was, lovelier than ever and so real I could smell her Jean Naté, making big plans for our future as if she'd never been away.

On with the shitty news: Janet Glidden called this morning to say she'd been having "problems in the lab" and that we might have to reshoot the video. I hit the ceiling and called her a "total incompetent" who didn't deserve to be working with "real professionals." Even as I said it, this sounded pompous, so I called her back a few minutes later and apologized. She was so shaken that my raging disappointment was instantly replaced by raging guilt. The project is a goner, obviously; I might as well face that now and be done with it. To spend another day lip-syncing in that stuffy greenhouse would only prolong the agony. I bowed out as nicely as I could, but Janet didn't take it very well. Too bad. The way I see it, if she has to start over again, she might as well start with somebody else.

I called Neil to fill him in, figuring Janet would probably call to cry on his shoulder. He was more than sympathetic and even tried to take responsibility for the whole mess. I can't believe how nice he is.

We've had no gigs for a week and won't for another two or three. Neil says not to worry about it, that things usually slow down in the fall. He seemed to be enjoying the break, actually. His kid was there for the weekend, and I could hear him romping and giggling in the background.

Aunt Edie called a little while ago, but I didn't pick up. How the woman does it I'll never know. The moment my life begins to fall apart, she homes in on me like a buzzard circling dead meat. She left a message on the machine about running into Lanny March at a gas station in Baker. Lanny March was a boy I hung out with in high school and haven't seen since. We played Clue together after school and went to the occasional movie, so Aunt Edie regards him as a vaguely romantic figure in my life, which he wasn't at all. He was probably a big homo, come to think of it, given his sweetly bemused demeanor and his enduring passion for Bernadette Peters. Aunt Edie only mentioned him to remind me that everyone who *really* cares about me still lives in Baker.

Aunt Edie is Mom's slightly younger sister, though you'd never believe those two came from the same womb. Aunt Edie is so uptight she makes Marilyn Quayle look like the Whore of Babylon. Mom could be prissy, sure, but she had a streak of real wildness too, a latent individualism that redeemed her at the most unexpected moments. She grew up in the desert, after all, in the only Jewish family for miles around. Circumstances alone must have forced her to make up some of the rules as she went along.

Given the same baggage, Aunt Edie went totally bourgeois, joining forces with Betty Crocker and Barry Goldwater to build a life her neighbors could understand. She married a restaurant manager and had three large-economy-sized children, who grew up torturing cats and puking at the Burger King and regarding Baker as the center of the civilized world. When I came into the picture—and my father, in turn, went out—Aunt Edie made such a prolonged display of sympathy that Mom broke with her completely, resolving to cope with the future on her own. She rented a new duplex on the other side of town, dyed her hair honey blond, and worked overtime at the power company to buy me my own set of encyclopedias. (I was reading voraciously by the time I was four.) To hear Mom tell it, Aunt Edie actually envied her sister's newfound freedom, but she never copped to it, ever. Not even when Mom and I moved to Hollywood and began sending home pictures of the celebrities we'd met.

Mom used to insist that Aunt Edie wasn't a wicked person, just a frightened one. So frightened, apparently, that whenever she visited her gynecologist, she took a special bag with her to wear on her head during cervical examinations. The theory, according to Mom, was that Aunt Edie's dignity wouldn't be compromised if she didn't actually *see* the doctor while he was looking up her pussy. Mom swore to the absolute truth of this and permitted herself a brief disloyal giggle before swearing me to secrecy. "I mean it now, Cady. Edie would be mortified if she knew that you knew."

Ever since then I haven't been able to look at Aunt Edie without thinking of that damn bag. I don't know whether it was paper or what, so I make up my own versions. Sometimes I see it as a pointy quilted thing with nose holes—a head cozy, if you will—or made of creamy linen and elaborately monogrammed, like her favorite handbag. Even at Mom's funeral, when Aunt Edie came decked out in the world's soberest navy-blue suit, I flashed on her in the stirrups again, her head shrouded in a matching navy bag, those skinny Nancy Reagan legs propped open like pruning shears. The image simply refuses to die. It was Mom's final revenge on her sibling.

Actually, *I'm* the final revenge. When Mom phoned Aunt Edie to report that I'd landed the lead—sort of—in Philip Blenheim's new fantasy film, it was the sweetest of victories, the ultimate payback for twenty years of simpering, uninvited pity. Mom never actually voiced her resentment, but her real message to her sister was there in the subtext of my success: *See what you can do when you refuse to be frightened.*

I hope I'm not making Mom sound like some sort of pushy stage mother, because she wasn't. The dreams of stardom were all mine; Mom simply adapted to them. She was baffled and often repelled by much of what I love about show business, but she knew what I wanted more than anyone on earth, and she did more than anyone to see that I got it.

I read a book once that said that the bond between a little person and her (or his) mother is one of the most inviolable in nature. Since the child remains child-sized for life, the weaning process is sometimes postponed and dependencies can develop that persist until death. When Mom was still alive, I worried about this a lot, terrified of becoming her permanent baby.

Now that she's gone, I just miss her.

Before I forget: Lya Graf.

Mom learned about her years ago, when she first started reading up on little people. Lya Graf was a Ringling Brothers performer in the late twenties and early thirties—a figure of great charm, from all reports, and only twenty-one inches tall. ("Almost a foot shorter than you," Mom would remind me tartly, just to keep me from getting too swell-headed.) One day on a promotional tour, Lya visited the floor of the Senate in Washington. As luck would have it, J. P. Morgan was there at the same time, about to testify before the Senate Banking Committee. A canny photographer, recognizing a great photo op, deposited the dainty Lya on the not-so-dainty lap of the famous financier, and the resulting shot made front pages around the world.

Because of that, Lya became a bigger star than ever. She continued to tour with the circus, finally earning enough money to fulfill her dream of returning home with her parents to their native Germany. Alas, Hitler was in power by then, and the unique imperfection that had won Lya the hearts of children everywhere didn't play as well in the Third Reich. Both she and her parents were consigned to the death camp at Auschwitz—and eventually to the gas chambers—in the interest of a more perfect race.

Mom fixated on this story as if it were personal lore, rattling it off with gusto to anyone who'd listen. For years I wondered if it contained an object lesson for me, a subliminal warning that might somehow spare me from Lya's fate. What was the moral, anyway? Don't sit on a rich man's lap? Never try to live with your parents? I was almost a teenager before I realized that the story was merely Mom's way of linking littleness and Jewishness, of relating her own early experience of outsiderdom to the one I had suffered. Lya Graf was *us,* rolled into a neat little fable about the supreme unfairness of the world.

12

THIS STRANGELY OFF-KILTER DAY STARTED WITH A WEIRD PHONE call from Neil. My first thought was that he'd finally drummed up a gig for us, but that bubble burst as soon as I noticed the peculiar note in his voice. He seemed cowed somehow, unnaturally subdued. After the briefest of preliminaries, he asked if he could come over. When I told him of course he could, he said he just wanted to make sure I was there.

"As opposed to what?" I said. "Skiing in Gstaad?"

He gave me the lamest little laugh, clearly in great discomfort.

"What's up?"

"I think it should wait," he said, "until I'm there."

As soon as I hung up I began manufacturing calamities. Leading the list was the notion that I was no longer of use to PortaParty, that an old and valued customer, repelled by my presence, or maybe just my singing, had specifically requested that I not be in attendance at her little Ahmet's, her little Blake's, her little Zoe's birthday party. Neil's uncomfortable task, as I imagined it, was to break this news to me as gently as possible, hence the need to talk to me in person.

If the ax was to fall, I decided, I would handle it like Mary,

Queen of Scots—looking my best. I shucked off my stretched-out mauve-period T-shirt and climbed into a deep-green sailor suit that brings out my eyes. My hair was beyond redemption, but I slapped on a quick coat of powder and lipstick, then arranged myself artfully on the living room sofa, a back issue of *Premiere* next to me, opened to an article about Jodie Foster. When Neil arrived, he knocked quietly once or twice, then poked his head through the doorway.

"Cady?"

"I'm here. C'mon in."

He slouched into the house wearing khaki trousers and a Hawaiian shirt, looking just as hangdog as he had sounded on the phone. Everything about him said supplicant. If he'd been wearing a hat, he'd have held it in both hands.

I gestured to the armchair. "Take a load off."

He lowered his rangy frame onto the worn velveteen. His eyes made a brief, anxious flight around the room before settling on me again. "Nice dress," he said.

"This ol' thing?"

He smiled feebly and asked if Renee was here.

"At work," I told him.

"Oh."

"Some people keep regular hours, you know." This remark was meant to be chummy, a breezy acknowledgment of our common gypsy bonds, but it was much too close to the subject of employment. I regretted it instantly.

Neil nodded distractedly and let it go. "Sorry I was so vague on the phone."

"Hey." I shrugged, unable to manage another word. Looking back on it, I think my breathing had stopped completely.

"It's about Janet Glidden," Neil said at last, fixing his eyes on the rug.

"What about her?"

He swallowed hard. "She's dead. She shot herself last week."

I can't tell you what a surge of relief I felt. Well, I *am* telling you, but I certainly couldn't tell Neil, or let it show on my face, since he was looking as if he'd just brought word of something truly heartbreaking. What I ended up saying was "Oh, no," or words to that effect, while I brought my hand to my cheek and left it there for a beat or two.

Neil nodded. "Linda called this morning."

"I'm sorry...?"

"My ex-wife. Janet's old friend."

"Oh, yeah."

"She didn't know the details." He scuffed the arm of the chair with the flat of his hand, filling dead air. "I wanted to tell you in person, to make sure you didn't feel ... you know, responsible."

I nodded slowly, letting that sink in.

"Linda said she'd been depressed for weeks. Janet, I mean. So anything you might've said to her on the phone wouldn't really have made that much ... Well, you could tell how fucked up she was that day at the greenhouse."

"Yeah," I said. "I guess so." I suppose I was rattled by then, but more than anything, I was touched by Neil's instinct to protect me, to spare me the guilt. Was guilt warranted? I wondered. Had my little diatribe about Janet's "incompetence" come at entirely the wrong time? What if she had told someone about the tantrum? Or left a note. Christ, a note. *Goodbye, cruel world. The dwarf made me do it.* "Does Linda know that Janet and I ... had words?"

Neil shook his head. "She didn't mention it, anyway."

"Did she call you?"

"Linda?"

"No, Janet. After I cussed her out. I thought she might."

Neil said she hadn't called.

"I called her back, you know. I tried to be really nice about it."

"I know. I remember. I really don't think it had anything to do with ..."

"What was she depressed about? Did Linda say?"

"No. Just ... general stuff."

"General stuff." I echoed him flatly, beginning to be annoyed by his vagueness.

"Janet had a few wheels in the sand, Cady. She always did."

I asked him if he'd known this when he'd fixed me up with her.

"Well ..." He picked his words carefully. "I knew she was neurotic. Lots of creative people are. It comes with the territory."

"Yeah," I said numbly. "I suppose."

"I'm really sorry, Cady. If it hadn't been for me ..."

"Oh, c'mon now." I wanted to be magnanimous, to brush it off as nothing, but my mind kept lurching back to the scene of the carnage, sifting through the wreckage for clues, the black box of Janet's personality. "She didn't leave a note?"

"Apparently not."

"What day did she do it?"

Neil chewed on that for a moment. "Tuesday, I think."

The day after, I thought. "Where?"

"At home. Her place in Brentwood."

I had already pictured her at the greenhouse, the setting of her final failure, that pale, angular body sprawled across the stage like a broken marionette, the lighting next to perfect. What if she *hadn't* been in dwarf panic that day? What if she had just been in panic, pursued by some entirely personal demon? ... And what if she had managed to keep that monster at bay until yours truly stepped in to destroy her defenses with a few lethal words?

You're a total incompetent, Janet. You don't deserve to work with real professionals.

Neil must have noticed the stricken look on my face, because he left the chair and sat on the floor next to the sofa, taking my hand in his. "Look, Cady. There are lots of people thinking the same thing right now. There's no way you can take the blame for this. You hardly even knew her."

"I suppose."

A moment of weighty silence passed, broken only by the piglet squeals of the Stoate kids, running amuck in their backyard. Neil gazed up at me with a sleepy, ironic smile. "There's more."

"Oh, shit. *What?*"

"It's not bad. It's sort of nice, actually. They've invited us to the funeral."

I couldn't have been more stunned. *Who?*

"Janet's parents."

"They didn't."

He nodded. "They specifically requested you."

"They don't even know me."

"They knew about the video, I guess."

"Did they know I *walked out* on the video?"

"Doesn't sound like it. Linda just said they were trying to reach some of Janet's film friends. They want the funeral to, you know, reflect her life."

Yeah, I thought, but what if Janet had told her mother about the Incident? And what if her mother had invited me to the service just to lure me into an ugly confrontation? I could already see her weeping hysterically, flinging her pale, gawky, Janet-like body across her daughter's coffin as she thrust an accusing finger (long and white, like Janet's) at the wicked actress in the front row.

"I don't know," I said.

"I think it would mean something if you were there," Neil countered. "They think of you as Somebody."

"Who does?"

"Janet's parents."

"C'mon."

Neil shrugged. "They know about *Mr. Woods,* at least. Linda said they did."

"Oh, swell. Do they expect me to wear the suit?"

Neil smiled benignly, refusing to buy into my cynicism. "It's next Saturday," he said. "I thought we could make a day of it. I've never seen Catalina myself." He was almost coy about the way he dropped the locale, a frisky light dancing in his eyes while he waited for it to register on me.

"Catalina? The island?"

He nodded.

"They're having the *funeral* there?"

"That's where they live," he explained, enjoying himself immensely. "In Avalon. Janet grew up there."

"Nobody grows up there."

"Janet did." He widened his eyes at me teasingly. "Ever been there?"

I had to admit I hadn't. I know the place mostly from a couple of old songs and that line of swimsuits. The island is largely wilderness, I've heard, and Avalon is a toy town, a tourist mecca that enjoyed a boom in the twenties and thirties and hasn't been the same since. They still have glass-bottom boats and salt-water taffy and that huge circular ballroom, the one so often depicted on sheet music, presiding over the harbor. As one of the songs goes, it's just "twenty-six miles across the sea," but no one I know has ever set foot there.

Neil was waiting for my answer. "So what do you say?"

"God, Neil. I just don't know."

"It would help me a lot if you came."

"Why?"

"Aside from the pleasure of your company?"

"Yeah. Aside from that."

"Well … Linda's gonna be there."

"Oh."

"I don't wanna get stuck with her all day. On an island."

"What a thing to say about somebody you married."

"Yeah … well … what can I tell you?"

"How fierce is she, anyway?"

"Not too."

I gave him a dubious look.

He laughed. "Not at all. It would just help to have someone there."

"A buffer."

"No, a friend."

"A friendly buffer. Is it a day trip?"

"It can be."

"A boat or something?"

"Or a plane," he said, "if you want."

I told him I preferred the boat.

I'm writing this in bed. Renee is out at the movies (*Bill and Ted's Bogus Journey*) with her friend Lorrie from The Fabric Barn. I feel truly shitty, but it's nice to have the house to myself, to be able to play my Nino Rota albums without provoking one of Renee's oh-poo-not-again expressions. There's a nondescript little breeze stirring my curtains, and the moon has just popped into view, red as a pumpkin. A scoop or two of rum raisin ice cream would lift my spirits considerably, but I'm just too tired—or too drained, maybe—to make the trek into the kitchen and haul out the ladder to the freezer.

Jeff called about an hour ago. We had the longest talk we've had in ages. They've started shooting Callum's film, and it's a closed set, so I think Jeff is on his own these days, except for a few stolen late-nighters at the Chateau Marmont. He seems as smitten as ever with Callum, but he's surprisingly ungenerous with the particulars. I guess he's superstitious about blowing a good thing. So to speak.

When he asked about my own schedule, I told him that so far I'd only been booked for a funeral.

"Oh, yeah?" he said blandly. "Anybody I know?"

I explained to him briefly about Janet, identifying her simply as "the woman who was doing my video." He said almost nothing in response, and I wondered if her death came across as self-indulgent (if such a thing can be said about suicide) in the harsh light of his own experience. Most of the people Jeff knows are just trying to stay alive.

"So what happens now?" he asked.

"About what?"

"The video."

"Oh, it was pretty much of a disaster already."

No, I didn't tell him about my tantrum. Don't ask me why. Maybe I *am* feeling guilty.

"Too bad," he said. "Sounded like a good idea."

"Well ... ya lose some, ya lose some."

Jeff laughed ruefully. "That's the fucking truth."

"Are you writing?"

"Some."

"That means none, right?" That settled it: he had to be in love. He only writes when he's in pain.

"Cadence ..."

"*I'm* writing."

"Good for you."

"I've got a snazzy new journal and everything."

"So what are you writing about?" He made a real effort to sound pleasant about it, but I could tell he found it impertinent that a rank amateur was frolicking so carelessly in his chosen field.

I did my best to reassure him. "Just ... stuff that happens. Nothing really important."

"Mmm. Well, it's always good therapy."

"It is," I said.

"And how's your love life?"

"Well ... the batteries are running low, but ..."

He snorted. "C'mon. You know what I mean. The guy you work with. The African-American."

I tried not to let him get to me. "He's not my love life, Jeff. He never has been."

"Well ..."

"He's not an African-American, either."

"I thought you said ..."

"I did, and he is. But he would never use that term. He'd sound too much like a white liberal."

That zapped him nicely. He retaliated with a long, aggrieved silence.

I didn't want to start a fight, so I added playfully: "You don't even use it yourself. What were you doing? Trying it out? Seeing how it tripped off your tongue?"

He informed me, icily, that he'd used the term for weeks.

Yeah, I thought. Ever since you read that interview with Spike Lee in which "Afro-American" was declared unacceptable. I kept my mouth shut, though. Even in jest, I know not to dick with him when it comes to matters PC.

"I didn't know he was a sore subject," Jeff said.

"He's not. He's just not what you think."

"OK, then."

"He's a good friend."

"Glad to hear it."

I had half intended to tell him about Janet's funeral being in Catalina—and the trip with Neil and all—but I knew Jeff would just turn it into something it wasn't. I gave myself a break and avoided the subject completely, rattling on about work and the lousy business we've been doing lately.

"Well," Jeff remarked darkly, "we are in a recession."

"You think they feel it in Beverly Hills?" I wasn't being bitter; I really wanted to know. It would be way too easy to blame this career slump on the crappy economy. If my battered little star is finally sinking in the west, I prefer to face the facts and be done with it.

Jeff replied that even rich pigs have to tighten their belts sometimes and that "cutesy birthday parties" would probably be the first thing to go.

"Cutesy?" I protested.

He chuckled. "You know what I mean."

"Yes, I believe I do."

"C'mon, Cadence. Don't pull that shit. You know you're better than that job."

"It's my *career,* Jeff. It's what I do."

He just scoffed at that. "It's not your career."

"Then what the fuck *is?*"

"Cadence…?"

"What is, Jeff? I'd really like to know. I'm not a real singer. I'm certainly not an actress. After a while you have to look at a few realities, don't you?" I have no idea where this came from, but it came with a holy vengeance, boiling out of me like toxic waste. "That cutesy little job of mine, as you call it, is what I do. It's all they'll *let* me do. I'd like to be flip about it, but I have to be proud of something, don't I?"

Poor Jeff was struck dumb for a moment. Finally, he said: "Who is they?"

"What?"

"They. You said it's all *they* will let you do."

I saw what he was getting at immediately and wanted no part of it. "They, Jeff. *Them.* The fuckheads who run the universe."

"Ah."

"And don't give me that shit about how there aren't any thems, because that's *all* there is in my life, and that's all there ever will be. I've got thems out the asshole."

"Nicely put."

"Fuck you. You know what I mean."

After a long silence, he stepped in gingerly: "Would this by any chance be …?"

"No, it wouldn't. I had it a week ago. This is pure unadulterated me."

In recent years Jeff has developed the nasty habit of attributing everything to my all-powerful menstrual cycle: mood swings, earthquakes, Amtrak derailments …

"Want me to come over?" he asked.

"What for?"

"I dunno. To slap you silly?"

I was glad he couldn't see me smile. "Just be thankful you didn't call last week."

"I am," he said, "believe me."

"I could be cracking up, I guess."

"Yeah, sure."

"I'd like to be. I'd like *something* to happen."

"Then something will."

"No it won't. Never again. I'm spinning my wheels, Jeff. Not even that; I'm *parked*. I'm parked in fucking Studio City and the lot is closed and nobody even comes around to kick my wheels any-more."

"Write that down," he said.

"Write it down yourself."

"What about Leonard?" Jeff suggested. "He might have some ideas. Callum talks to him all the time."

"Yeah, well, Callum is cute and has a pretty dick."

"Cadence ..."

"I only go by what you tell me."

He let it slide. "Do you need money? Is that it? Because I could ..."

"No. Well, I always do, but ..."

"Are you sure?"

"Yeah, Jeff. Thanks." He'd embarrassed me now, turning so unexpectedly sweet and sacrificial in response to my cattiness. There's no way he could lend me money. As far as I know, he makes even less than I do. "I'm all right," I told him. "It isn't a loan I need, it's a life."

A *longer* life was what I should have said, but I was afraid of the feelings I'd unleash and Jeff's proven inability to cope with them. Janet's death, if nothing else, has made me more painfully aware of my own mortality, which is only natural for a little person—or so Mom used to tell me—even on a good day. When you're a walking bag of organs like *moi,* you just can't help wondering how much time you've got left.

Suddenly, in spite of myself, I wanted Ned there instead of his surviving partner—big old easy uncomplicated Ned—because Ned would have understood these emotions without having them explained to him. In the last months of his life we spent hours together, playing cards and putzing in his garden and enjoying the unspoken irony that fate had made us equals of a sort. Ned and I treasured each other's company all the more, I think, because we both knew what it felt like to be living on a deadline.

13

So far, I haven't told anyone what happened on Catalina. It's not that I'm embarrassed; I just don't know *what* to think at the moment, and I'm wary about entrusting such fragile, half-formed impressions to other interpretations—especially Renee's and Jeff's—before committing them to paper. With any luck at all, there should be enough room in this journal (the one Neil gave me, appropriately enough) to tell the whole story. If not, I'll switch to something different.

The boat we took left from Long Beach, so we drove down late Saturday morning in the PortaParty van. The van was a sad sight, conspicuously unwashed and stripped of its usual jolly stock of props and streamers. It had all the poignancy of an empty stage. A cardboard box crammed with plastic beach toys rattled against the back door, but that was the extent of our cargo. I shuddered a little at this visual proof of the troupe's decline, but didn't remark on it to Neil, scared of what he might say.

"Are those Danny's?" I asked, indicating the toys.

Neil smiled out at the white blur of the freeway. "We drove down to Zuma last week."

I remarked that it was nice there.

He seemed a little surprised. "You like hanging out at the beach?"

"Sure."

"Same here." He grinned extravagantly, as if we'd just discovered something rare and wonderful in common.

"Where is he, by the way?"

"Who?"

"Danny."

"Oh. Staying with the neighbors. Linda's neighbors."

I told him I'd hoped I might meet Danny today, that I'd wondered if either he, Neil, or Linda might bring the boy along for the day. It seemed like a great trip for a kid, after all, in spite of the circumstances.

"Yeah," said Neil. "We talked about that."

"But?"

He shrugged. "We just weren't sure how heavy it might get. The funeral, I mean."

Great, I thought, and suddenly I was picturing Mrs. Glidden again, only this time she had me by the throat of my charcoal crepe de chine funeral frock and was shaking the bejeezus out of me. *Do you know what that video meant to my daughter? Do you? Do you have any idea?*

"Of course I'd like him to see the island, but ..."

"What? Sorry." I'd lost track completely of what he was saying.

"Danny likes it at the neighbor's," he explained. "They've got a pool with a water slide."

"Oh ... well ... that's good."

"Yeah. Gets him outa my hair."

You could tell he didn't mean that at all. It was just a man thing, mostly, a false gruffness designed to underplay his obvious devotion to his son. This embarrassment surprised me a little, since I've seen him be so unembarrassed around hundreds of children. I guess it's different when it's your own kid. "Is Linda taking the same boat?" I asked.

He shook his head. "She flew into Avalon this morning. She thought the Gliddens might need some help."

I pondered that one for a moment or two, discarding several possibilities, all of them ghoulish. "Help with *what?*"

Neil smiled at me languidly. "I think there's a brunch after the service."

"Oh." A funeral brunch, I thought. Only in California. As we barreled on down the freeway, bound for God knows what, the event grew more and more surreal in my head.

The dock for the *Catalina Express* was immediately adjacent to the *Queen Mary,* the classic thirties ocean liner, now dawdling away her declining years as a stationary hotel and all-round tourist trap. We had two hours to kill before our boat left, so we did the obvious, foolish thing and paid to go on board. The tickets were hideously expensive (Neil put it on his Visa card), and the approach to the gangplank alone nearly did me in. It seemed to wind along for miles, a grueling serpentine, routing us first through Ye Olde Phony English Village, then past a huge circular hangar containing Howard Hughes's preposterous wooden airplane, the "Spruce Goose." By the time I finally set foot on board the *Queen Mary* I was panting like a sheep dog in a heat wave.

"Are you OK?" asked Neil.

I fell back against a wall—a bulkhead; whatever—and swatted my chest several times with my palm. Neil hunkered next to me and offered me a handkerchief. I took a few broad swipes at my dripping brow and handed it back to him.

A squadron of children, accompanied by a haggard middle-aged female, came to a dead halt next to us, enraptured by what they must have taken to be the first of the ship's exotic attractions. The adult—a teacher, I guessed—gaped at us just long enough to embarrass herself thoroughly, then salvaged what remained of her composure and bustled the children away. I took a deep breath. Then another. Then counted to ten slowly. My heart felt like a small, desperate bird trying to escape from my rib cage.

"Better," I said at last.

"You sure?"

I nodded.

"Can I get you some water or something?"

"No," I said. "Just shade. And a place to sit."

We retreated to one of the big lounges, a calmly elegant space, all curves and gilt and cool green frescoes. Neil hoisted me onto a sofa, then gave the ship's brochure a hurried once-over. "This was a big mistake, I guess."

I told him we had no way of knowing that without seeing for ourselves.

"Everything's so far away," he said. "Unless ..." He looked down at the brochure again.

"What?"

"They have something called The Haunted Passageway. It's kind of a ghost tour. Like a fun house."

"Kids in the dark? I don't think so."

He smiled. "Good point."

"What sort of ghosts?"

"Oh ... some deckhand who got crushed by an iron door. Back in the sixties. According to this, they still hear him thumping sometimes."

I rolled my eyes, though I couldn't help admiring the cold-blooded genius of the marketing strategy. The owners of this enterprise had obviously learned from experience that a pretty ship alone wouldn't cut it with the American public; true Family Entertainment demands at least a smattering of gore. But that "ghostly" deckhand had been a real person, after all, who was mangled during my lifetime, a guy who probably still has a family somewhere, people who loved him and miss him and remember the real horror. Does it give *them* the shivers, I wondered, to know that he's been reduced to a thrilling special effect, a scenic attraction in a spook house? Do they get royalties?

"We could split," said Neil, reading my mind.

"We could."

Without further ado, we made our way back to the neighboring dock. The afternoon had turned unseasonably hot, and a gritty industrial haze hung over the harbor. A long queue of tourists, laden with scuba gear and ice chests and plastic tote bags, had already gathered for the *Catalina Express.* A vein in my temple commenced to throb in smart syncopation with my dread. I was beginning to think I'd made a terrible mistake.

The voyage to the island took a little over an hour and a half. Mercifully, the smog lifted and the temperature dropped as soon as we were out of sight of land. The seats on the boat were airline style, really quite comfy, but the view they afforded was completely lost on me. Sensitive to this fact, Neil led me out to the slippery deck several times, where I clung for dear life to the bottom rung of the railing and made appreciative noises about the color of the water. A whey-faced lady in a sundress and Barbara Bush beads watched this awkward ritual with smug, philanthropic glee, as if I were some midwestern orphan with leukemia catching my first glimpse of the mighty Pacific. "She must enjoy that," she said to Neil, apparently perceiving me to be deaf as well. For Neil's sake, I restricted my response to a brief, murderous glare.

Our first glimpse of Avalon was amazing. The town was almost ramshackle, miraculously un*done,* The Land That Time Forgot. Simple wooden cottages as random as shipwrecks tumbled down the dry hills to a pristine crescent-shaped beach, at the end of which stood the great circular ballroom, as natural there as the dot on a question mark. There were dozens of sails on the harbor. And dipping gulls. And *chimes,* so help me, as if to welcome us, ringing from a distant hillside. Neil and I both wore expressions of wordless wonder. Blink once, I remember thinking, and the whole damned thing disappears.

Up close, of course, it was easier to detect the chinks in the fantasy. The eroding crag above the boat landing had been repaired with sprayed-on concrete, and there were far too many lard-assed tourists like me (well, almost like me) slouching along the promenade in search of diversion. Even worse, some of the more recent architecture (a sort of faux-Spanish postmodern) had lost touch with the charming artlessness of the rest of the town. Still, I liked the place a lot, and Neil did too. We felt unreasonably proud of ourselves, as if we were the first people ever to discover it.

We had an hour or so before the funeral, so we camped out on a waterfront bench and let the motley parade of humanity pass us by. The people who weren't on foot were in goofy little white golf carts, since cars are *verboten* on major portions of the island. I couldn't help grinning at the sight of these Toontown vehicles. Here was one place, at least, where life seemed a little closer to my own scale.

Neil pored over a street map he'd bought at the landing.

"How far are we from the church?" I asked.

"Not far."

"Let's see."

He pointed to it on the map.

"That's far," I said.

"Is it?"

I nodded. "Unless you've got time for two funerals."

He chuckled. "We'll rent a golf cart, then."

I made a face at him. "You can't go to a funeral in a golf cart."

"Who can't? That's what they do here."

So that's what we did. We procured a racy little number with a striped canopy at a rental agency right there on the main drag and tooled up a leafy street called Metropole in search of the church. The suspension on the cart wasn't for shit, but Neil had strapped me in snugly, so my squeals whenever we hit a bump were more of exhilaration than of terror. Neil would glance at me each time with a look of real concern until I succeeded in reassuring him with a smile. It was the strangest sensation, riding along like that. I felt utterly ridiculous and utterly contented, all at the same time.

The church was a plain white frame structure hung with scarlet bougainvillea. An assortment of golf carts was parked in front, most of them fancier than ours and missing the telltale rental number painted on the side. These were locals, obviously, friends of the family. As we made our way to the door, I wondered if Neil and I were the only mourners from the mainland. Besides the dreaded Linda, that is.

Our progress was observed by a tall, gray-haired man in a navy suit standing guard just inside the door. When we finally reached him, he gave us a dubious once-over and uttered Janet's name softly, as a question. Neil nodded, following the man into the church. I came after them at my own pace, trying to look devout—or at least concerned—and acutely aware of all the eyes on me. Neil lifted me onto a pew and handed me a printed program bearing Janet's name, the minister's name, and the high points of the service. That piece of paper and the less-than-fascinating grain of the pew in front of us was all that occupied me for the next half hour; I couldn't see for shit.

The service was your basic Protestant understatement, so devoid of specifics that the honoree might just as easily have died from natural causes at eighty. We sang a few tired hymns and received a few tired words of comfort from the reverend. At one point, about halfway through, Neil glanced at someone across the room, acknowledging her presence (I was sure it was Linda) with a thin smile. I couldn't help wondering if the deceased was there, too, but decided not to put the question to Neil. My voice has a way of carrying sometimes.

To avoid the rush, we left before the last hymn was finished, then waited outside on the lawn for Linda. When she emerged from the crowd she gave Neil a chaste peck on the cheek and, without waiting for an introduction, extended a long, dry hand down to me. "Hello, Cady. It was sweet of you to come."

"Hey," I said stupidly. "No problem."

The ex–Mrs. Riccarton was tall, lean, and oval-faced, several shades lighter than Neil. Not exactly pretty, but elegant, and enormously self-possessed. She wore a chic-looking gray silk suit, and her hair was pulled back in a modified Wilma Flintstone. Neil had never painted her as a monster, and she certainly didn't seem to be one. What was it he had said? Unsentimental? Too organized?

"Have you met the Gliddens yet?" she asked.

I told her I hadn't.

"I think they're …" She craned her graceful neck. "Yes … over there."

The Gliddens stood together on the sidewalk, receiving the consolation of friends, so identically pear-shaped and shaggy-headed that they might have been salt and pepper shakers. Both of their plain, open faces wore the same expression of wistful stoicism, and you could tell at a glance they were one of those couples who do everything together. I just knew they owned matching nylon windbreakers.

"Maybe we should wait," I said. "There's sort of a crowd."

Linda nodded, then looked at Neil. "I know a shortcut to the house, if you feel like a little walk."

Neil looked confused. "Isn't there going to be…?"

His ex finished the thought for him and shook her head. "The ashes are at the house."

Neil glanced to me for guidance. "How do you feel about a walk?"

"Fine," I said, sounding as casual about it as possible. I was determined not to look like a pussy in front of Linda.

So we followed those long, efficient legs through the dusty shrubbery to the Gliddens' house, about three backyards away. It was part of a row of houses, cottages really, each the same, yet each in some way different, facing another such row across a palm-lined walkway. They reminded me of the company houses that mill owners once built for their workers, only nicer, with tile-studded birdbaths and rose trellises and perfect little postage-stamp lawns. To my surprise, there was already a small group of people assembled in the Gliddens' backyard.

"Is this where Janet grew up?" I asked Linda, after Neil had gone off to get us punch.

"I believe so," she said. "She was third generation, Mary says."

"And Mary is…?"

"Her mother."

"Ah." I tried in vain to picture Janet here, she of the acrylic-look hair and artsy ways, living in this simple house with these simple salt-shaker people, this matched set that couldn't be broken. Maybe that had been the problem, come to think of it. Maybe Janet couldn't picture it, either. Even as a kid.

"Her grandfather worked down at Catalina Pottery," Linda continued. "He was one of Wrigley's original employees."

I had no idea who she meant.

"The chewing gum guy. The big millionaire from Chicago. He sort of invented Avalon. Half the people in town worked for him."

I nodded.

"Neil says he really likes working with you."

I was rattled for a moment by the abrupt change of subject. "Well," I said eventually, "I'm flattered."

"You should be. He doesn't make friends all that easily."

This was so out of left field that all I could say was: "Doesn't he?"

"No." She offered me a tiny, sisterly smile as if to say: it's the truth.

I was so flummoxed that I glanced around me in search of distraction, which came in the form of Neil himself, returning with two cups of punch. The stuff was lime green, with vanilla ice cream floating in it. I'd seen nothing like it since junior high school. "Festive," I deadpanned. Then I hoisted my cup in a silent salute to Neil, which he returned with a flicker of a smile. I just wanted us to be alone again. His ex had already struck me as the sort of woman who could say something incredibly mean in the name of just-us-girls intimacy.

"I met the Gliddens," Neil said. "They're nice."

"Aren't they?" said Linda.

"They're coming over, Cady. They really want to meet you."

"Well … good."

Even as we spoke, I could see them approaching. I could feel myself wobbling a little too, so I moved my legs apart slightly to gain a steadier stance. Moments later, the ever-attentive Linda spotted the Gliddens herself and moved in swiftly to take charge of things. "Mary, Walter ..."

The couple greeted her in unison.

"Such a sweet service," Linda said.

"Wasn't it? We were just saying that to Bud Larkin—the reverend." Mrs. Glidden was smiling graciously, but her eyes were swollen from crying. It was touching to see her make such a valiant effort to be social in the midst of her pain.

"I think you've met Neil," said Linda.

"Yes." Mary nodded. "And this must be ..."

"Cadence Roth." I held up my hand before Linda could usurp the introduction. I didn't want to risk how she might define me to the Gliddens.

"And what a pleasure this is," said Walter.

I thanked him.

"It certainly is," Mary put in.

Looping his arm through hers, Walter drew his wife closer. "You know, Mary here reviewed you."

Mary looked instantly embarrassed. "Oh, Walter, for Pete's sake!"

I had no idea what they were talking about, but my guilty heart was lodged firmly in my throat again.

Walter patted his wife's hand. "Don't be so modest, Mary. I'm entitled to brag about you."

Mary gave her husband an affectionately reproving look, then turned back to me. "I used to write a little column here. Just chitchat, really. For our local paper. I thought *Mr. Woods* was delightful, so ... I said so in the column."

"It was a rave review," Walter declared.

"It wasn't actually a *review* as such." Mary addressed me sheepishly, clearly embarrassed by her husband's hyperbole.

"Must have sold a few tickets, though."

This time Mary was firmer. "Walter, please. I don't think they needed my help. It was the top-grossing movie of all time."

I was beginning to like this lady a lot, so I sent her a faint, private smile, just for the two of us. "Second, I believe."

"Really? What was first?"

"Star Wars."

"Oh, well. I liked you *much* better."

I thanked her as earnestly as I knew how.

"Janet was just thrilled to be working with you."

"That's so nice."

"It's not nice," she insisted, "it's the truth."

"Well, it was mutual," I said, biting the bullet. "I thought your daughter was a supremely gifted artist."

The Gliddens were far more touched by this monumental lie than I'd expected them to be. Almost instantly, they tightened their grip on each other, like riders on a roller coaster bracing for another heart-stopping dip. Mary's lower lip began to quiver slightly, but she managed to retain her composure. Her husband staved off the tears by gazing woodenly at the ground. I didn't record Neil's response, or Linda's, for that matter, because I couldn't bring myself to look at them.

Walter was the one who finally spoke, his voice cracking pitifully. "We're ... awfully proud of her."

"You should be," I said.

An excruciating silence followed. I waited for Neil to fill the void, but he just left me there, the sorry bastard, flailing in the quicksand of my own hypocrisy.

Finally, Mary said: "We looked for that film, you know. We couldn't find it anywhere."

"What film?"

"Of you. Janet's film."

"Oh, really?" I squeaked.

"Isn't that odd? As much as she talked about it."

"It is."

She destroyed it, I told myself. *Burned the sonofabitch. Tossed it off a cliff. Right after I told her what a loser she was.*

"Did she give you a copy, by any chance?" Walter asked.

"Not really."

"What a shame," said Linda.

I shot a quick glance at her to see if she meant this maliciously, but I found her face utterly unreadable. Turning back to the Gliddens, I said: "It wasn't really finished, you know."

"Still," said Walter pleasantly, "you'd think there'd be something."

"You would." A clammy trickle of sweat had begun to work its way down the inside of my crepe de chine.

"What did you sing?" asked Mary.

"'If,'" I told her.

"I don't believe I know that."

Linda's face became animated for the first time that day. "The old David Gates song? You're kidding? Janet didn't tell me you were doing that."

I sincerely hoped that wasn't all Janet hadn't told her, like what a roaring bitch I'd been when I quit. I didn't particularly want Linda for a friend, but I didn't want her for an enemy, either.

"Why didn't you tell me she was doing that?" This time Linda was addressing her ex-husband, and he, in turn, was looking awkward beyond belief. I wondered suddenly if the song had once meant something to them. If, perish the thought, it had been *their* song. It was Neil, after all, who'd suggested that number, who'd included it in our repertoire in the first place. It gave me the willies to think that all this time I might have been acting out some sort of postmarital delusion for him.

Walter spoke up before the question could be resolved. "Say, I don't suppose you'd mind...?"

"Walter ..." This was Mary, admonishing her husband with a stern glance, having read his mind. "I'm sure Miss Roth didn't come prepared to sing today."

I was struck dumb for a moment.

"You're right," said Walter. "We wouldn't dream of asking you that."

"We certainly wouldn't."

Linda was giving me a plaintive, cow-eyed look that said: Think how much it would mean to them.

Neil was studying his shoes, no help at all.

"The thing is," I said, "I'm used to working with accompaniment."

"They've got a piano," Linda burbled. "Neil, you could play."

At this new development, Walter gazed hopefully at Mary, Neil gazed at me, and I gazed into another dimension, where I was just tall enough to reach out and throttle Linda's scrawny neck.

"It isn't as strange as you might think," Mary informed me, clearly beginning to warm to the idea. "We have a little program planned. Janet's grandmother is singing a few of her favorite hymns." She smiled at me sweetly. "Funerals are really for the living, aren't they?"

Lucky Janet, I thought, to be missing all this.

"Well," I said finally, "if you don't mind a few rough edges."

"Of course not!" The Gliddens spoke in unison, united in their joy.

Linda was positively ecstatic at the prospect of something new to organize. She offered her services to Walter and Mary on the spot, then engaged them in a brief discussion about folding chairs and placement of the piano. Charged with purpose, the three of them scuttled off toward the house, leaving me and Neil alone on the lawn.

"You're dead meat," I said.

Neil chuckled.

"I mean it."

"Well ... it's the least we can do."

"Oh, yeah?"

"For such a supremely gifted artist."

I gave him the evilest eye I could muster.

"I think you're wonderful," he said.

There must have been thirty people crammed into that tiny living room—including Janet, who now resided on the mantel, I was told, in a piece of vintage Catalina crockery. My opening act, as promised, was Janet's grandmother, who did a creditable job with those hymns of hers, despite a brief dental mishap. The audience rewarded her with polite applause and several dutiful pecks on the cheek.

Then Walter took the floor.

"And now it's a great honor for me to introduce a special guest, a person our Janet was working with when—uh—this year. Some of you know this young lady starred in *Mr. Woods,* the—uh—second, I believe, most popular movie of all time, *and* went on to star in Janet's most recent movie … film; excuse me." He displayed a tepid smile. "Janet preferred the term 'film.' *Anyway,* before I mess this up … Cadence Ross."

He made an ineffectual flourish toward the ancestral upright, where Neil and I were both seated—him on the stool; me, rather precariously, on top. Feeling oddly like a saloon girl, I explained to the audience that I had sung this song in Janet's brilliant but sadly unfinished film, that it had always been a personal favorite of mine, that I hoped it would mean something special to each and every one of them.

I was surprised by how well it worked. I was in decent voice— thanks to all that fresh air, no doubt—and Neil played with a tenderness that seemed perfectly tailored for the occasion. It was easily our best performance, far better than anything we'd ever done for that stupid video. Something just clicked that had never clicked before. And the music seemed uncannily appropriate. Especially the soaring part at the end that sounds like an ascent into heaven.

As that last wistful note lingered in the balmy air, I closed my eyes and let my head drop humbly to my chest. There was a moment of total silence before the audience could convert its rawedged emotion into thunderous and sustained applause. I basked in it at my leisure, soaking it up like sunshine after too many weeks of rain. When I finally opened my eyes again, Neil was beaming up at me, every bit as stunned as I was.

★ ★ ★

"We killed 'em" was the way he put it later, when we were down on the beach at an open-air café.

"Fuckin' A," I said. "Miss Ross can sing." I'd had a few margaritas by then.

"We should do funerals more often."

"We should do *something* more often."

"Hey."

"Oh, c'mon. We're washed up, Neil. Aren't we?"

To my horror, he didn't even bother to deny it. He just shrugged and twitched a little and shook the ice in his glass.

"That's what I thought."

"Things could change," he said. "The whole economy's lousy."

"Yeah, right. Want another one?"

He looked down at his empty glass. "Well …"

"Waitron!" I made an elaborate semaphore signal across the deck at the girl who'd been serving us, then turned back to Neil. "I owe you at least a round or two."

"What for?"

"The journal, remember?"

"That was a present."

"You said I could buy you a drink sometime."

He smiled. "That was a figure of speech."

"Well, I, for one, plan to get shitfaced." I polished off the tangy remains of my margarita and plonked the glass down. "That's another figure of speech."

He chuckled, studying me for a moment, then looked up as the waitress arrived.

"The gentleman would like another gin and tonic," I informed her grandly. "And I'll have my usual."

"Coming right up," said the waitress.

"I think that should be my last," Neil said after she'd gone.

"Why?"

"I have to drive, remember?"

I snorted. "You couldn't kill anybody with that dinky thing if you tried."

"Just the same."

"You wanna hear my theory?"

"About what?"

"Us," I said. "The business."

"OK." He wove those long mahogany fingers through each other and laid them on the table in front of me.

I could never have said it without the booze, but I did say it: "I think the problem is me."

"Oh, shit."

"No, hear me out …"

"Look, Cady, we did a record number of gigs after you came on with us."

I told him I was aware of that.

"Then, why would …?"

"Just listen, OK?"

"I'm listening."

"I think the clients liked me at first because … it was a novelty, and everybody wanted to see what it was like. But the novelty has worn off now, and they're just left with sort of, you know, a creepy aftertaste."

"For Christ's sake."

He looked so annoyed that I winced a little. "It's just a theory," I said.

"Were you *conscious* back there?"

"Back where?"

"The Gliddens' house. Those people adored you, Cady. You let them look into your soul, and they worshiped you for it."

As much as I enjoyed hearing this, I felt compelled to remind him that it *had* been, after all, a funeral, that the audience had been emotionally primed for the moment.

He wouldn't buy it. "They weren't primed for the old lady. They barely clapped for her at all."

"Well, her teeth fell out, for God's sake. She lost the momentum."
He threw back his head and groaned in exasperation.

"Besides, I wouldn't exactly call that …"

"One margarita and one G and T." Out of nowhere, the waitress had returned with our drinks.

We both thanked her sheepishly and waited until she'd left before resuming.

"Did it ever occur to you," said Neil, more softly this time, "that business just might be shitty, period? It's a big world, Cady. Everything doesn't have to be about *you*."

"It doesn't?"

"No."

"Well, that sucks."

He laughed wearily. "I hate to be the one to break it to you."

"I need a drink," I said, grinning at him over the salty rim.

The boat back to the mainland didn't leave for several hours, so we paid for an extension on our golf cart and took it out for a spin. Neil seemed relatively sober, thank God, but I was feeling very little pain. We followed the coastal road past the original pottery works, long ago demolished, then hung a right at the water conversion plant and climbed into the hills. There wasn't another vehicle in sight, so the road was all ours most of the way. It snaked along through spicy eucalyptus groves and huge forbidding clusters of prickly pears, affording random glimpses of the blue-green water below. A fine red dust danced in the slanting afternoon light, so that everything around us seemed rendered in sepia.

"I wonder if we'll see buffalo," said Neil.

I gave him a half-lidded look. "Sure thing, kemo sabe."

"They have them, you know."

"Yeah, right."

"Not here, maybe, but they've got them."

"Real ones, you mean? Wild?"

"Yep. They just keep multiplying."

I asked him how they got there in the first place.

"Somebody brought a few of them over for a movie and forgot to take them home. Back in the twenties."

"I didn't know buffalo went to movies."

I thought this was a brilliant witticism, but all Neil could manage was a tiny smirk. "They used to shoot Zane Grey westerns here."

"Aha." In my drunkenness I conjured up my own version of a Gary Larson cartoon—a retirement home for aging buffalo actors, where the inmates sit around reminiscing about the big stampede scene that brought them their only fame.

"He lived here, in fact."

"Who?"

"Zane Grey. His house is a hotel now, sort of pueblo style. Across the harbor there."

"No kidding."

He swung the golf cart off the road and parked it.

"What's this?" I asked.

"Stretch my legs. Wanna get out?"

I told him I was fine right there.

He climbed out and shook the stiffness from his limbs, then he fished a cigarette from the pocket of his blazer and lit it, took a drag, surveyed the picture-perfect scene beneath us. I wasn't used to seeing him so dressed up, I realized. He looked nice like that. One more thing to thank Janet for.

After a while, he came and stood next to the golf cart, still holding the cigarette and staring down at Avalon.

"You know what?" he said.

"What?"

"There's no way I wanna get back on that boat."

I had no earthly idea what he expected to hear from me, so I kept it as pleasantly neutral as possible. "It's pretty nice here, all right. I'm surprised."

"Yeah. Me too."

"Who'd've thunk it?"

He took another drag. "We don't have to, really."

"Have to what?"

"Go back." He shrugged, then looked at me directly, those amazing eyes probing mine. "What's the rush, anyway? It's not like we're working. I bet we could get rooms at the Zane Grey."

Rooms. Plural. I can't remember when a single letter has mattered more to me.

"Yeah," I said carefully, drawing out the word to cover my confusion, "we could, but ..." I didn't manage to finish the thought.

"But what?"

"I'm broke, Neil."

He laughed it off. "Forget it. It's on me."

"You're broke too."

He shrugged. "That's what credit cards are for."

"Don't you have to get back to Danny?"

"Nope. Linda's got him. She's picking him up at the neighbor's right about now."

"She's gone back, then?" I don't know why I had to know this, but I did. Linda had vanished completely after thanking me for my performance and spending an agonizingly inaudible moment or two with Neil.

He nodded. "Took the plane. Right after the reception." He smiled ruefully. "After she helped 'em clean up, I'm sure."

Surprised by how relieved I was, I kept from betraying myself by changing the subject. "How much does that cost, anyway? The plane."

He rolled his eyes. "More than *we've* got, believe me."

Oh, how I wallowed in the sound of that *we,* the way he'd lumped us together so casually, so naturally, as a functioning unit—in distinct contrast to Linda. And now, separate rooms or not, we had a whole island to ourselves. A whole night, too, and another whole morning.

The Zane Grey was so high up on a ridge that it looked across at the carillon we'd heard on our way into the harbor. A small parking space next to the road was as close as we could get to the place without walking, so I waited in the golf cart while Neil climbed the stairs through the cactus garden to inquire about accommodations. He came bouncing back down less than five minutes later.

"Two singles," he said, beaming, "next to each other, just off the swimming pool. With a view you won't believe."

"Great."

"It's a climb."

"Yeah, I see."

"Why don't I carry you?"

I declined this time, because the operation struck me as a little too public and undignified, and because I didn't want him to think of me as helpless. Also, I'd begun to pit out my funeral frock. "You go ahead," I said. "I'll meet you up there. They don't sell T-shirts, by any chance?"

"I think they do. Why?"

I told him I needed a new gown.

He smiled. "What size?"

"Large."

"Coming right up. Any preference as to design?"

I shook my head. "Long as it doesn't say 'Eat Shit' or something."

"Right." He started up the stairs, two steps at a time.

"Wait," I said. "What's my room number?"

He thought for a moment, then said: "'Western Stars.'"

"That's the number?"

"They're all named after Zane Grey novels."

"Cute."

"It's the row just past the pool. You can't miss it."

I asked if he'd take my purse with him and leave my door open and turn the shower on, please, medium warm. He smiled and said, "Yes, ma'am," took my purse and bounded up the steps out of sight.

It took me almost fifteen minutes to get up there. In the absence of railings, I negotiated most of it on my hands and knees, cursing the faceless housekeeper who'd neglected to sweep the grit off the tile. Just before I reached the top, a pair of bare male legs appeared in front of me, white and unrecognizable and definitely going down.

"Lovely day," I said.

"Uh … yes. Can I…?"

"I'm fine," I assured him. "Just pretend I'm not here."

So the poor, confused thing stepped around me and left me to manage the rest on my own. There was a low rail, thank God, where the steps ended, so I hoisted myself to my feet again and caught my breath. I was standing on a small poolside terrace over-looking the harbor. The view was spectacular, all right; it looked as if this might be the highest point in town.

Somewhat to my relief, the pool area was completely deserted, if you ignored the pride of house cats skulking around the AstroTurf. There must've been a dozen, at least, of every age and coloration, and they seemed to regard me with overt suspicion as I set off in search of my room.

"Nice kitties," I murmured. "Just passing through. Stay the fuck away."

The sound of showers running led me to a motel-style row of rooms perched on the very edge of the drop-off. The first shower belonged to Neil, I decided, since the door was shut. The second one shushed invitingly behind an open door that was indeed marked "Western Stars." The room was hardly bigger than its dou-ble bed, adorned with southwestern murals and a huge plastic cac-tus stuck in a pot of gravel. A blue-and-gray plastic electric fan droned away on the bedside table. On the bed, arranged neatly next to my purse, lay my new T-shirt—an ad, not surprisingly, for this very establishment.

I pushed the door shut and shucked off my dress with a sigh of relief, then made a beeline for the bathroom. Neil, bless his heart, had thought to take the soap and shampoo off their way-too-high ledge and leave them on the rim of the shower stall. It felt wonderfully rejuvenating to wash away the grime of the journey, not to mention the sweat of my various exertions, both physical and mental. I never feel fully at ease in a new place until I've had a nice hot shower.

I was toweling dry my hair in front of the electric fan when he rapped on my door. "Hang on," I hollered. "Almost done."

"No problem," said Neil.

I pulled on the T-shirt—which was white, with just enough green to do something for my eyes—gave my bouncy, apricot-smelling ringlets a final fluff, and made a hasty effort at applying lipstick.

"OK," I yelled. *"Entrez."*

Neil was wearing a T-shirt just like mine, only red, and the same khaki pants he'd worn with his blazer. "All riight," he crooned. "A new woman."

"We try." I did a little curtsy in the T-shirt. "Thanks for the smashing ensemble."

"My pleasure."

I stuffed my lipstick and compact mirror back into my purse. "I *think* I'm ready."

"You want me to turn off the shower?"

"Oh, yeah, would you? Thanks."

When he came back from the bathroom, he said: "I made dinner reservations for us."

Us. For us.

"It's down on the water, and they serve seafood," he added. "That's all I know. I hope it's OK."

"I'm sure it is."

"The guy at the desk recommended it."

I smiled at him slyly. "It's probably run by his brother-in-law."

"Yeah." He looked distressed, suddenly. "If you'd rather wait and ..."

"Hell, no. I'm just kidding. I could eat a horse right now. A *buffalo.*"

He laughed and led the way out the door. As we passed the swimming pool, with its battalion of cats, he said: "Have you noticed how empty this place is?"

"I have, yeah."

"The season must be over."

"Yeah, probably. I don't mind a bit. I like having it all to ourselves."

"Same here," he said.

This time I let him carry me as we went down the stairs.

The restaurant was very nice. I've already forgotten its name, but it was weathered and shingled and strung with lights and built out over the water on stilts. The food was nothing grand, your basic deep-fried seafood with iceberg lettuce and baked potato, but it tasted heavenly in the salt air, especially after two or three drinks with little umbrellas in them.

"This is all right," I told Neil, twirling one of the umbrellas as I gazed out at the moonlit sea. "I am one happy camper."

"Yeah," he said. "I think we owe Janet one."

I smiled a little, tickled that we thought so much alike, then plunged headlong into the only subject still eating at me. "Linda seemed to like the song."

"She did," he agreed.

"I mean, a lot."

He shrugged. "It's beautiful the way you do it."

"Yeah, but it seemed like it had ... you know, some significance. Just the way she reacted when I told her I was doing it."

Another shrug. "I didn't notice that."

"You didn't? I did."

"Lots of people like that song."

"Yeah, I suppose."

He looked completely confused. I decided maybe I *had* been barking up the wrong tree.

"She was much nicer than I'd expected, by the way." I didn't mean a word of this, but it was the only way I could think of to test him.

"Oh, yeah?" he said, tossing the ball back to me.

"Well, she was awfully sweet to the Gliddens."

"Janet was her friend," he said, as if that took care of it. "They were in the same sorority or something."

"Yeah, but she was so helpful."

"That's her," he said grimly.

I asked him what was wrong with being helpful.

"Nothing. Unless it's a substitute for ever showing any real feelings."

I closed the little umbrella, opened it, closed it again and set it aside. I'd wanted him to be philosophical about Linda, a little blasé even. This maelstrom of unresolved emotions just beneath the surface was bad news indeed, confirming my worst suspicions.

"She's a cold fish," he added.

I nodded.

"What are you getting at?" he asked.

"I haven't said anything."

"No, but you're thinking something."

"Doesn't matter."

"Yes it does. What?"

"OK ... just that ... you don't seem to be over her yet."

"Don't I *look* over her?"

I told him I wasn't sure what that looked like.

"Like this." He framed his face with his big pink palms and mugged at me.

I smiled at him faintly, unconvinced.

"Why would you even think that?"

"Just the way you're talking now," I said. "Your bitterness. If you didn't still feel something, you wouldn't resent her so much."

He was genuinely aghast. "I resent her," he said with calm deliberation, "because she's still in my life. We share a little boy, and she's been one lousy influence on him."

Some people, I reminded myself, have kids in the equation.

Neil loved his kid more than anything, so it was only natural to resent Linda for forcing him to subdivide that love. It made perfect sense. *Of course* he was over her. I felt like jumping off the pier in celebration. With one of those tacky little umbrellas over my head.

"How," I asked soberly, "is she a bad influence?"

"Like I said, she's a cold fish. She never should have become a mother in the first place. She does it now just because she thinks she *should,* because it's one more noble responsibility for her to shoulder. She's not even comfortable around Danny. She pats him on the head like he's a neighbor's kid or something. It's a real crime, Cady. He's shut down for days after he gets back from her."

"How awful."

"It is. You should see him. He has to pretend she loves him. He makes up stories about the nice things she does for him. You can tell he makes them up."

I nodded.

"I don't talk about it a lot, because it sounds ... you know, typical. Fighting over the kid."

I reached out and squeezed his hand—or as much of it as I could manage: a finger or two. Neil squeezed back, looking straight into my eyes. "I just think he deserves better," he said.

I told him I thought so too.

We got a lot merrier after that, practically closing the place. How we made it back up the hill safely in that golf cart will remain a mystery to me forever. We were both giggling like stoned teenagers when we reached the daunting stairs at the Zane Grey. Neil composed himself briefly, then hoisted me to his chest with an exaggerated groan and began the climb. "Jesus," he muttered. "Who knew a few scampi could weigh that much?"

"Just shut up and drive," I said.

"Yes, Miss Daisy."

That got us both giggling again, more hysterically than ever, until it struck me that Neil had begun to sway ever so slightly, like an oak in a high wind. "Stop," I said. "We're gonna fall."

He came to a halt and steadied himself. "Just trust me, OK?"

I gazed down at the necklace of lights along the beach, the black silhouettes of the palms, the luminous white carousel that was the casino. Even at this height, it was far too beautiful to be scary. And what a way to go, I thought, to tumble heedlessly into that mystical landscape in this man's arms. It would almost be worth it.

"Just take it a little slower," I said.

So he did, and we made it, congratulating ourselves with simultaneous sighs of relief. The little pool was lighted now, the same glowing green—or so I imagined—as the eyes of the cats who slept in the shadows around it. Wisps of vapor shimmied along its surface, beckoning to us. Neil stood stock-still at the edge, as if momentarily hypnotized, then shucked off all his clothes and dived in. His body shot through the pool like a projectile, a dark steel torpedo, surfacing in a soft-spoken explosion at the other end. "It's really warm," he said. "Go for it."

I glanced around briefly to make sure we were alone, then kicked off my shoes and shed my T-shirt, leaving it on top of Neil's. My entrance into the water wasn't nearly as graceful as his, but after dropping like a rock, I managed to flutter-kick my way back up to the surface and catch my breath. I gave Neil a game smile, which he returned from across the way, bobbing merrily above the surface, on the same level as me for once.

"Nice," I said.

"Mmm."

I wasn't sure where to look at this point, so I looked up, found the moon, studied it as a newfound object, huge and pale and perfectly round. It glinted back at me in amazement, like a monocle inserted in haste by an old man who couldn't believe his eyes. When I looked down again, Neil was paddling closer.

"Maybe they could use an act."

"Who?" I asked, still treading water.

"This place. Then we'd never have to leave."

"Right."

"I could play, you could sing 'Feelings.'"

"Where? Next to the Ping-Pong table?"

He chuckled, closer still, walking on the bottom now, though his head remained level with mine.

"My legs are tired," I said. "I think I'd better ..."

"Grab hold," he said.

"What?"

"Put your hands around my neck."

I did that without protest, and my buoyancy increased instantly, lifting me like a giant's hand, up and forward, into the sleek porpoise flesh of Neil's chest. As my feet dangled free, relieved of their task, my muscles relaxed completely. I felt the cedary caress of his breath across my cheek.

"How's that?" he asked, holding me by the waist and drawing back a little.

"Fine."

He bounced a little on the balls of his feet. "Where would you like to go?"

"Nowhere."

He studied me for a moment, then kissed me on the mouth. I kissed him back.

There was a clink. Then the whir of machinery and a final kerplunk. Somewhere in the darkness behind us, a can of soda was removed from a machine.

We froze in that absurd bouncy-baby position, silent as burglars, with only our eyes to register alarm. Neil was facing the wrong way, but I could make out movement in the shadows, a fragment of something pale. It hissed at us, snakelike, as a pop-top was released, lingered there for a moment, then retreated down a concrete path, to the slapping sound of flip-flops.

"Damn," said Neil, grinning. "How long you think they were there?"

"Who knows?"

"Oh, well."

"Yeah."

Still holding his neck, I began to tread water again. I wasn't altogether surprised when something poked against the bottom of my foot. "What's this?" I asked, feigning shock.

He gave me a sheepish look.

"How long have you had that?"

"Long enough."

I couldn't resist. "Seems to be."

He chuckled.

I moved my foot in tight against his sculpted belly, then down into that sweet Velcro wonderland until it rested on the base of his cock, making it spring out from his body. Then I traced its length slowly with my toes, enjoying the silken feel of it—my own private diving board.

He began moving us toward the shallow end.

"Where are we going?" I asked.

"Somewhere where we're *not* the resident act."

"Oh, c'mon. Think of the fun we'll be spoiling." It was booze and nothing else that made me this playfully brazen. I can be as trashy as the next girl, but I'm not an exhibitionist. At least not the sexual kind.

We gathered up our discarded clothes and made our dripping way back to Neil's room. It was a miracle we didn't run into any of our neighbors in the process, but we didn't, so the poor souls were deprived of cocktail chatter that would have lasted them well into the next millennium.

Neil's room was exactly like mine, except that the closets were reversed and his plastic cactus was of a different variety. He switched on a little lamp on the dresser, then brought towels from the bathroom and dried us—first himself, hastily, then me—blotting away gingerly as I stood on the nubby chenille of the bed, my cool skin all taut and tingling, my knees weak from the exercise and the raw, unobstructed sight of him. "You OK?" he asked softly as he put down the towel.

"Fine."

"Lay back, then."

He scooched both pillows against the headboard and eased me back into them, stroking me lightly, smoothing me into place. Then he knelt on the floor next to the bed and moved in close to me, his head so huge and unbelievable it might have been on a movie screen. The lamp behind him produced a sort of coppery nimbus around his hair as his velvety lips covered mine. His tongue slipped into my mouth, filling it momentarily, then roamed off to my ears, my neck, my nipples, which he lapped at with teasing expertise before finally devouring my tits, one after the other, completely enveloping them in liquid warmth.

Before long, though, his mouth had wandered off again, swabbing its way across my belly and between my legs. I reached down and buried my fingers in the thicket of his hair as his tongue continued its exploration, charting in precise terms a territory it seemed to know already. When he looked up again, smiling at me with half-lidded pleasure, he said only one word—"Nice"—and returned to the business at hand.

"Hey," I whispered.

"Mmm?"

"Come up here."

He hesitated briefly, then rose somewhat clumsily to his feet, his cock swinging into sight. "Where?"

"On the bed."

I wiggled closer to the wall to make a space for him.

"Like this?" he asked, lying down.

"No. Kneel." I had spoken his name, of course, which was funny to me, but I didn't remark on it, since it was hardly the time for word games.

So he knelt in the middle of the bed and I knelt in front of him, a pilgrim before the Wailing Wall. From there I could reach up to pet the thick-skinned planes of his chest and stomach and, moving lower, trace the thin ridge of hair descending from his navel. I hoisted his balls with one hand, feeling their weight spill over the sides, then nuzzled the shaft until it began to stir in fits and starts, jerking to life again, the foreskin rolling back with lazy majesty to reveal flesh as shiny and pink as the heart of a conch shell.

In no time at all, my hand couldn't encompass it, so I used two to steady him as I went down on him. Actually, *around* on him would be more like it, since I had to tackle the job in stages, a bit at a time, like licking a large manila envelope. He made gentle growls of encouragement while I worked, stroking my hair and leaning into me for easier access.

When I finally got the head in my mouth, he bent even lower, propping himself up with one hand, sliding the other across my tits and belly and into my bush, where his middle finger pushed deeper and deeper as I bounced on my haunches. In the process his cock slipped from my mouth and banged against the side of my head like a boom on a sailboat in a storm at sea. I wanted his lips on me again, but they were miles away by then, somewhere just below the ozone layer. He must have sensed this, because he stretched out full length on the bed and pulled me up into the crook of his arm, still wearing me on his hand like a bowling ball. Then his mouth covered me again, and a second finger joined the first, and the circle was miraculously complete.

I lay there panting, a pat of butter melting into him, as much there as everywhere. Those chimes were back again, doing their silly thing, and a kitten was mewing plaintively somewhere outside.

"What about you?" I asked, glancing down at his cock to show him what I meant.

He took hold of it and slapped it once against his belly, making a wonderful sound. "You mind?"

"Of course not."

He smiled at me sheepishly and began pumping away, slowly at first, then building steam.

"What can I do?" I asked.

"Nothing. Just stay there. Stay close."

So I obliged, happily, nestling into his shoulder, enjoying the ripe, ferny smell of him, the rising heat of his body. Just before he came, I lodged my tongue in his ear and gave his nearest nipple a vigorous tweak. Jeff told me once that men like that too—or at least some of them—and it seemed to work, because Neil groaned even louder the moment I did it. His sperm shot so far that gobs of it caught us both in the face.

"Whoa," I said, laughing.

He rolled his head toward me, wiped some of the stickiness off my temple. "I'll get a washcloth."

"No. Stay put."

"OK." He observed me with startling tenderness, then added: "Those eyes."

We stayed sprawled there for the longest time, blissfully debilitated. As I nestled into his shoulder, he reached down and held my foot for a while, rubbing it idly, as if it were a smooth stone, all but engulfing it in one of his palms. Something about the gesture got me to thinking again. Worrying.

"Neil?"

"Mmm?"

"This wouldn't be ... a black thing, would it?"

"Huh?" He turned his head toward me again.

"Don't take it personally, OK?"

"What wouldn't be a black thing?"

"This," I told him. "Us."

"What are you talking about?" He let go of my foot at this point, not angrily, but certainly distracted.

"Well, some black people see little people as ... sort of enchanted. Like a good luck charm or something, someone who can grant wishes. They'd do anything for you. Just because you're there."

He propped himself up on his elbow suddenly, separating us. "I am *not* believing this."

"It's the truth."

"According to who? David Duke?"

"I know how it sounds, but it's not just blacks. Norwegians are just as bad. Or good, depending on how you look at it. And some of the Eastern Europeans. It's cultural, really."

"And you thought …?"

"I didn't think anything. I'm just asking."

"What? If I think you're a leprechaun?"

"Well … yeah." I tried to soften it with a smile. "More or less."

He laughed more bitterly than I'd hoped.

"Please don't be mad."

He brooded for a while, then asked: "How long have you been thinking this?"

"Not long. Just then, really. I'm trying to … explain it to myself."

"Explain what?"

"Why you would … you know."

"Cady …"

I knew where he was heading, or thought I did, and did my best to stop it. "I'm not fishing for compliments, Neil."

He grunted. "More like handing out insults."

"I'm sorry. I've had it happen before, that's all."

"You have?"

"Uh huh."

"Somebody black."

"Yeah, sure." Reading his expression, I amended that as quickly as I could. "I mean, not like this, not with someone I really … not in bed or anything … Oh, fuck, just fuck it."

My confusion made him laugh, at least. "Relax," he said, sliding in next to me again. "Tell me about it."

"No, it's stupid. I shouldn't have mentioned it."

"C'mon, tell me."

So I told him about the time Mom and I stopped at a market in Watts to use the telephone, how the kindly old proprietor had grinned at me and followed me through the store, heaping me with frosted doughnuts and Baptist blessings, how we'd returned there repeatedly when money was low for bags of free groceries, with nothing expected in return except the touch of my hand on the old guy's arthritic elbow.

"Was he the only black person?" Neil asked.

I told him there'd been a few others.

He chuckled, absorbing it all, more fascinated now than offended.

"I shouldn't have brought it up," I said. "I was just being insecure." I smiled at him wanly. "Which is a Jewish thing."

"I know," he said somewhat ruefully. "This whole thing could be a Jewish thing."

"What do you mean?" The way he punched the J-word made me put my guard up.

"You having sex with me. It could be Jewish guilt, for all I know. Your version of a freedom ride."

"Well, that's pretty nasty."

"No nastier than comparing it to a couple of free doughnuts."

"It wasn't a *couple*," I said, thumping him on his sticky stomach. "It was lots. And bags and bags of groceries."

"Oh, well ... in that case."

"I wasn't comparing, either. I just wondered ..."

"Yeah, yeah. Did it work?"

"What?"

"Did you cure his arthritis?"

I gave him a guilty smile. "I got a movie about that time. We never went back."

He issued a little murmur in response—disapproving, I thought—then left the bed, snatched a towel off the floor, and wet it in the bathroom sink, mopping himself up. When he came back a minute or so later, he worked on me, dabbing delicately at my face and shoulders as he held my head with the other hand.

"I'll tell you one thing," he said finally.

"What?"

"You granted *my* wish."

★ ★ ★

I sailed along on that thought all night, willing myself awake sometimes just to prove that he was there, warm and real and breathing beside me. Once I even left the bed, so I could stand by the window and feel the breeze and memorize the look of it all: that enchanted ballroom, the dwindling constellation of lights along the shore, the miracle of Neil's body beneath the sheet. I knew that whatever happened from then on would never be quite the same as this, never as pure and rich and bracingly new. I wanted to save it somehow, to store it away somewhere to be treasured again when I needed it most.

The feeling lasted well into the next morning, but I never gave words to it, for fear of frightening him. He had hoped this would happen, I reminded myself; he had planned on it even, much more than I had. His actions that morning gave witness to that, since he held my hand at breakfast (a sweet little greasy spoon straight off a sound stage) and romped with me in the clear blue-green waters of our own secret cove. Even as we sailed back to the smogbound mainland and watched with mounting melancholy as our special island shrank back into nothing, he stayed close to me always, touching, smiling, speaking with his eyes. There was nothing to dread, I realized. Everything about him said this was a beginning, not an end.

He dropped me off at my house a little past six. We kept our goodbyes brief and unsensational, sealed with a couple of pecks on the cheek. Renee watched us from the door, giving a little wave, obviously bursting with curiosity, since overnight funerals are not all that common a phenomenon. Once Neil was gone, I told her something vague and half-assed about missing the last boat and went directly to my room.

That was yesterday. Now it's night again, late, and I've been writing nonstop since who-knows-when, practically to the end of the journal. Renee has been in and out all day, both excited and vaguely unsettled, I think, by this burst of literary activity. She had a date last night with "a serviceman," she says, though she seems unclear about exactly which branch of the service it was. They went to a taco place in Burbank and then out for beers somewhere. I have a strong suspicion she fucked him in his car.

She's in bed now, talking ladylike in her sleep, delivering her Miss San Diego acceptance speech. I melt a little whenever she does that; don't ask me why. I'd hoped that writing this all down would eliminate the need for a listening ear, but it doesn't seem to have worked at all. This one takes a girlfriend, I think.

Maybe I'll tell her in the morning.

THE THREE-RING NOTEBOOK

14

I'VE SWITCHED TO THIS KIND OF NOTEBOOK, WHERE I CAN ADD pages at will, since life is getting weirder by the minute and I'd rather not be restricted by space considerations. Renee lobbied zealously for another journal with a Mr. Woods motif, insisting it would mean something to future historians, but I put my foot down and told her the elf was history. The cover is quite plain this time, clean white vinyl, in the hope that the stuff on the inside will speak to my future, not my past.

Neil and I have been having a thing—for want of a better word—for over three weeks. We aren't cohabitating, but we talk on the phone almost every night. When we're together it's usually early afternoon, when Renee's at work and Danny's in school. Neil comes over here (the logistics are simpler), and we squeeze fresh orange juice and make humongous sandwiches and curl up on the rug in front of the afternoon movie. Sometimes we have sex; sometimes we don't.

My eagle-eyed neighbor, Mrs. Bob Stoate, is absolutely consumed by this latest turn of events, though she hasn't worked up the nerve to ask me about it. I'm sure she will, sooner or later; several days ago she initiated a completely pointless conversation about the state of our respective drainpipes in an obvious effort to reestablish communications. I guess she's forgiven me for the Yellow Ribbon Incident, the Gulf War being last year's ball game in her squalid version of the world. Keeping her in suspense about my gentleman caller is sweet revenge, to say the least.

We've had two gigs since I last wrote—an improvement, but not exactly a turnaround. When the take is divided between Neil and me and Tread and Julie and whatever clowns we're using at the time, it's hardly worth the effort. Neil thinks we may have to let the others go, if PortaParty is to survive at all. He hasn't told them that yet, for fear of demoralizing them, and we both felt it best to keep quiet about Us, for roughly the same reason. I'm intrigued by the idea of a duo with Neil, but I can't help feeling fretful about the others. Where would they work, after all, if they didn't work for him?

Last week I finally told Jeff about me and Neil, and he was predictably smug about having "known all along." Looking back, I'm not sure why I didn't see it myself, since Neil claims he was sending out signals months ago, waiting for even the slightest response from me. Maybe I was too self-protective to pick up on them, or maybe the signals weren't as clear as he thinks they were, or maybe it just helps him to believe that something more complicated than unadorned friendship existed between the two of us before we went to bed with each other.

This much I do know: it's not about charity. Neil is just as flabbergasted about this as I am. And just as insecure about motives. The week after we returned from Catalina was spent convincing him that I'd slept with him out of affection and respect, not out of Jungle Fever. I howled when he suggested this, since weeks before we'd both agreed that the movie was a crock of shit, that it made hay of a so-called controversy, then ran screaming for cover behind a cop-out ending that neither Jesse Helms nor Jesse Jackson would find in the least offensive. But Neil was so obviously sincere in his doubt that I did my best to put his mind at ease, assuring him time and again that I was above such things—or below them, perhaps—that I found him no more or less sexually exotic than any other man with three and a half feet on me.

One morning last week, while I was painting my nails a snappy new shade of rust, I received a phone call that utterly baffled me. Since it continues to do so, it's worth recording, I suppose:

"Hi, doll. It's Leonard."

My long-lost agent. Calling *me,* if you please, for the first time in years.

"Hi," I said as colorlessly as possible, waving my wet nails in the air. For better or worse, I have a career of my own now, no thanks to Leonard Lord, and I wanted my tone to convey that. I also haven't forgotten for a moment how he lied to me about Callum Duff being back in town. The scumbag.

"How's it goin'?"

"Fine. Great."

"You working, then?"

"Oh, yes."

"Well, that's good."

"Mmm."

"Look … are you around for a while?"

"At the moment, you mean?"

"No," he said, obviously unsettled by my chilliness. "For the next month or so."

"Hang on." I made him wait for over half a minute, while I wagged my nails around some more. I'm pretty sure he wasn't fooled, but it was worth the effort, I thought. "Looks OK," I told him finally. "What's up?"

"Well … maybe nothing. Maybe something kind of big."

Well, that narrows it down, I thought, but I didn't say it, because the bastard had me going again, just like that. Was there a property out there with my name on it? I wondered. Had somebody finally written a fully human role for a little person? A long shot, of course, but why else would Leonard be calling me? Especially after he'd dumped me in Arnie Green's low-rent stable.

Before I could think of anything to say, he'd jumped in again. "So lemme ask you something, doll."

"Shoot."

"It'll piss you off, probably."

"Go ahead."

"How's your weight these days?"

If you remember, the last time Leonard mentioned this, it was just a generic cheap shot, an easy excuse for my unemployment, callously disguised as a friend's concern. This time it felt different, fraught with significance, completely pertinent to that "something kind of big" percolating out there in the pipeline.

"It's good," I lied. "Down a lot."

"Great."

"I've been on a diet that Cher uses." This felt like much less of a lie somehow, even though I haven't touched one of those god-awful shakes for at least three months now. "I've got a real waistline now ... and a boyfriend." The second part was way out of line, I know, since Neil likes me the way I am, but I thought it would help convince Leonard of my total dedication to the New Me. Anyway, I can always go on a diet, if something really important is at stake.

"Well, look, doll, I'll get back to you, OK?"

"I'm singing now, you know. I have an act and everything. In case they can use that, I mean."

"Hey, good for you," he said, but I could tell he was only half listening. His secretary, the latest of a long line of male bimbettes, was murmuring to him solicitously in the background. My time was obviously up.

I asked him, a bit too desperately, if he could give me at least a hint.

"'Fraid not, doll. I'll get back to you soon, though."

Soon, in Leonard's lexicon, can mean anywhere from a week to never.

I thanked him and hung up and went back to painting my nails.

Three days ago Renee and I had Jeff and Callum over for dinner. I'd been meaning to do this for weeks, partly out of curiosity about the progress of their relationship and partly because Renee hadn't stopped badgering me for another session with her second-favorite movie star. When I finally told her that Callum liked boys—and Jeff in particular—I thought she might lose interest in a reunion, but she rallied admirably and threw herself headlong into preparations. She made spaghetti and a nice salad and surprised us all at dessert with rum raisin ice cream—the very thing, if you remember, that Jeremy used to lure Mr. Woods from his hiding place in the oak tree.

"It's Baskin-Robbins," she announced shyly as she set a bowl in front of Callum. "I wasn't sure what brand it was in the movie."

"It looks great," said Callum.

"It wasn't any brand," I told her.

"How come?"

"Because it was wax, Renee. Or some synthetic shit. Real ice cream would melt under the lights."

"Oh." She was openly crestfallen. "I didn't think of that."

Callum, being a good sport, told her he preferred the real stuff, anyway, but shot a subtle glance to Jeff after he'd said it that made me think they'd already discussed Renee at length and found her lacking in the smarts department. She didn't catch it, thankfully.

"What was that you ate, then?"

I thought she was addressing me in my elfin persona, so I told her they'd used the robot in that particular scene, that I hadn't been on the set at all when it was shot.

"I meant him," she said, indicating Callum. "You tasted it before you gave it to him, remember? To show him how good it was?"

"Oh, yeah." He nodded. "You're right."

"That wasn't wax, was it?"

"No." He smiled at her without malice and scratched his boyish head, now becomingly short and fuzzy for his new movie. "I can't remember what it was, actually. Ice cream, I guess. It was a long time ago."

"Yes," I said, and gave Renee a pointed look that said to please spare us any further strolls down Memory Lane. I was pissed at her about the ice cream stunt, since she'd promised me repeatedly she'd keep the fawning to a minimum. She widened her eyes in exaggerated innocence, then stared down bleakly into her ice cream.

Callum picked up the slack by turning to me. "Jeff says you stole the show on Catalina."

"Stole the funeral."

He chuckled. "Wish I'd seen it."

I replied with a shrug and a modest smile. I wondered how much Jeff had told Callum about me and Neil and whether he, Callum, found our affair droll or, worse yet, bizarre. He grew up in New England, after all, in a family that would make the Bushes look Jewish. I'd almost asked Neil to join us all that night, until I realized he'd have to bring his little boy along. I haven't met Danny yet, and a dinner party for five adults didn't strike me as the ideal setting for our first encounter. It would be tough enough managing the social intrigue among four of us.

"She used to sing on the set," Callum told Jeff.

"I'll bet she did," said Jeff.

"Fuck you."

Callum chuckled at our phony friction and kept going. "Remember the time you sang 'Call Me' for Mary's thirtieth birthday?"

I nodded.

"Mary Lafferty?" Renee perked up again at the mention of another star from the film.

Callum confirmed it for her and continued. "I'd never heard your mother play before. She was great."

"She used to teach it," I told him, recalling how Mom had come into her own that day the moment she sat down at the piano. Up until then, I think, the other cast members had seen her simply as my handler, a soft-spoken, slightly ridiculous lady from the desert with no particular claim to their attention. She got a little drunk on all that unexpected glory, not to mention the champagne brought in for the occasion. Remembering all that, I couldn't help thinking how much Mom would be tickled to know that there's a pianist in my life again.

"Whatever happened to her?" asked Jeff. "Mary Lafferty, I mean."

I shrugged. "Not working, I guess."

"Yes she is," said Renee. "I saw her on *Matlock* a few months ago."

"Oh, well." I rolled my eyes just for Jeff. "I stand corrected."

Renee lunged ahead, oblivious. "She was such a neat mom in *Mr. Woods.* I wanted my mom to be just like her."

"She *was* good in that," said Callum, being gracious again. "She sort of established the prototype, didn't she?"

Having no idea what a prototype was, Renee nodded.

"You know," I told Callum, "she was free-basing in her trailer." My co-star nodded soberly.

"How did you know that?"

"I knew," he said.

"You were ten years old, you little fucker!"

Everybody laughed, even Renee, who usually has a big problem with "dirty" words in mixed company. Jeff gave Callum a jaundiced glance and said: "Why am I not surprised?" There was enough edge to the remark to make me wonder what sort of preexisting tension might have provoked it. It didn't take long to find out.

"Mary auditioned for *Gut Reaction,*" Callum told us.

"Oh, really?" I said.

"What's *Gut Reaction?*" Renee asked.

I told her it was Callum's new movie.

She lit up and turned back to Callum. "Did she get the part?"

"I'm afraid not."

Renee frowned. "Aw. Why not?"

Callum shrugged. "It wasn't really right for her. She's at the stage where she's not young enough to be a mom anymore and not old enough for good character parts. My agent said she looked a little beat up too."

I could just imagine the relish with which Leonard had proclaimed the poor woman toast.

"Well," said Renee, "if she's doing drugs …"

Callum shook his head. "She got clean years ago."

"Oh."

"It's a shame," said Callum. "Really."

"Yeah." Renee mourned Mary's career demise for a solemn moment or two, then asked brightly: "What's the movie about?"

I noticed Jeff twitch a little in his chair, but he didn't say anything, just turned to Callum and waited.

"Well," said Callum somewhat sheepishly, "it's your basic action thriller."

"I love those," said Renee.

"I'm a rookie cop in L.A. whose fourteen-year-old brother gets kidnapped. The chief doesn't want me on the case because I'm too young and too emotional to deal with it. So I track the guy down in secret, when I'm off duty. It's just something I have to do. Hence the title. Marcia Yorke is my girlfriend, who works at the DMV, and she ends up more or less solving the case." Callum smiled. "There's a strong feminist slant to it."

Renee wouldn't know a strong feminist slant if it walked up and bit her on the ass, but she made a face, anyway, to show how much she approved. "Is that the part Mary Lafferty tried out for?"

Callum shook his head. "A smaller one. Another cop's wife."

"Oh."

I almost reminded Renee that Mary had played Callum's mother in *Mr. Woods,* so she would hardly have been a logical candidate for his girlfriend ten years later, but I thought better of it, seeing the nasty little storm cloud that had just gathered over Jeff's face. "Tell 'em about the kidnapper," he said.

Callum looked at him blankly.

"Go ahead," said Jeff.

"I don't see how it's of interest."

"Well, I do."

"He's just a psychopath." Callum shrugged and gave me and Renee an amiable, bemused look that said: What got into him?

"A queer psychopath," said Jeff.

"That's your interpretation."

Jeff wheeled around to argue his case with me. "He wears eye shadow, OK? He has a fucking Judy Garland poster over his bed. How tired is that? And his hair"—he looked around urgently for a moment, then held up a corner of Renee's electric-yellow tablecloth—"is this color."

"You've read the script, then?"

"What else? You can't get on the goddamn set. I can't, anyway."

I wasn't about to touch that one, so I turned back to Callum. "And this psychopath … molests your little brother?"

He shook his head, remaining remarkably serene. "It never comes to that. It's never clear what he's going to do."

"It's clear," said Jeff. "It's clear to me."

"Well, your imagination is highly political."

"And something's wrong with that?"

Callum shook his head, smiling dimly. "Unless you're talking about entertainment."

"Yeah, you're right. What could be more entertaining than a good old-fashioned queer-killing?"

"Jeff …"

"Well, that's what it is."

"I don't think so."

"You push him out of a helicopter, don't you? We see the guy being nellie all the way to the ground. Jesus, I can hear the cheers already."

"He's the villain, for God's sake."

"The *gay* villain. And they never let you forget it. I could handle that if there had ever been a single gay hero, or even a regular person, but there never is. We're only visible when we're killers or objects of ridicule." Jeff looked at me again. "Don't you think it's a little twisted that a gay man is playing a straight cop who greases a fag?"

Callum laid his napkin on the table. "I think we're boring the ladies, Jeff."

"Oh, really?" Jeff kept his eyes on me. "Am I boring you?"

I waited a beat before replying calmly: "Not quite yet." For all I knew, he could have a valid point, but he'd picked a crummy time to make it. Renee was looking mortified, and I was getting sick and tired of playing middle woman.

"Fine," said Jeff. "I'll shut up."

Callum tried to placate him. "That was an old script you saw. I should've shown you a new one."

"Yeah, I guess you should have."

"Other people thought that was a sensitive area too. They made some major changes."

"What did they do?" asked Jeff. "Lose the Judy Garland poster?"

"Kassabian, chill out!" This was me as I hurled my wadded napkin—lightheartedly, I hoped—in Jeff's direction. It landed short of the mark in his empty salad bowl. He scowled at it briefly, then at me, but said nothing further, apparently secure in the knowledge that the last word had been his and that all I'd provided was the punctuation.

"There's lots more ice cream," Renee offered meekly.

After dinner we retired to the parlor—as Renee insists on calling it when we have company. I stretched out on my tapestry pillow at Callum's and Jeff's feet, and Renee took the armchair, where she proceeded to kill four glasses of "cream dement" and hold the guys in thrall with an unconsciously gothic account of her kiddie pageant days. She was so delighted by their response that, as a grand finale, she sprang to her feet and recited a poem about world peace (complete with hand gestures) that she used to perform in the competitions. To me, it felt a little like *Whatever Happened to Baby Renee*, but the guys didn't let on if they found it ridiculous.

There was no further tension between Jeff and Callum that night. At least not around here. They even got affectionate at one point, Callum rubbing the back of Jeff's neck and squeezing his knee when I talked about the day we rented That Movie so Jeff could see if Jeremy and Callum were the same person. The more I'm around them, though, the more hopelessly different they seem. Jeff is open and vulnerable, but also abrasive and hyper, while Callum is affable and coolheaded and unrevealing to a fault. Opposites attract, sure, but there has to be *something* in common, doesn't there?

Jeff called later that night, after Renee had gone to bed. I knew he'd do this, so I'd waited up for him. As usual, he just began talking without announcing himself.

"You asleep?"

"No."

"Is Renee in the room?"

"No."

"Are you mad at me?"

"Not a bit."

"Sorry I fucked up your party."

I told him he hadn't, so he shouldn't expect an absolution anytime soon. Then I asked him where Callum was.

"Back at the Chateau. He has to be up at five. There are movies to be made and psychotic queers to be put in their place."

I sighed at his renewed ranting. "Didn't you guys make up?"

He made an unreadable grunt.

"What does that mean?"

"That I was gutless," he said, "and let it drop."

Touched by this attempt at compromise, I slipped into my

Pollyanna mode. "Maybe it won't be a problem, Jeff. I mean, if they fixed the script like he says ..."

"They haven't fixed shit. He just said that to get off the hook."

"C'mon now. He sounded concerned enough."

"Yeah. About his own ass. That's the only reason he even thinks about this. He's petrified he'll be outed if this becomes an issue."

I digested that for a moment. "You think it will? Become an issue?"

"It could. Very easily. It's the meanest script I've ever read, Cadence. It cost two and a half million dollars, and it's just one more lousy cheap shot at fags. I'm not the only person who's gonna be pissed off."

I asked him what he expected Callum to do.

"He could raise a stink. If he won't come out, he can at least tell the press the movie's homophobic. He's the star, for Christ's sake. What if Wesley Snipes took a role in a film that turned out to be racist?"

"But didn't he see the script before he accepted the role?"

"Yeah, well ... let's not get into his ethics."

I hesitated a moment, then said: "Maybe we should."

"What do you mean?"

"I don't get it, Jeff. Why are you still seeing him if he's such a scumbag?"

"I didn't say that."

"You just said he didn't have any ethics." There was no response to this, so I added: "How pretty can a dick be?"

"You know," he said quietly, "I'll always be sorry I told you that."

I told him maybe so, but the information was nonetheless pertinent to our discussion.

"He has other qualities," he said.

"Like?"

"He can be very ... personal and tender. When we're by ourselves."

Personal and tender. I could imagine the sway that would hold over Jeff. Especially now. If Callum had been the first person to make him feel human again after Ned's death, it would be tough for Jeff to renounce that sensation completely, even for political reasons. It would mean starting all over again from rock bottom.

"Personal and tender is good," I said. "Maybe that should be enough."

"I tried that," he said. "I kept the whole damn thing in a vacuum for at least two months. No demands on his conscience, no expectations, nothing."

"And?"

He snorted bitterly. "I ended up in a closet at the Chateau Marmont."

"Pardon me?"

"OK, it wasn't a closet; it was a fucking kitchenette or something. But it felt like one."

"Jeff ..."

"Leonard showed up unannounced at the suite one night, and Callum asked me to hide in the other room."

"You're joking."

"I wouldn't joke about something that humiliating."

"But Leonard is gay."

"So what? He gave Callum explicit instructions not to get laid until the movie's over, and Callum promised him he wouldn't. You know how this crap works. There's big money riding on that piece of cryptofascist dreck."

I giggled just a little. "So you hid?"

"Don't rub my nose in it, Cadence."

"I think it's kind of sweet."

"Well, it wasn't; it was degrading. All I could think was: Here I am, the fifth or sixth best-known gay writer in L.A., this fucking *elder statesman* of Queer Nation ... and I'm acting out some Feydeau farce, cowering in a goddamn closet—"

"Kitchenette."

"—from a couple of other fags, for Christ's sake. One of whom, need I remind you, is an official self-loathing shithead of the Hollywood establishment."

He meant Leonard, I presumed. "I thought he knew about you and Callum."

"Not as far as I know, he doesn't." He brooded over that in silence for a moment. "You haven't talked about it, have you?"

I told him I hadn't dared even mention Callum to Leonard ever since Leonard lied to me about Callum's being back in town, since it was never prudent to embarrass Leonard in the act of spinning a big one—he was liable to turn poisonous on the spot.

"He might pump you," said Jeff. "So play dumb. Callum thinks Leonard smells a rat."

"Why would he pump me?"

"Well … he knows you know Callum."

"Yeah, but he thinks I think that Callum's still back in Maine."

"No he doesn't. Callum told him he ran into you at Icon."

"Oh."

"Leonard even called a few days ago, asking what you were up to."

You should've seen me perk up at that one. "Leonard called Callum about me?"

"Yep."

"Why?"

"He didn't say. Or at least Callum didn't bother to tell me if he did."

"He called me too," I told him. "Just about the same time. He said he might have a role for me. Something big, apparently."

"He didn't mention Callum, did he?"

I was annoyed, frankly, that Jeff had skated so blithely around the news of my Big Break. He was the one, after all, who'd insisted that birthday parties weren't my real career, and here he was, in all his self-centered glory, ignoring the first hopeful light to appear on my horizon in months. "I told you," I said curtly. "We didn't discuss your snuggle bunny."

"What's the matter?" he asked.

"Nothing."

"I knew you were mad at me."

"I'm not mad at you," I told him wearily.

"But you think I'm being a fool, don't you? Or a hypocrite."

"No."

"It's not like he can't change. I was closeted once myself. It's all just a process, really. If I'm there to encourage him and influence him in that direction, just think how it could be, Cadence. This wholesome kid that everybody loves like a little brother, who grows up to be an all-American heartthrob—a *homo* heartthrob, thank you, who doesn't care who knows it. It would rock the world if he did it with a little class. He'd change the course of history."

This altruistic speech reminded me of one Mom used to make about Paul Newman. She loved him above all other actors, worshiping at the shrine of those amazing eyes, even unto death. It was always a guilty pleasure, though, because Mom believed "her" Paul to be a secret Jew, a man who'd concealed his heritage to become a matinee idol. Still, she clung to the hope that one day he would declare himself, stand up somewhere, and proclaim, "I am a Jew" and justify all her years of belief in his potential as a mensch. She was certain that day had arrived when he started pushing popcorn and salad dressing and turning the proceeds over to liberal causes. Any moment now, Mom insisted, Paul would break the news the easiest way—through delicious food—with the introduction of Paul Newman's Gefilte Fish or Newman's Own Family-Style Matzo Ball Soup. She waited and waited for that moment of truth, reading labels religiously, but all she ever got for her faith was marinara sauce.

I couldn't help thinking that was exactly what lay ahead for Jeff, but I tried to be gentle about it. "What you say makes sense," I said, "in an ideal world."

"Meaning?"

"Well ... Callum can't change the course of history if they won't hire him in the first place."

"Who says they won't? Who wrote this rule?"

"It's just there, Jeff."

"It's there because creeps like Leonard Lord won't get off their asses and challenge it."

"In part, yes."

"Well, we have to start asking why not. Why can't there be gay movie stars?"

"Maybe so." I let him hear me yawn, since I was ready to turn in. Frankly, I wasn't sure whether this brave new crusade was for real or just his impromptu justification for an affair that seems to be going nowhere fast.

He got the message and let me go, after asking me to thank Renee for dinner and bidding me a civilized good night. I dropped the phone on the floor, snapped off the lamp, and beat a retreat into dreamland, burrowing into sheets that still smelled of Neil and the musky remains of our afternoon delight.

15

Something ugly happened to Renee last night, so she's taken the day off from work, at my urging. She's on the sofa now, stretched out in her ragged pink nightgown, all that yellow hair tangled up like last year's Christmas lights, pressing an ice pack against her cheek. I made the ice pack myself, from a Ziploc bag and an old kitchen mitt. It seems to help a little, though Renee's expression remains gloomy. Her depression has less to do with the incident, I think, than with the sudden, unflattering snapshot it provided of her life.

I've been pampering her all day to the best of my ability, dispensing her favorite instant coffee (Irish Mocha Mist—gag) and reading out loud from trashy magazines. I knew she required attention more than anything, so I called Neil this morning and canceled our lunch date, filling him in on the details. He got it immediately, as I knew he would, and even offered to swing by with takeout and leave us to our girl talk. Tempted though I was by a chance to see him again, I thought it best he stay away for a day or two. This is no time for Renee to be reminded of Neil's surpassing sweetness.

Like most of Renee's calamities, it happened on a date. This one was set up by Lorrie, her ditzy pal from The Fabric Barn, who knew a guy who had a friend who'd been "out of circulation for a while" (whatever that means—prison, if you ask me) and wanted his ashes hauled in the worst kind of way. Lorrie didn't know this, of course, or claims she didn't, and had no misgivings about leaving Renee alone with this dude after the four of them went out drinking in Venice. Renee insists he was "a perfect gentleman" all the way back to the Valley and didn't show signs of actual derangement until they got here and parked in the driveway and she informed him as nicely as she knew how that the date was over.

At first he pleaded with her, she says, playing pitiful. When that didn't work, he exploded in righteous anger, depicting himself as the victim of false advertising—Renee's poor jiggly bod being the billboard, I suppose, and he the innocent motorist who'd been conned into taking the wrong exit off the freeway. From there it degenerated into "dirty words," the shortest of which—"Cunt!"— slashed through the shrubbery like hedge clippers and invaded my bedroom, waking me from a light sleep. I heard a car door open and close, then another, and a sickening, high-pitched scream, unmistakably Renee's. I flipped on the light, rolled out of bed naked, and bolted—or my own best imitation of that—to the front door.

Yanking the cord that enables me to open said door, I eased out onto the little brick porch. Renee lay on the lawn next to the drive- way, propped up on one elbow and whimpering softly, having just been hit. Her dream date stood over her, snarling and cursing under his breath, a surprisingly skinny creature considering the ferocity of his voice. He had a pale, chinless, ferrety face that might have struck me as pitiful under other circumstances. Under these, it seemed like depravity itself.

"OK, cowboy, get the fuck outa here!"

This was me, thank you very much. I don't know *where* that cowboy shit came from or who I thought I was—Thelma and/or Louise, I guess—but the sheer audacity of the act produced the desired effect. The guy wheeled around to find the source of this angry chipmunk voice and discovered under the porch light a fat child with tits and pubic hair, watching his every move.

"I mean it," I said. "I've already called the police."

As if in response to this invocation of authority, a light came on at the Bob Stoate residence. Renee's date glanced toward it, then back at me, then down at Renee, who was stumbling to her feet finally, no longer whimpering. The mere sight of her naked rescuer had apparently been enough to stun her into silence.

"Do you know this asshole's name?" I asked as she hobbled toward the stoop.

She made a feeble sound that meant yes.

"Get inside, then."

She slumped past me into the house. Her assailant muttered something unintelligible—I doubt seriously that even he knew what it meant—and climbed into his car, slamming the door shut violently. By the time the little worm had scratched off into the street, spewing gravel, Mr. Bob Stoate, the Toyota salesman, had appeared on his own doorstep, wrapped in a terry-cloth Lakers robe and brandishing a pistol.

"It's OK," I yelled to him. "He's gone."

He peered at me, aghast, across his driveway.

At this point modesty seemed superfluous. "Sorry about the outfit," I said.

"Did he hurt you, Cady?"

This is just about the nicest thing anyone from that house has ever said to me, and I came close to being touched and responding in kind, except that I wasn't really dressed for it. "No," I told him. "I'm fine. I think he hit Renee." And I retreated into the house, feeling exposed for the first time.

Renee was crumpled on the sofa, sobbing.

"Did he rape you?" I asked.

She shook her head.

"I'll run a tub," I said.

★ ★ ★

I stood by the tub and scrubbed her back with a sea sponge. She had finally stopped crying, but she was still a mess.

"I think you should call Lorrie," I said.

"Why?"

"Because that prick tried to knock your head off."

"It's not *her* fault," she said.

"I'll call the cops, then. What's his name?"

"Skip."

"Skip what?"

"I don't know."

"Renee ..."

"Well, I don't."

"Lorrie will know."

"No she won't," she said. "She only knows Barry."

"Her date?"

"Yeah."

"We'll call Barry, then."

"No." Renee shook her head dolefully. "Just leave it, OK?"

"He hit you, goddammit."

"I know." She started to sniffle again. "What's the matter with me, Cady?"

"Nothing. Jesus, Renee, it's not your fault."

"I should've never went on a stupid blind date. They never work out."

"Well ... yeah. Maybe that's true."

"And the regular ones don't, either."

"Oh, c'mon. Some of them do. You've met some nice guys." I couldn't name any right offhand, but it seemed like the thing to say. Fortunately, Renee didn't challenge me.

"But they never last," she said.

"Well ..."

"I have to find somebody."

"Why?"

"Because ... never mind."

When Renee resorts to "never mind," you know the truth is

about to surface in some convoluted form or other. "C'mon," I said, biding my time as I swiped the sponge across her spacious pink back. "You're twenty-three years old. You've got all the time in the world."

"Not if …" Again she cut herself off.

"Not if what?"

"If you move out."

"Why should I move out? This is my house." I saw it now, of course, ever so clearly.

"Yeah, but you've got a boyfriend now."

"Not," I said emphatically, appropriating one of her more asinine pop phrases.

"But I thought …"

"We're seeing each other, Renee. That doesn't mean we own each other."

"You sleep with him."

"So?"

"Well, I thought …"

"He has a kid, honey. It's his whole life. He's not gonna ask me to come live with him."

"Maybe he will."

"Yeah, and maybe the moon is cheese."

"But if he came to live here …"

"With the kid?" I rolled my eyes for her. "I don't think so."

She giggled, mostly out of relief, I think. I wondered how long she'd been dwelling on this desertion/eviction fantasy and if it had actually driven her to go shopping for shitheads. I began to feel guilty about the lump rising on her face. "We're a team," I told her. "I thought you knew that."

"Well …"

"Nobody else would put up with me, honey."

"Oh, Cady!" In a rush of pure emotion, Renee pivoted toward me like an overaffectionate baby elephant, making me drop the sponge.

"Don't hug me," I said, stepping away. "You're wet."

★ ★ ★

So we've been bonding today, us girls. Renee's spirits have lifted considerably since I started writing, but she still hasn't left the sofa. Now that she sees Neil as less of a threat to us, she's begun to extol his virtues, how nice he is and how talented and how cute.

"You should get Denzel Washington," she said at one point. "He'd be so perfect."

I looked up from this notebook. "For what?"

"For the movie."

"Huh?"

She sighed as if I were the thickest person in the world. "You're writing about him, aren't you?"

"Some," I said, feeling slightly invaded.

"Well ..."

"I don't think there'll be a movie, Renee."

"Why not?"

"Trust me on this, OK?" I had tried to picture me and Denzel playing the big love scene on Catalina, under the directorial eye of, say, Penny Marshall or Ron Howard or any of those seventies kids currently making sensitive movies, and I just couldn't do it. Times had changed, true, but not that much. Besides, the real thing had been too perfect, too exquisitely internal, to imagine its cinematic counterpart. Maybe that's what happens when you're having a life: the real thing *is* the movie.

The phone just rang, and Renee says it's for me.

16

I've been at Icon all day—the actual studio, not the theme park—where weirdness followed weirdness until I'm no longer sure of anything. It started yesterday with a phone call. Not the one that interrupted my last entry—that was from Neil, saying he missed me—but another, later at night, when I was almost asleep. It was Callum, asking if I'd like to be his guest on the set of *Gut Reaction*. They were shooting a crucial scene, and he thought it might be fun for me to observe. That's what he said, anyway.

And get this: he sent a limousine for me. This vulgar white barge that looked as if it could accommodate a Jacuzzi pulled up outside the house after breakfast. Renee cooed and swooned over it, then ran back to my room to get my sunglasses. I put them on just to please her, but they felt so right somehow that I left them on for the ride to Icon. The driver was a buff blond named Marc, who pumped me shamelessly about my function at the studio. I wasn't about to bill myself as a sightseer, so I took the easy way out and played mysterious. "Played" is the wrong word, really; I was beginning to *feel* mysterious.

I could tell we'd reached the gate when I heard Marc talking to the guard. In an eerie flash of déjà vu, I conjured up the days when

Mom and I had done this very thing in the old Fairlane, bound for Stage 6 and the green plastic realm of Mr. Woods. It wasn't the same guard, of course—the voice seemed younger—but I got a little shiver, anyway. I remembered my maiden visit: the first time I'd seen a backdrop stacked against a building (a piece of snow-covered alp) and spotted a star's name (Mary Steenburgen) on a trailer and caught the rich, tarty scent of gardenias growing in the dust outside the commissary.

The driver took me to Stage 11, where I was met by a young production assistant named Kath—not Kathy, but Kath, she told me after I got it wrong—who led me into the dim, cavernous building and helped me into a deck chair near the action. Callum was in this scene, she said, which was taking way longer than expected, which, of course, was nothing new in this business. Her sweetly condescending tone annoyed me, so I nodded solemnly to show her I already knew a thing or two about this business, thank you, and the delays it entails. I wondered what Callum had told her about me.

The set was the psycho's apartment, a city loft stocked with fifties furniture and barbells and—yes, Jeff—a poster of Judy Garland. It's night. The only light comes from a Lava lamp and a strip of green neon blazing beyond the big, grease-streaked windows. Callum kneels outside the door, jimmying the lock in his cop's uniform. The psycho hears him and rushes to open a hatch in the floor, revealing the coffin-sized space where Callum's terrified kid brother lies captive.

In mounting panic, the psycho gags the boy with something that looks like an S & M device—a black-leather-and-chrome hood—then closes the hatch and pulls a Persian carpet over it. Clad only in a jockstrap, he shinnies up the wall into the shadows. Callum enters cautiously and crosses the shadowy room, stopping over the very spot where his brother struggles to be heard. The set is revealed in cross-section, so that the camera can move in one seamless, stomach-churning motion from the boy in the box to his oblivious brother to the fiend crouched above them both, watching it all from the rafters.

So far, according to Kath, there had been over a dozen takes, for reasons apparent to no one except the director. He was a real stickler, she said, a perfectionist of the old school. The cast was punchy as a result. When the psycho accidentally demolished a statue of David with a lethal flourish of the Persian rug, the kid under the floor—who, remember, had been munching leather all morning—broke into an all-out giggling fit. It spread rapidly, catastrophically, as those things do, first to the psycho, then to the crew and almost everyone on the set. Only the ever-cool Callum was a model of composure when the director finally called glacially for "a little professionalism, please."

He got the shot he wanted on the nineteenth take. When they finally broke for lunch, Callum exchanged words with the guy in the jockstrap, then came over and crouched next to me. "Remind you of anything?"

"Oh, God," I said, rolling my eyes.

"Exciting business."

I glanced at the director, hunched over a clipboard as he gave notes to an assistant. "And I thought Philip was anal."

Callum smiled without showing teeth, committing to nothing, remembering where his bread was buttered. "Feel like a bite to eat?"

"The commissary?"

He nodded. "It's not so bad these days, believe it or not."

"Your taste has diversified, that's all. You never ate anything but macaroni and cheese."

He laughed. "You remember that?"

"I remember everything," I said.

I barely recognized the commissary. There were new chairs and tables and a witty new mural, rendered in bright ceramic tile, that depicted all the great stars of Icon standing, one after another, in the cafeteria line. Mr. Woods was there, of course—the shortest diner by far, except for the cartoon stars—predictably elated over a bowl of rum raisin ice cream. Callum picked up trays for both of us and led the way down the line, telling me what was available. I settled on chicken Kiev with mashed potatoes and Key lime pie.

"You need something green," he said.

I pointed out that the pie was green.

"The asparagus looks nice," he said.

"Don't be my mother, OK? It's obnoxious when you're dressed like a cop."

He paid for the food and got a table for us next to the window. After a brief foray around the room, he found something for me to sit on: scripts on loan from a reader across the room. I settled onto them with a chuckle. "They call this coverage, don't they?"

He chuckled too and took a sip of his iced tea.

"Who's here?" I asked, looking around. "Anybody good?"

He shrugged. "Bridget Fonda."

"Where?"

"In the corner over there."

Sure enough, there she was, entirely recognizable, but smaller than I'd imagined. I wondered if she could say the same of me.

"She's hot, isn't she?" Callum, to my amazement, was managing a reasonable facsimile of a leer. "I'd punch her ticket in a minute."

I gave him a friendly but pointed look. "You and who else?" Something flared up behind his eyes, but he extinguished it and reached for his iced tea.

"I know you're on the lot," I said, tucking a napkin into my Peter Pan collar, "but it's just ol' Cady here, remember."

He was reddening noticeably. "You don't know all there is to know about me."

"I'm sure I don't," I said, and pointed at his plate with my fork. "The asparagus do look nice."

He gazed down at them.

"I should've gotten those," I said. "You're absolutely right."

We stayed off the Subject after that. I didn't even bring up Jeff, though I was dying to get Callum's angle on the affair. I called Jeff this morning, by the way, thinking he might have been invited to Icon, too, and wanting his take on my own invitation, but he wasn't home. I left a message, but so far there hasn't been a peep out of him. For all I know, he and Callum are already kaput.

Over dessert, Callum said: "I had a nice visit with Philip and Lucy in Malibu last week."

Lucy is Philip Blenheim's wife of six or seven years. He was still a bachelor when I knew him, so to me Lucy is just another drawn shiksa face I see sometimes in paparazzi shots. She stays in the background as much as possible, dropping babies with long Old Testament names and decorating their three—count 'em: three—local mansions.

"Everybody says she's nice," I said.

"She is. Really down-to-earth. You'd like her a lot. She'd like you."

"Well … if her husband did."

Callum frowned. "What do you mean?"

"Oh, you know. All that business."

"What business?"

I filled him in briefly on my spat with our director: how I'd granted one lousy interview to a local trade sheet and Philip had put me on his shit list forever. "Everybody on the set knew about it," I told him. "I can't believe you don't remember."

"I guess I do," he said, "barely."

"Let's just say we aren't chummy anymore."

"But he likes you, Cady. We talked about you a lot."

My mouth went completely slack. "When?"

"Last week in Malibu."

"You and Philip talked about me?"

He mocked my amazement. "Yes, Cady."

"What did he say?"

"He's very fond of you."

"Oh, right."

"I'm telling you, he was delighted I'd run into you. He said he'd lost track of you."

I'm listed, of course, but I didn't bother to point that out; I was too bowled over by what I was hearing.

"I'm sure he'd be hurt," Callum added, "if he thought you were mad at him."

"*Me* mad at *him?*" All I could do was laugh. "Have we just stepped through the looking glass or something?"

Callum laughed with me. "I wish you'd heard it, Cady. He had this elaborate theory about what you'd done for the character. Especially in the last scene. He said people were moved then because they realized—on a subconscious level, at least—that something had been in there all along, a living being that conveyed all these complicated emotions. He said you couldn't do that with a robot, no matter how advanced the technology."

I was eating this up. I put down my fork, in fact, and stopped eating my pie—something of a first for me. "And you didn't record this? You didn't call me from the nearest gas station?"

He chuckled. "I was sure you'd heard it a million times."

"Not from Philip."

Not from anybody, really. Not in those words.

"Well, he doesn't hate you," said Callum. "Anything but."

I just sat there shaking my head.

Not only that, but five minutes later, who should saunter into the commissary but Blenheim himself! I examined him thoroughly before alerting Callum, just to make sure I wasn't hallucinating. All the familiar elements were there: the shiny bald dome; the ancient letter jacket and corduroy pants; the big, furry, slope-shouldered body. He stood just inside the doorway, surveying the room in a way that was both casual and precise, like some shrewd big-city antiques dealer at a roadside rummage sale.

"Guess who's here," I said.

Callum jerked his head around, spotted Philip, and immediately began signaling him.

"Wait!" I said.

"Why?"

I couldn't think why; I was filled with panic.

"It's OK," Callum assured me. "I swear."

Philip, I decided, hadn't seen me when he started toward us, since he did a real doozy of a double take when he reached the table.

"Cady? Good God—Cady?"

I hate to think what a goofy look I must have given him.

"I can't fucking believe it," he thundered. "This is so time-warpy! The two of you together again! Jesus, you look terrific."

"Thanks," I said lamely. "You too."

"What are you doing here?"

"Just"—I glanced over at Callum—"hangin' with the stars."

"Shit, this is wonderful!" Philip regarded me like a benevolent bear, then pulled out a chair and sat on it backward, turning abruptly to Callum. "You don't mind, do you, kid?"

Callum smiled and shook his head.

Philip turned back to me. "He told me he'd seen you. I was so fucking jealous."

I was tongue-tied.

"You're singing now, huh?"

"Yeah. Some."

"That is so cool. I told you your voice was something special. Didn't I always tell you that?"

"Yeah, you did." I just didn't happen to remember it, that's all.

"You should come out to the beach sometime. Meet Lucy and the kids."

I told him I'd like that.

"Your mother passed away, huh?"

I nodded.

"Gee, I'm so sorry." He ducked his head and let it swing a little, dolefully. "What a fine lady she was."

"Yeah."

"Really fine."

"Mmm."

"Well, kids ..." He sighed and slapped his hands on his knees and stood up again. "I've got a script meeting across the lot. I better get my fat ass in gear."

I laughed in a last-minute effort to seem friendly, suddenly annoyed at my own passivity. He was getting away, I realized, this legendary titan of film who had suddenly become my dear old friend again. "What's the project?" I asked, throwing tact to the winds.

"Oh, a period thing." He was already two tables away. "Sort of a musical. Gotta run, *tantele*. I'll be in touch, OK? Does Callum have your number?"

"I'm in the book," I yelled, as he made his exit, stumbling through a maze of grips eating doughnuts. They gazed up at him in weary, undemonstrative awe, like biblical shepherds beholding one more holy vision in the clouds.

Callum was tremendously pleased with himself. "You see?" he said. "Does he love you or what?"

What, I decided.

Definitely what.

I knew something was funny before lunch was over, right about the time Callum told me I could keep the limousine for the rest of the afternoon. The driver was booked for the day, he said, so I might as well make use of the limo, since Icon was paying for it and wouldn't care. Anyway, the scenes of *Gut* to be shot after lunch would be boring as batshit, so there was no reason to hang around if I had places to go. I'm sure he wasn't trying to get rid of me, either—just being nice. As unbelievably nice as Philip had been.

Marc was waiting for me where I'd left him, reading a *Silver Surfer* comic book on a bench in the sunshine, his biceps round as cantaloupes under the black polyester of his chauffeur's jacket. He sprang to his feet when he saw me.

"Oh, hi. All done?"

"All done," I said.

"Where to?"

I gave him Neil's address in North Hollywood.

"You got it."

He opened the door and lifted me into the back seat, following Renee's example earlier. "Is that a production facility?"

"An apartment house," I told him. "My boyfriend's."

He nodded.

"He's not expecting me, so you might have to ring his doorbell for me."

"Sure," he said. "Or you can call him. We've got a phone."

I hate to admit it, but this basic fact of modern life hadn't even occurred to me, lowly pauper that I am. "Of course," I said. "Silly me."

So I called Neil as we were cruising off the lot, mostly to record the moment.

"Guess where I am?"

"Where?"

"In the back of a limo at Icon."

He chuckled. "What happened?"

"I'm not sure exactly. Feel like a little company?"

"The littler the better," he said.

It took us over half an hour to get there, inching through terrible traffic. When we arrived, Neil was already out by the street, obviously curious as hell.

"Well, well," he said, as Marc helped me out.

"Marc, this is Neil. Neil, Marc."

The guys shook hands jovially, their forearms getting hard over it. There's something really sexy about two guys holding each other off like that, sniffing each other out. I wondered if Marc had expected another little person, instead of someone like Neil, or if he was simply trying to picture the two of us—me and Neil, that is—having hot, pyrotechnical sex. I, for one, was picturing it already, since Neil was in a T-shirt and purple gym shorts and looked like a million bucks. Or whatever that sort of gorgeousness is going for these days.

"Want me to wait?" asked the driver.

I looked at Neil. "Do we?"

Neil's lip flickered. "Oh, I think so."

"How long can you wait?"

"Well," said Marc, glancing at his watch, "you've got me until six."

"Then, maybe ... an hour or so?"

The driver smiled prettily, catching my drift. "Whatever."

Upstairs, I kicked off my shoes and crashed on Neil's bed. Neil lowered the matchstick shades until the light in the room was the color of iced tea. Then he unlaced his high-tops, tugged them off, and flopped down on the bed next to me. Rolling onto his side, he touched the tip of my nose with his forefinger and studied me with mild amusement.

"OK, where'd you get the footman?"

I told him briefly what I've just told you, except for the part where I called him my boyfriend.

He smiled when I was done, smoothing my hair back from my forehead. "What a morning," he said, as if that were all the comment required.

"Don't you think it's weird, though?"

"What?"

"Philip showing up like that. Just after Callum had said all that stuff."

"Maybe."

"And maybe not?"

"It's a small world there, isn't it?"

"Not that small. Not usually. Philip walked in like he was looking for somebody. It's like the whole thing was a setup from the beginning."

"For what?"

"I dunno. So we could make up gracefully, I guess."

"Yeah." He didn't sound too convinced.

"Look," I said. "Remember that call I got from my agent a few weeks ago?"

"Oh, that's right."

"Yeah, well, he said something big was about to happen."

"He did. Jesus, you're right. I hadn't thought of that."

"And then Callum, who has the very same agent, invites me to the studio, sends a limo for me, butters up my ass like it's corn on the cob ..."

Neil chuckled.

"*And* tells me how Philip never stopped loving me—which is a lie, let's face it—and then Philip comes strolling in with a shit-eating grin on his face, tells me how fabulously I sing, how great my dear old mother was, and just happens to let it drop that he's working on a musical. It's so obvious, Neil. He wants me for something."

Neil nodded slowly. "Sure seems like it."

"Doesn't it?"

"But why wouldn't your agent just call you?"

"Because he knew there was bad blood between me and Philip. He got Callum to be go-between to spare Philip the embarrassment. That way Philip didn't have to apologize. It took a few minutes out of his day, and we all just pretended that everything was hunky-dory. It's the way they do things. If they need you badly enough, you're their new best friend again."

Neil's eyes widened, taking it in. He was finally looking as excited as I felt. "What's the musical about?"

"I don't know. He left in a big hurry, as usual. Period was all he said. Think of that: a Philip Blenheim musical!"

"Maybe you should call your agent."

"No."

"Why not?"

"Let him call me."

"Don't be too proud, now."

"I'm not. I just think it's the smartest way to handle it. He'll call, you watch. Tomorrow or the next day."

He looked at me for a moment, then kissed me on the fore-head.

"How was your day?" I asked.

"Oh … I let the others go."

I grimaced sympathetically. PortaParty felt like ancient history already—at least since lunch—but I couldn't help identifying with the other performers. We'd been a family of sorts, once upon a time, driven by the same dreams. Until Neil and I narrowed it down to two.

"It was pretty grim," said Neil.

"I guess so."

"Julie was OK, but Tread flipped out."

"Poor guy."

"He even offered to work for nothing."

"Oh, no."

"I feel rotten about it."

"Don't, Neil. It's not your fault."

"I know."

I was beginning to feel a bit guilty myself. I'd come galumphing in there, after all, flaunting my good news, on what could well have been the worst day of Neil's whole year. "What happens now?" I asked.

"Check in with Arnie, I guess. See if there's any lounge work available."

I winced inwardly, not only at the sound of "lounge work" but at my own fading memory of Arnie Green's office. The morning I had thrown myself on the agent's mercy suddenly seemed so long ago. I hated to think of Neil, with all his talent, starting from scratch in that seedy little room.

"You know," I said, "if my movie happens, they might need a pianist."

He shook his head, smiling faintly. "I don't think it works like that."

"It might."

He wiggled closer to me and began unbuttoning the front of

my dress. "Lots of things *might* happen. Ever done this with a limousine waiting?"

"Nope."

"Me either."

"That was the idea," I said.

When we were naked, we had our first all-out fuck. Neil was reluctant at first, largely on my account, so I took the bull by the horns, so to speak. I rolled a condom onto his cock with leisurely precision, as if working clay on a slow-spinning wheel, then eased myself down a bit at a time until that sweet certainty filled me so completely that it became more mine than his, part of my own skeletal system, next-door neighbor to my heart. When I hit bottom, he smiled languidly, then cupped his hand against my cheek and began to move inside me.

I actually had visions when I came, Technicolor images that whipped and roiled through my consciousness. In one I was a ragged peasant girl, a dwarf revolutionary manning the barricades at the Bastille. In another I was the plucky star of a small traveling circus in the forties. In both I was singing with such bell-like brilliance, such total conviction, that everyone on the sound stage, even the director himself, was stunned by my performance. Just as I was taking my bows, Neil came, arching into me with a growl of primal release. Maybe it was just me, but it felt remarkably like applause.

17

THERE WAS A SMALL FIRE AT THE FABRIC BARN LAST NIGHT, SO Renee has three days off while they clean up the mess. With all that time on her hands, she's as frisky as a kid sent home from school after a bomb threat. She tried to organize a shopping trip first thing, but I told her to go it alone, thinking I should stay near the phone in case Leonard called.

He didn't, of course.

Not so far, anyway, and it's almost four o'clock.

This makes two days and counting.

Fuck him. Just fuck him.

18

F<small>IVE DAYS SINCE THE BIG LUNCH, AND STILL NO WORD FROM ANY-</small>body.

Renee is back at work, so I'm rattling around alone in my suburban cage.

Jeff came by this morning, misery in quest of company. Three days ago, over a grimly efficient little dinner at Musso & Frank's, he and Callum called it quits.

Jeff sprawled on the floor next to me and waved an obese joint in my face.

I rolled my eyes at him. "At ten o'clock in the morning?"

He looked at me blankly for a moment, then lit the joint with a Bic, sucking in smoke, holding it, letting it go, handing the joint to me. "You'd have an excellent point, if your period weren't coming on."

I gave him an irritated look, my slowest burn, then took a few tokes.

"I gather no one called," he said.

I shook my head.

"What do you think that means?"

I told him I didn't know anymore, and left it at that. I couldn't put words to my darkest doubts. I'm prepared to face them like a big girl, but not yet, not officially. Part of me still hopes against hope that Leonard is just dragging his feet again. I'm small potatoes in his client stew, after all. He could be tied up in negotiations for someone more important than I, maybe even someone who's wanted for the same musical.

"You know," said Jeff, "I could call Callum and ask him what he knows."

This threw me. "You parted that amicably?"

"Well, no. But I don't mind calling."

I told him that was sweet, but I wouldn't think of imposing. Frankly, I was worried that Jeff's failed romance might rub off on my fledgling deal, screwing it up for good. I wasn't sure I could trust him to stay cool about it.

He took another toke, staring contemplatively at the ceiling, then pinched off the roach and deposited it in the pocket of his jeans jacket. "You know what pisses me off?"

"What?"

"Ned warned me about this. He described the whole thing."

"Described what?"

He shrugged. "How it would feel."

"How *what* would feel?"

"Sleeping with a movie star ... a closet case."

"Well, I guess Ned would know."

"Too bad I wasn't listening."

"What did he say?"

"He said it could start a million different ways. But you always ended up feeling like a mistress."

I studied his face to see how seriously he expected to be taken. "Is that how you feel?"

He nodded. "More or less."

"Get any nice lingerie out of it?"

"Hell, no." He laughed ruefully. "Nothing."

"Well, fuck that."

"Exactly."

"When did Ned say this?"

"Right after we met. When he told me about living with Rock. I used to quote it to everybody for years, and then I met Callum, and the whole thing just flew out of my head."

"Yeah, well … a pretty dick is like a melody."

"Just shut up, OK?"

"OK."

My docile response amazed him. "When did you get to be so easy?"

"Since you anesthetized me."

Jeff smiled and was silent for a moment. Then he said: "You know … I never met anybody on that movie."

"Really?"

"Not one soul. I never even met anyone he knew."

I shook my head sympathetically.

"What was it like?" he asked. "You never told me."

"The movie?"

"Yeah. Did it seem homophobic?"

I told him the killer seemed queer, but I didn't see that much of it.

"They're gonna picket it, you know."

"Who?"

"GLAAD."

I giggled. "The sandwich wrap people?"

He wasn't amused. "The Gay and Lesbian Alliance Against Defamation."

"Oh, yeah."

"This shit's gotta stop sometime."

I asked him if he had plans to picket.

"I dunno. It's too early to tell."

I hate to admit it, but I was thinking about myself again, wondering if Jeff's politics would alienate Leonard and if Leonard would take it out on me. "Does Callum know about the GLAAD protest?"

"Oh, yeah. That's what started the last fight. I told him about it, and I said I thought it was valid. He said I was being a hothead just for the sake of it, because my lover had died and I had no place to vent my anger. So I told him I felt this way long before Ned died and that I was sick and tired of pricks like him who were willing to live a lie in exchange for stardom. He called me a fascist and accused me of trying to sabotage his career, and I told him so be it, if the career is corrupt to begin with. Why should I give a shit about a system that keeps insisting I don't exist? This isn't *my* fantasy."

I flashed on that day in the commissary and Callum's clumsy salacious remark about Bridget Fonda. "Do you think he might be bi?" I asked Jeff.

"Is that what he told you?"

"Not in so many words."

"Well, he's not, however he said it."

I nodded.

"Trust me."

I smiled at him faintly. "I do."

"He is definitely a member of the greatest show on earth."

"Too bad it wasn't enough."

"Well … there are all kinds of queers."

"Mmm."

"Just because you suck cock doesn't mean you're perfect."

"That's my motto."

"I bet it is," he said.

We both started giggling, rolling on the floor like puppies. Jeff's seizure was more purgative, though, lasting longer than mine and playing itself out in a resonant sigh.

"You'll get over it," I told him.

"I know."

"Did you leave him … or vice versa?"

He thought a moment. "Both, really."

"How does that work?"

"Well … I told him it was over, and he looked relieved."

"I see."

"He looked *very* relieved."

I hesitated before asking: "You think there's somebody else?"

"Oh, hell no," he said, and then thought about it and smirked. "Unless you count Billy Ivy."

"Who's that?"

"This porn star, a local kid. He plays college boys in skin flicks … wrestles in jockstraps, gets fucked with a tie on, that sort of thing."

"Of course."

"Callum's obsessed with him. Back in Maine, he used to jerk off to him in *Honcho*. Then he moved back here and got the video, which, I swear, never left his VCR at the Chateau Marmont."

"You watched it together?"

He nodded. "I got off on it the first time, but it turned into a real thing with Callum. After a while he never had sex with me at all without Billy Ivy's preppie butt on the screen. It got to be almost insulting. Then one night Callum came to Silver Lake—the only time he ever did—and flipped through one of my *Advocate*s and found out that Billy Ivy has his own eight hundred number for outcalls in L.A."

"Phone sex, you mean?"

"No. The real thing. If you're tired of his movies, you can call up and order *him*."

I smiled at him. "You think Callum did?"

"I know he did. He says he didn't, but he did."

"Does that bother you?"

"It bothers me that he lied."

"Nothing else?"

"No. I'm a sex-positive person."

I gave him a dubious look.

"OK," he said, "it bothers me a little."

"Thank you."

"That wasn't why we split, though. He just panicked because I told him he should come out."

"Ah."

"I didn't bully him or anything, if that's what you're thinking."

"I'm sure you didn't."

"I was really gentle about it. I told him just to think it over … how much more peaceful he'd be, how much it would mean to millions of gay kids who're still struggling with it."

"What did he say?"

"He didn't. The blood just drained out of his face, and he changed the subject." Jeff traced a pattern on the carpet with his forefinger. "That was it. I became the enemy after that."

He seemed so filled with sadness that I refrained from comment.

"You know," he added, "I thought I could fix him."

"Yeah."

"My first mistake, right?"

"Maybe not."

"Yeah. It was. Nothing ever changes here, and you can't do shit about it. That kid is twenty years old, and he might as well be Rock in 1949. They just keep making 'em."

"Someday it'll change."

"Right," he said. "In the meantime, Ned would be laughing his ass off." He stroked the carpet slowly, soothingly, as a form of punctuation. There were tears blurring his eyes, but whether they were for Callum or some dim, resurfacing memory of Ned was far beyond my powers of observation.

19

I'M SO MAD I COULD SPIT. ONE WEEK AND TWO DAYS AFTER THE lunch at Icon, Leonard finally called. I don't much feel like writing about our conversation, but I'll do it, anyway—in the interest of thoroughness, if nothing else.

"Doll."

"Leonard."

"How are you doing?"

"Swell."

"Terrific. Look, this thing is on."

"What thing?"

"The thing I told you about. You free a week from Saturday?"

A low-grade dread began to seep through my system like pale-green poison. Blockbuster musicals are not generally described as being "a week from Saturday." I sat down on the floor, took a deep, cleansing breath, and collected myself. "Just tell me what it is, Leonard, and I'll tell you if I can do it."

He didn't answer right away, obviously conscious of my fragile state. "OK ... how does this grab you? Meryl Streep, Whoopi Goldberg, Jay Leno, Candy Bergen, Sly Stallone, Elizabeth Taylor,

Michael Jackson, Annette Bening, Warren Beatty, Madonna ...
Stop me when you've had enough."

"No, go ahead. Keep jerking my chain."

"I'm serious."

"Right."

"It's a tribute, doll."

"To what? My gullibility?"

He laughed. "To Philip Blenheim."

I said nothing.

"You still there?"

"I'm listening, Leonard. Keep talking."

"Well ... the UFL is giving Philip their Lifetime Achievement
Award, so they're having a big blowout at the Beverly Hilton. It's
like the night of nights. HBO is televising it, *ET*'s gonna cover it. I
haven't seen a roster like this in years. Bette's gonna sing, Patrick
Swayze's gonna dance. Barbra might even sing, for Christ's sake...."

What can I tell you? I tried to stay cool, but my face had
already gone up like a baked Alaska, flaming in early celebration.
"And they want *me*?"

"Who else?"

"To perform?"

"No, to bus tables. Of course to perform."

I laughed extravagantly, because Leonard suddenly struck me as
the wittiest man in the world. "You're really serious?"

"I'm really serious."

"Jesus."

"No need to thank me," he said. "Your ecstasy is my reward."

I hooted. "My ten percent is your reward."

"Well, that too."

"It does pay, doesn't it?"

"Does it pay? the woman asks. Does it pay?"

Suddenly the pieces fell into place. I flashed on Philip at the
Icon commissary, that strange new respect in his eyes, telling me
how exquisitely I sang, how he'd recognized my talent even in the
old days. Then I remembered Leonard's inquiry about my weight

when he'd first teased me with that "something kind of big." Then, with no effort at all, I saw myself onstage at the Beverly Hilton before an all-star black-tie audience, singing "If," or maybe something entirely new, while Meryl and Madonna listened from the wings in rapt amazement and jaded producers scrambled for the phone.

"So," said Leonard, "they're giving the suit a thorough overhaul."

"Come again?"

"Mr. Woods. They're disinfecting him. Spraying him with poly-whatsit." He laughed gleefully. "He's been on the shelf for ages, but he'll be nice and fresh for you."

In a matter of seconds I was sick with despair, suffocating on the truth. Words just wouldn't come.

"Cady?"

"Is that all this was about? Somebody to wear that fucking suit?"

"Not just somebody."

"Well, you can find yourself another dwarf."

"Doll, doll. You act like it's nothing. This is historic. It's a moment for the ages. Nobody's even seen Mr. Woods since the movie was made."

"Horseshit. I saw hundreds of them on that goddamn ride."

"What ride?"

"At Icon."

"Those are robots."

"Then hire yourself a robot. I'm an actress."

"They *need* an actress, Cady. That's why they're asking you. You *are* Mr. Woods."

"Yeah, yeah."

"You know what he requires, Cady. How to give him life and personality. You're the only one who does."

"What about Philip's sacred rule?"

"What rule?"

"About the elf never showing up in public."

Leonard heaved a condescending sigh. "That's what I'm trying to tell you. This'll be the first time. Nobody'll be expecting it, so they'll go nuts when it happens. It'll bring down the house. You'll be the one who gives him the award."

"Mr. Woods, you mean, not me."

"But don't you see? It'll make every front page in the world."

As angry and disappointed as I was, this pronouncement stopped me short for a moment, causing me to consider another possibility, one that just might work. "OK, what about this?"

"Yeah?" Leonard sounded wary.

"What if I did that, the whole elf thing, and then came out later as myself and ... sang, maybe?"

No reply.

"That would *really* surprise them. Talk about the crowd going crazy."

"I really don't think—" He cut himself off abruptly.

"What?"

"Don't take this wrong, Cady, because it's not about you."

Of course not, I thought, it never is.

"I just don't think that's the way Philip sees the evening."

"Oh." All sorts of stuff had begun to register. "So Philip is actually organizing this?"

"Well, he's a consultant. He has to be. They want to get it right."

"Of course."

"He really wants you to be there, Cady. He told me so himself."

"Is that why he kissed my ass at Icon last week?"

Leonard feigned ignorance. "You lost me there, doll."

"I don't think so. You set this up through Callum, didn't you? You knew Philip and I weren't speaking, so you arranged for us to meet and make up. Just so I'd put on that fucking body condom one more time and give a trophy to the prick who—"

"Cady, look—"

"Callum's part of this tribute, isn't he? He must be."

"Well, sure, but—"

"So you boys all chipped in and sent me a limo, and … Oh God, it's so clear now. Why didn't I see it? I'm such a jerkwad."

Leonard offered me a hurt silence. Then: "I can't believe you're being so hostile."

What *I* couldn't believe was that Leonard hadn't blown a fuse and hung up. He'd taken more abuse from me in ten minutes than I'd dared to dole out in ten years. His moderation could mean only one thing: he needed me too badly to risk alienating me. Philip had obviously put the screws to him. "What's the matter?" I said. "You fresh out of wee people?"

No answer.

"That's it, isn't it?" I laughed bitterly. "You can't find anybody to fit that damn suit."

"That's not true, and you know it."

"Try Arnie Green, why don't you? He's got some terrific midgets. You might have to chop them off at the ankles or something, but what the hell. Or maybe a child. That would work. Homeless, preferably, so you don't have to answer to SAG or anything."

"This is so unlike you."

"No, Leonard, this is exactly like me. This is me. This is what you get when I don't have to be careful anymore, when I don't give a fuck what you think."

And *that's* when he hung up on me.

At least an hour has passed, so I'm calmer now, if a little numb. Leonard called back a while ago, as I suspected he might, given the apparent urgency of his mission. When I answered, he didn't even bother to announce himself, just started talking, assuming the tone of a long-suffering parent.

"How long have we known each other?"

I groaned.

"Have I ever steered you wrong? Have I ever betrayed you? Have I ever acted against your best interests?"

"Save it, Leonard. I'm not doing it."

"Just tell me why not."

"Because it hurts too much."

"You mean the suit? I'm sure they could—"

"Not the suit. The whole twisted thing. I'm sick and tired of it, that's all. I have to be myself sooner or later. I can't keep doing this."

"Doing what?"

"Being invisible."

After a pause he said: "It's had its rewards, hasn't it?"

"Not enough."

"Think of the people you've met. Think of the life you've led."

"I *am* thinking of the life I've led."

"C'mon. It hasn't been that bad."

"Oh, really? *You* try it sometime."

"Yeah, well ..." He laughed uneasily. "You've got a point, I guess."

Even at this late juncture, that dazzling lineup of stars kept coming back to taunt me. It took all my strength to stifle the whiny child within who kept telling me to stuff my principles, for God's sake, Meryl and Bette and Barbra would be there, and I would probably get to meet them. But I couldn't forget my years of exile from Philip's life or the silence he'd imposed on me from the beginning. It was better to take a stand, I felt, to make an exit with my dignity intact. I needed to know that I could do that, I guess, that I could take control of my own destiny no matter how much empty glitz they threw my way.

"I'm wasting your time," I said.

"Look ..."

"I'm a singer and an actress, Leonard. If you can help me with that, fine. If not ..."

"You won't do this for Philip?"

"Why should I? He won't do shit for me."

"That's not true."

"Has he cast his new musical yet?"

You better believe *that* stopped him cold. "Well, uh ... I don't know much about it, really."

"I bet you don't."

"It's just a script. If there's anything right for you, I'm sure he'd ..."

"Oh, blah, blah, blah ..."

"Why are you acting like this?"

"Because you're a liar, Leonard."

"I've never lied to you."

"Bullshit."

"When? When have I ever lied?"

"When I asked you if Callum was in town. You told me he was back East in college."

"Well, he was—then."

"He was not, Leonard. He was blowing a friend of mine in Griffith Park."

There was an audible intake of air. Most satisfying.

"Not in the park, really. Back at the house. They met at the park."

"What is your point, please?"

"That he was here in town and you knew it. And that you lied to me. Why did you lie to me?"

"I barely remember this."

"Then why do you think you *might* have lied to me? Because you knew I'd try to reach Callum?"

"Maybe ... I guess."

"Maybe?"

"The kid needed his space, Cady."

"And I was just gonna pester him, beg him for jobs, make your life complicated."

He considered that for a moment, then said: "Something like that."

"So you lied."

"Yes ... OK, yes."

We shared a moment of silence over that one.

Finally, Leonard said meekly: "You can be pretty ... persistent, you know."

I grunted.

"I admire that, though. I admire it a lot. Don't get me wrong."

I was beginning to think I could make Leonard say or do any-thing, confess to the sins of the whole sorry town. I felt a little giddy with the power of it. Nothing makes you stronger, I guess, than saying no and meaning it to someone who really needs you for something. Given time, I might have found other ways to tor-ment him, but I suddenly felt bone tired, drained of energy. I'm ready to be done with this for good, I realize. All I want now is to lie in Neil's arms and have a good cry.

"I have to go," I said.

"I want you to think about it," Leonard said. "I don't want you to turn it down yet."

"I just did, Leonard."

"I'll call you back in a day or so. You've had a lot thrown at you at once. I won't talk to Philip about it yet. He can find somebody else, I'm sure, but that's not what I want. I want you to be there, playing the role you created. It's just good karma all the way around."

Good karma? All else had failed, so Leonard was stooping to metaphysics. I might have felt sorry for him, if the approach hadn't been so patently out of character. Everything Leonard knows about karma he learned from an afternoon of shopping at The Bodhi Tree with Shirley MacLaine.

Two hours later.

I just got a call from Callum—the first in ages. I let the machine take it:

"Hi, Cady, this is Callum. Leonard told me about—uh—your reaction to Philip's tribute. I just want you to know that I'd really like for you to be there. I'm sure Philip would too. He really does have great admiration for you. It looks like an incredible evening too, and it wouldn't be the same without you. I hope I didn't do anything to upset you. Leonard seems to think I might have. I'm still at the Chateau. Call me, OK?"

Yeah, right.

After supper.

I tried to reach Neil several times this evening, but there was no answer. Renee, meanwhile, thinks I've gone off my gourd. When I told her about turning down the tribute, she stared at me in open-mouthed horror. "Gah, Cady ..."

"Save your breath. I've heard all the arguments."

"But if he said he was sorry ..."

"Who?"

"Blenheim."

"He hasn't said shit. He let Leonard and Callum do his dirty work."

"He must not be mad at you, though. He wouldn't have asked you."

"I don't give a shit whether he's mad or not. *I'm* mad."

Seeing the truth of this, Renee let the subject drop, but her expression has since grown more and more petulant. She just sits there on the sofa, stuffing her face with Mini Oreos and sulking into her magazine. The message is clear enough: I've been a fool and a hothead, guilty of excessive pride. What's more, I'm being punished by her silence because I willfully deprived her of a glamorous evening.

We have a weird relationship, Renee and I. Sometimes I'm her parent and sometimes she's mine. I'm not sure which mode we're in at the moment, but I resent her attitude. If she wants a little glamour in her boring existence, she can find it on her own for once. I've had it up to here. All I want is a life I can live on my own terms.

Neil just called, so I told him what happened. He offered to come by and pick me up, take me back to his place.

Sounds like a plan to me.

20

IT WAS RAINING HARD WHEN NEIL BROUGHT ME TO HIS APART- ment. The white brick building had turned the color of dishwater in the downpour, grim as an old Kleenex, while the AstroTurf lawn shimmered brighter than ever, a glossy, nuclear green. I'd left home in a hurry, without a raincoat, so Neil made me walk under his as we headed to the elevator—a peculiar four-legged, two-armed, one-headed creature lumbering along under a leaden sky. From where I stood, about knee-high to Neil, it was a place of safety and peace: my own little terrarium, toasty warm, smelling deliciously of denim. I could have stayed under there for hours.

Upstairs, he made me cocoa. He had learned of my favorite comfort food a week or so earlier and had gone out and bought a big can just for me, as if he'd sensed somehow my impending need for comfort in large quantities. In the van on the way over, he'd listened to my tale of woe with sympathy but without comment. I knew that would come, but I thought it best not to push it, so I didn't raise the subject again until we'd finished our cocoa and were under the covers, face-to-face, in bed.

"You think I fucked up?"

"How?"

"Telling them no."

He smiled at me faintly. "Not if it feels better this way."

I told him I wasn't sure how it felt.

"Well," he said, "if you were degraded by wearing that suit, then it was the right thing."

"I was degraded by the fact that they refused to see me as anything else."

"Like yourself."

"Like myself." My eyes clung to him with a grip all their own, grateful for his placid understanding. "Tell me something."

"What?"

"Why is Mr. Woods cute and I'm just disturbing?"

"C'mon."

"That's what they think, Neil. They won't say it, but that's exactly what they think."

"You're just depressed."

"No. Don't bullshit me. I count on you for the truth."

He blinked at me for a moment, assembling his thoughts.

"Is it because I'm a woman?"

He chuckled. "You sound like Streisand."

"Be serious. Would a little man be easier to take?"

"I don't know."

"How do they see me, then?"

"Who?"

"People."

"I'm not sure," he said after a pause. "Once they get to know you—you're just Cady."

"Do they pity me?"

"I don't," he said. "I admire you sometimes, for what you put up with, but I never pity you. I couldn't be with you if I felt that way. You're the strongest person I know, Cady, and the most forgiving. That's what makes you so beautiful."

In spite of my best efforts, a tear rolled out of my eye. Neil smoothed it away with his thumb as rain splashed against the windows by the bucketful. I heard the squeal of tires on wet pavement, then a car alarm shrieking in the distance like a teenage banshee caught in the storm.

After a while, I asked: "Do you think I'm talented?"

"Cady …"

"Just tell me again, OK?"

"I think you're very talented."

"Am I mainstream?"

"I'm not sure what that means, but … I think everybody would love you."

"Leonard doesn't think I'm mainstream."

"He said that?"

"Not in so many words, but I know how he thinks. He thinks I'd frighten the horses, scare off the yahoos."

"What does he know?"

"Everything, when it comes to that. That's how he got rich. It's his job to second-guess the public. He's a pissy queen with his own Hockney and this fancy house in the hills, who is paid to think exactly like someone from Iowa."

"Who needs him?" said Neil.

"I'm not sure he even knows I can act."

"Who cares? He's just an agent."

"I can, you know. I'm a really good actress when they let me do it. I'm not just selling my size."

I must admit, I'm a little sensitive about this. In the early days, when Mom and I first hit town, we used my stature as a calling card to the haunts of the rich and famous. We'd go to The Comedy Store, say, when Robin Williams was performing, and slip the security guard a handwritten note to take backstage: "Hi, Robin, I'm the shortest woman in the world and I love your work. If you'd like to meet me, I'm outside." It was shameless, but it worked almost every time—Diana Ross being the notable exception—and Mom chronicled our conquests on a monthly basis in long, heavily embroidered, eat-your-heart-out letters to Aunt Edie in Baker.

The way I saw it, my height was a means to a worthy end, so I worked it like a carny scam, always knowing, deep down, that I had the talent and the drive to back it up. Actually, Mom was more of a fanatic about this than I was. I'll never forget the night she chastised me for wearing my hair up in a bun to a big premiere. "It's spoiling the whole effect," she told me. "It adds a good two inches. You're almost as tall as that girl in North Dakota." Mom kept track of these things.

"I've been thinking," said Neil.

"Yeah?"

"What if we talk to Arnie, get some glossies made of the two of us?"

"And?"

"Start our own act. Riccarton and Roth. I think it's time, don't you?"

"Riccarton and Roth?"

"Sounds good, doesn't it?"

"If you like second billing."

He laughed. "OK. Roth and Riccarton."

I rolled it around for a while, testing the rhythm of the words. "No, you're right. Works better the other way."

He stroked my hair. "I know a guy with a club just around the corner. He might not book us right away, but we'd steal the show on Open Mike Night. After that, who knows?"

"Well ... it's a start."

He frowned. "Hate it, huh?"

"No. Sounds good." Not as good as an evening with Meryl and Bette and Barbra and Madonna, but I was trying like hell to lower my sights for once. I have to do that, I realize, if I'm to survive in this town at all. All things considered, an Open Mike Night in North Hollywood sounded preferable to, say, phone solicitations in Reseda or another idiotic infomercial where you can't see my face. I'd sunk lower than this, after all, and still managed to hold up my head about it.

Neil got out of bed, lit a cigarette, returned to stretch out and stare at the ceiling. "We need a classy look," he said, warming to his subject. "I'll get a tuxedo, maybe, with a bow tie the same color as your dress."

"That'd be nice."

"You can sit in one of those tall stools with a back. With a pin spot."

I told him I sounded better standing up.

"OK, then, we build a little box, like a pedestal. I can roll it out with me before you make your entrance. It would announce you, sort of—like a trademark."

"Can we put steps on it?"

"Sure."

"It's better if you don't have to lift me. People aren't as nervous."

"No kidding?" He acted as if he'd never thought of that before.

"Absolutely," I said.

"OK."

"The pedestal's nice, though. I like that."

"I thought you might."

I smiled, but warily. "Are you sure about this?"

"Completely. Never surer." He touched my cheek. "Can you spend the night?"

I told him I'd planned on it.

"Good."

"We can do this, Neil, but I don't want a Svengali."

"I know that."

"I'm my own Svengali."

"Hey," he said, "I'm just the piano player."

"We aren't gonna sing duets?"

"If you want," he said, laughing.

"Duets would be nice, I think."

"Then we'll do them. As many as you want."

I told him not to be so easy, that I'd take advantage of it.

"I'm just glad you're staying," he said.

He made a nice dinner for us—beef stew and garlic bread and salad—while the rain kept pounding away. I watched TV from the bed, comforted by the circling smells of the stew, the muffled clatter and clink of his movement in the kitchen. The tube, meanwhile, was full of the Thomas hearings, recap after recap of the weirdest day of testimony yet.

"I am *not* believing this!"

Neil arrived from the kitchen wearing a white butcher's apron and holding a soup spoon like a scepter. "What now?"

"He told her he has a dick like Long Dong Silver!"

"Who's that?"

"This porn dude."

"You've heard of him?"

"I've seen him. My friend Jeff showed me a photo once years ago in a magazine. He's got this long, skinny shlong that hangs down to his knees. It looks like a piece of garden hose or something—a really useless piece of garden hose. It was tied in a knot when I saw it."

Neil grinned. "You're shittin' me."

"No, sir. And if *we're* having this conversation, they must be having it at the networks."

Neil chuckled.

"They've got that photo as we speak, and they're racking their conscience, wondering if this is something America *really* needs to know. I say show it. Show the world exactly what a pig Clarence Thomas is."

"How can you be so sure she's not lying?"

"Why should she, Neil? Why should she sit there and say the words Long Dong Silver?"

"Because he jilted her."

"*Jilted* her?"

"Well, rebuffed her. She was obviously hot for him once."

"Oh, please." I threw up my hands.

"Plus he married a white woman."

"Oh, now, there's a good reason to get him."

"It is to some black women. It's the worst crime you can commit."

"Look at her," I said, gesturing toward that strong, cool, dignified face on the screen. "Does she look like a racist to you? She taught civil rights law, for God's sake!"

"At Oral Roberts University."

"Well …"

"That's not a credential *I'd* brag about. That's like … teaching ecology at Exxon."

I absorbed that for a moment, then gave him a grumpy look. "Go back to your stew."

We ate dinner on the bed. The media in all their tongue-lolling sleaziness made poor Anita Hill say the words Long Dong Silver no less than four hundred times in the course of the evening. You couldn't hit the clicker without landing squarely on that moment in time and the attendant shabby spectacle of all those middle-aged white men—Teddy Kennedy especially—trying their damnedest to keep a straight face.

After another hour or so, we tired of the spectacle and turned off the set. I felt lulled by the rain and my pleasantly full stomach. Seeing me begin to drift off, Neil doused the light and slid into bed next to me, pulling the covers over us. I snuggled against him and fell into a solid sleep.

I woke up alone to sunlight streaming through his matchstick shades. Hearing activity in the kitchen, I slid out of bed in the T-shirt I'd slept in, gave my hair a quick fluff, and went out to join him. He was tidying up with a vengeance: scraping plates over the disposal, sponging the countertop, bagging garbage.

"I hope you're not doing that for me."

"I must be brain dead," he said. "I completely forgot something."

"You've got another date, and she'll be here in five minutes."

His laughter was short and sour. "Linda's bringing Danny by."

"Oh."

"It's not his usual day, but she called a few days ago and asked. I just forgot about it."

"That's cool."

"I'm really sorry."

"You want me to call a cab or something?"

"No. Not at all."

"I don't mind."

He shrugged and gave me a sheepish look. "There's not much point. They get here in ten minutes."

In other words, we had to deal with it now, and that was that. No wonder Neil was panicked. I was suddenly annoyed that his negligence had turned this fairly significant confrontation into a rush job.

"Do you need anything?" he asked.

"No ... well, maybe a wet washcloth."

"You got it."

"Do you still have my green T-shirt? The one I left here last time?"

"Sure."

"I'll take that too, then."

He left me alone in the bedroom with my requirements. I shucked my grungy T-shirt and gave myself a quick sponge bath in front of the closet-door mirror. Then I put on the green shirt—which was freshly laundered, at least, and a fairly becoming color—slapped on lipstick and powder, and spritzed myself with Charlie. After a futile effort to repair my sleep-dented hair, I flung down the brush in exasperation. It was Linda I was doing this for, but don't ask me why.

I returned to the living room, where Neil was snatching scattered newspapers from the floor.

"Need a hand?" I asked.

"No. It's fine. You look nice."

I grunted.

"Sorry about this."

"What the hell."

"She won't stay. She's just dropping him off."

"You need some time alone with him. Let's just call a cab now and—"

"I'll drive you home, OK? In a little bit."

I shrugged.

"He's a nice kid. He doesn't bite."

"Maybe *I* do," I said.

He laughed and dropped the newspapers on the dining table—just as the doorbell rang.

I jumped a little in spite of myself. "Is she always on time?"

"Always," he replied, and headed for the door.

I smoothed out my T-shirt and waited from a distance to give him as much opportunity as possible for explanations and introductions. He swung open the door to reveal an informally garbed Linda—pink slacks, gingham blouse, sunglasses—and, hard by her right leg, the handsome, stormy-eyed seven-year-old who made these meetings compulsory. Danny was dressed in vinyl cowboy boots and Levi's, with a bright aqua corduroy shirt. While his mother greeted his father, the boy gazed across the room at yours truly, having sensed on some primal level, as I had, another living creature in the room at his eye level. I guessed him to be about a foot taller than I am.

"We aren't late, are we?" asked Linda.

"No, no," said Neil. "Just on time. Hi, Skeeter."

"Hi, Dad."

"Look who's here." Neil beamed. "We were just rehearsing."

"Oh, hi," said Linda. "How are you, Cady?"

"Great."

"Danny, this is Ms. Roth …" Linda began.

"… the lady I sing with," Neil finished.

The kid hadn't stopped staring at me, so I walked toward him, looking friendly, letting him see how this apparatus works. "Hi, Danny." I gazed up at Neil. "What's this Skeeter business, anyway?"

Neil smiled. "Just a dad name."

I stuck out my hand to the kid. "I like Danny better. Unless it's short for Danforth."

The kid shook my hand dutifully, if lamely, without meeting my eyes.

Linda laughed, getting my little joke. "Don't worry, it isn't."

"I had a feeling."

"Here's his eardrops." The ex–Mrs. Riccarton handed Neil a brown paper sack. "The directions are on it."

"Gotcha."

"You can reach me at Vonda's after six tonight."

"Fine."

"Nice to see you, Cady."

I told her it was nice to see her.

"Behave yourself, now."

For one creepy moment I thought she was talking to me, until I saw her patting her son on the head. Three mechanical pats, evenly spaced. It was the gesture Neil had once described to me, one of cold economy and bloodlessness, the gesture I've always imagined my father to have made the last time he laid eyes on me.

Linda left without ever setting foot in the apartment. I wondered if this was their usual practice or if she was conveying a message to Neil about my presence there. As soon as the door was shut, Danny made a beeline past me into the hallway, bound for his bedroom.

"Hey, Skeeter, slow it down!" Neil yelled after his son, with a look of jovial exasperation. I knew he was trying to keep it light on my account. "He has to check on all his shit," he said, "make sure it's still there."

I smiled at him.

"I'm sorry about this."

"Is it usually that quick?"

"What?"

"The changing of the guard."

"That was pretty good," he said. "She used to let him go on the sidewalk and wait till I waved from the window."

I took that in for a moment, then said: "He's cute."

He nodded.

"He's lucky to have a dad like you."

He shrugged. "I just do the regular stuff and hope it's right."

"Like I said, lucky. Lots of people don't get that. I certainly didn't." I smiled at him. "Must be why I go for big guys." I made myself blush with this little display of self-analysis, so I didn't give him time to respond. "I should go, Neil. This is too much for him at once."

Neil looked cowed. "He knows who you are, Cady."

"The lady who sings with you."

"That," he said, nodding, "and a friend."

"Whatever." I began looking for the portable phone, thinking I'd call the cab myself. Neil usually keeps the phone on the carpet while I'm around, but he'd returned it to its cradle on the bar in his feverish preparations for Linda's arrival. I was about to ask him to hand it to me, when Danny emerged from the hallway.

"Oh, hi," I said.

"Hey."

"Your dad tells me you play keyboard too."

"Yeah. A little."

"He says you're terrific."

He shrugged sullenly.

"Danny, look at people when they're talking to you." This was his father, beginning to crack under the pressure. "He's a great keyboardist. You wanna show Ms. Roth, Skeeter?"

"No."

"Why not?"

"I'm tired."

"Neil, I think it's best—"

"Tired? It's ten o'clock in the morning."

"Well, I don't wanna do it!" The kid spun on his heels and stomped off to his bedroom.

Neil gave me an apologetic look.

"I don't blame him," I said.

"No. He knows better than that. I have to deal with this. Hang on, OK?"

Neil left in pursuit of his son. I heaved a sigh for all of us and leaned against the end of the sofa, suddenly realizing I had to pee. Luckily, the bathroom door was open, so I slipped in and pulled it shut after me—as much as I could, at least—by gripping the side of the door.

Once inside and seated, I discovered that I was adjacent to the room where the father-son drama was unfolding. I heard only snatches of their dialogue, like that on a car radio when you pass through a long tunnel, but there was no mistaking the stern but reasonable drone of a modern parental reprimand. I made out the words "rude and unkind" and "not how I raised you" and "not her fault she's that way." And then from Danny: "I don't care" and "weird" and "grosses me out."

I peed and beat a retreat as fast as I could. My purse was in Neil's bedroom, so I went there and picked it up and returned to the living room. Neil came out a minute or so later, with his hand laid lightly on Danny's shoulder, as if the poor kid were a mini-mum-security prisoner being taken into custody.

"So," said Neil, much too cheerfully, "time to boogie, huh?"

"You bet."

"Looks like it's cleared up out there."

"Mmm. It does."

"Maybe we can stop for ice cream or something."

I told him Renee was expecting me back at the house.

"OK ... well ... whatever."

So we headed out—the three of us—father and son taking the lead and waiting for me at the van. Neil lifted me into the back seat with more chipper talk about the suddenness of that thunderstorm and how clean the air had become overnight. Then, on the way back to my house, he told his son what a fine singer I was and how I'd played Mr. Woods in the movie and how I'd dropped by his apartment that morning, eager for an early start, to begin rehearsing our new act.

Danny just sat there, saying nothing.

21

A DAY LATER, THANK GOD.

Neil called this morning, apologizing for Danny's behavior. "That wasn't like him at all," he said.

"That's OK."

"All I can think is that Linda may have told him something."

"About us, you mean?"

"Maybe."

"Have you told her about us?" I asked. I felt certain he hadn't told Danny—and probably never would tell him—but I still wasn't clear about how much he'd conveyed to his ex.

"She knows we're friends."

"That's not what I asked."

"Well … no. Not that."

"Then how could she tell Danny?"

"I dunno," he said. "She could've guessed."

"And that bothers you?"

"No."

"Bullshit, Neil. If you're worried about the kid finding out …"

"I'm not worried about anything. I'm just trying to explain why he acted that way."

"I thought he was fine," I said. "He did the best he could with what he'd been given."

Neil caught my meaning, I'm sure, but chose not to address it. He took the manly way out and changed the subject. "I called Arnie Green yesterday," he said.

"Oh, yeah? What about?"

"You know. Riccarton and Roth."

"Oh."

"He thinks he can book us, Cady. He thinks it's a great idea."

"Yeah, well, he thinks dancing poodles is a great idea."

Silence.

"Let's just forget it," I added. "OK?"

"Cady, look … if you wanna try another agency …"

"No. I just don't wanna do it."

"OK, then." His voice was as small as I've ever heard it.

"I've got some other ideas," I said. "I'd rather not blow them on somebody as small-time as Arnie Green." Since it was Arnie who'd brought me to Neil in the first place, I knew this would sting, but I didn't care. I wanted it to sting. I wanted him to feel at least a fraction of the pain I felt.

"Well," he said meekly, "if you need any help …"

"No. Thanks."

"You wanna do a movie this week? Or dinner somewhere?"

"Not really, no."

"Cady, if I said anything …"

"Just drop it, OK?"

"But I don't want you to …"

"Look, Neil, I haven't got the energy for forgiveness. I really don't. Work it out on your own. I've got better things to do."

I hung up on him—or rather pushed the little button on my cordless receiver—banishing him from my life with a single petty, melodramatic act. Almost instantly I burst into tears, crumpling into a lump on the floor. I cried until I couldn't cry anymore, until my eyes were an angry red mess. When it became perfectly clear he wasn't calling back, I pulled myself together and marched into the kitchen to boil some eggs.

When the phone finally did ring, just before noon, it was Jeff. It seems I unleashed the furies when I told Leonard about Callum and Jeff and their meeting in Griffith Park. Jeff said Callum had called him in a snit, because Leonard had called him, Callum, in an all-out rage, accusing him of "totally uncool behavior at an extremely ticklish time." The times are ticklish, apparently, because GLAAD has mounted an all-out media campaign against *Gut Reaction,* citing it as a prime example of homophobic filmmaking. Leonard told Callum that activists have threatened to disrupt a crucial scene to be shot on location next week.

As you might imagine, Leonard is beside himself. What if the tabloids—or, worse yet, some activist—had discovered the virile young star of said movie wagging wienie at the local meat rack? According to Jeff, who's enjoying the flap no end, Callum had to assure Leonard repeatedly that he had not frolicked in the bushes more than once or twice tops and had given it up completely after he'd met Jeff. Though Jeff didn't believe this, he claimed not to care, and for once I believed him.

Apparently Callum also accused Jeff of mobilizing the GLAAD protest, which Jeff denied both to Callum and to me. There were lots of loose scripts floating around, he said, lots of fed-up queers infiltrating the studios these days.

I asked him if GLAAD knew that Callum was gay.

"Of course."

"You told them?"

"Cadence." He sounded miffed. "I slept with the guy for months. I don't live in a vacuum, I have friends, I have a life. He's the one who's supposed to be invisible, not me."

"Does Callum know they know?"

"He didn't say, and I didn't ask."

"What did he say?"

"Just that you had blabbed to Leonard about Griffith Park and he'd appreciate it if I'd talk to you nicely and ask you to be more careful in the future."

"What did you say?"

"I told him to talk to you if he had a bone to pick."

"He won't do that."

"Why?"

"Because he has to be nice to me."

"Why?"

I explained about the tribute and how Philip and Callum and Leonard had jerked me around for days and how, ultimately, I'd aborted the return of Mr. Woods. When I was finished, Jeff responded with a dumbfounded silence, and then: "You really aren't gonna do it?"

"No."

"Are you sure that's wise?"

I released a long sigh. "Jesus, Jeff, if *you* don't get it, who will?"

"I know, but Bette Midler *and* Madonna."

"Jeff …"

"I understand the principles involved. I see what you mean, believe me …"

"But?"

"I don't know."

"Well, I do."

"What if they find somebody else to wear the suit? They're bound to try that."

"As short as me? I don't think so."

"You never can tell."

I told him I'd just have to live with it if they did.

"You're right," he said eventually. "Forget it. Fuck the bastards. This is exactly the way to go. It's the only way you can have any power at all over them."

"Thank you."

"Unless ..."

"Unless nothing."

"No, wait a minute ..."

"Jeff ..."

"What if you didn't wear the suit?"

"I just told you ..."

"No. I mean, what if you wore the suit, or agreed to, and went ahead with rehearsals and all that, and then took off the suit ... you know, just before you go on."

I met this with the stony silence I felt it deserved.

"They couldn't stop you then," Jeff added. "They'd look like monsters."

"OK, Einstein. And then what?"

"You sing. Or whatever."

"With no rehearsal, no prior communication with the orchestra, just grab a mike off a five-foot stand and start singing."

"Somebody could help with the mike. And forget the orchestra—sing a cappella. It'll show off your voice even more."

"Jeff, read my tiny lips: Philip Blenheim will be standing in front of me, waiting for his award."

"So you sing to Philip Blenheim. It's your tribute to him. The audience will be charmed, and he'll just have to stand there and smile and take it." Jeff laughed triumphantly. "This is so brilliant I can't believe it! This is exactly what you have to do, Cadence!"

What I felt at that moment was the strangest mixture of irritation and terror and total exhilaration, because I knew instantly that Jeff was right. It was time I started thinking less like a victim in this unholy war and more like a guerrilla. Why skulk off in anger from my best shot yet at the big time? What good would it do to make a point for the sake of honor if the public never even knows I've made it?

"God, Jeff ... do you think?"

"I *know.*"

"But they'll introduce me as Mr. Woods."

"And out strolls this stylish little woman, totally herself, totally sure of who she is. I'm telling you, Cadence, I'm getting shivers already."

So was I, for different reasons. Like, for instance, what if I couldn't get out of the suit in time? It's a bulky and confining lump of latex and wires, not some flimsy veil I can fling off like Salome at a moment's notice. And what if somebody takes note of this striptease and puts a stop to it before I can escape into the public eye? On the other hand, this was only a live performance in a hotel ballroom, not the rigid and overpopulated environment of a movie set; with a few well-placed diversions and the right accomplice, it might not be that hard to pull off.

Jeff must have heard my wheels turning over the phone. "I know you can see this," he said.

"Oh, yeah."

"Then … what?"

"I don't know. Just being a pussy, I guess."

He laughed. "What can go wrong?"

"A million things."

"Do you give a shit?"

"No."

"Well, then …"

"Will you help me with it?"

"Sure, but … what about Neil? He knows a lot more about show business."

"If I wanted him, I'd ask him," I said.

"Oh. Sorry."

"Will you help me?"

"What would I have to do?"

"Oh," I said, "stand around a lot and cope with rubber."

"I can handle that."

"I'll bet."

He laughed, then turned sober again, obviously beginning to feel the weight of his impending responsibility. "I just thought of something," he said. "What if they want you to walk on with

Callum? As Mr. Woods, I mean. He'll have to hang out with you backstage."

"That won't happen," I told him. "It's too much at once: the grown-up Jeremy and the first sight of Mr. Woods. The audience wouldn't be able to absorb it."

"I don't know," said Jeff. "They might think it was touching or something—the height difference."

"Yeah, but that's not how Blenheim thinks. He'll want the elf to come out on his own. My guess is that Callum'll come on first and introduce Mr. Woods."

"Make sure you get your own dressing room," he said.

"All right."

"That way we can keep you hidden until the last minute."

"Good idea."

"And don't let him give you any shit about that. You're the one holding the cards here."

I got an actual lump in my throat, imagining my little nook between Bette's and Barbra's. "I should get off and call him," I said.

"Who?"

"Leonard."

"No. Wait till he calls back. And agree to it very reluctantly. You can't be enthusiastic all of a sudden. He'll be suspicious."

"Oh, yeah."

"But don't be bitter about it, either, or they'll see you as dangerous."

"What a good criminal you make."

"Attitude is everything," he said.

"I have to go now. I want to think about this."

"I thought you'd decided."

"I have decided. I just have to let it soak in. Tell me something."

"What?"

"You aren't doing this just to embarrass Callum, are you?"

He hesitated for a moment, then said: "Why should this embarrass him?"

"Well ... it's not what they planned on."

"No, it's a hundred times better. Nobody's getting stiffed here, Cadence. This'll work to everyone's advantage, whether they know it or not. You watch. Even Blenheim will see how much more human and interesting this is."

"OK," I told him. "You're the one who's responsible when the poo-poo hits the Panasonic."

"When the *what?*"

I giggled. "Leonard used to say that."

"Wouldn't he just?"

"I was trying to be Hollywood for you."

"Well, stop it."

"I'm hanging up now."

"Call me when you've heard from him."

"Don't worry."

"This is my best idea ever," Jeff announced.

For the next two hours, I paced the backyard in a state of near delirium, while disaster and triumph fought for top billing in my mental movies. On the dark side was the notion that Leonard had already told Philip about my refusal and Philip had become so enraged that he'd checked *The Guinness Book* under "smallest" and was sparing no expense to acquire the twenty-nine-inch title holder from Yugoslavia. She'd be flown in like a live lobster just in time to save the day. Philip would be so grateful he'd break his vow of secrecy over the functioning of the elf and unleash a torrent of publicity for his new "pint-sized discovery." I could see the little bimbo already, sitting prettily atop her luggage at LAX, blowing kisses to reporters as she recounts her life story in charmingly broken English.

On the positive side, I saw amazing things in my future: a spread in *Premiere* magazine, a record contract, a custom-made role in Philip's new musical, and, above all, Leonard, wearing his best shit-eating grin, taking credit for my success as if he'd believed in it all along. Neil would be so proud of me we'd end up frolicking openly on his AstroTurf for the "Couples" section of *People*. I could conjure up almost anything in those queasy hours in limbo, because I knew for sure—perhaps for the first time in my life—that almost anything was possible.

When Leonard finally called, I adopted a weary, affable, slightly defeated tone as I agreed to crawl back into rubber one last time for the sake of friendship. He was so elated that he promised me my own dressing room the moment I requested it, a clear indicator that I should have asked for more. There will be a preliminary fitting next week at Icon, in case "adjustments" are required, which I took to be another reference to my weight. Mr. Woods will have only one line of dialogue (no prize for guessing which), which will emanate—prerecorded—from a tiny speaker in his head. He will make his entrance all alone, Leonard assured me.

22

Five days to go.

Maybe it was a mistake, but yesterday I told Renee about my coming-out party. It was just too hellish keeping the secret any longer, seeing as much of her as I do, and frankly, I needed a fashion consultant for the big night. When I explained the plan, she screamed even louder than she had when I told her I'd decided to wear the suit. What's more, she thinks it's a brilliant idea—absolutely foolproof—which some people might regard as reason enough to be worried.

This morning she took me to The Fabric Barn so we could select the material for my debutante gown. We settled on green bugle beads, very dark and shimmery, in a sort of half-assed nod to Mr. Woods. (Also, as you know, it's a color that looks great with my hair and eyes.) We bought Velcro too, so the gown can be breakaway, capable of being donned in seconds. I'll be in the rubber suit for an hour or more, so there's no way I could wear the gown underneath. And, as Renee keeps reminding me, my hair and makeup will need attention after confinement in that sweatbox. This will take a pro, she says, someone who can work fast—someone like her, for instance.

It's true that her pageant skills might come in handy for this, but I've got my doubts about her ability to stay cool in the midst of all those stars. She was ditzy enough around Callum. On the other hand, the more henchmen I have, the easier it'll be to pull off the switch. I'll just have to play it by ear, I guess.

Meanwhile, I've got a brilliant idea for the song I'll sing to Philip on stage: "After All These Years," from *The Rink*. It's Kander & Ebb—frisky and up-tempo enough—yet the lyrics have a definite edge of sarcasm, especially when applied to me and Philip:

> *Gee, it's good to see you*
> *After all these years*
> *Gee, you've really lifted my morale*
> *Kept it all together*
> *After all these years*
> *What's your secret, old pal?*
>
> *I can see that fortune has been kind to you*
> *Guess you've had no obstacles to climb*
> *Gee, you look terrific*
> *After all these years*
> *Completely unchanged by time!*

That line about "obstacles to climb" just might get a laugh, which would be all right with me. Anything to keep the audience loose. In any event, the message won't be lost on Philip.

Jeff drove me to Icon early this week for the fitting. Seeing that suit again was like viewing the embalmed remains of an old and bitter enemy. It was arrayed on a table in its own room—Lenin in his tomb came to mind—while technicians glued and snipped and soldered with offhanded, clinical calm, bringing the creature back to life. There was new, lighter-weight circuitry attached to his eye and facial muscles, which allowed more breathing space, but not enough to make a real difference. His insides, having been recently overhauled, were gaseous with epoxy, though one of the technicians assured me the smell would be gone by Saturday night.

For a terrible minute or two—just as I staggered, arms forward like a sleepwalker, into the breach again—I considered the possibility that the motherfucker might not fit. When I made it all the way in and they snapped me shut, my ass and waist were a little snug, but the rest felt fine. I was so relieved I made a nervous joke about my weight to the technician, who laughed and said not to worry, they'd already enlarged the suit, at Philip's request, in the event of just such an emergency. This was not what I needed to hear.

I'd halfway expected Philip to make an appearance that day, but he didn't. According to the technician, Philip keeps in close contact with the shop but has expressly asked not to see Mr. Woods before the tribute, to keep from diluting the impact of the experience. "Like the bride before the wedding," said the technician, chuckling, as if this were the very sort of quirky, unpredictable thing that makes Philip so darned lovable. I would have blown lunch then and there if the circumstances had been more amenable.

When Mr. Woods was on his feet again, testing his functions, word of his resurrection seemed to spread telepathically through the studio. Office temps and ADs and perky publicity minions begged admission, one by one, to the crowded hallway where the elf strutted his stuff. After a few seconds of experimentation, I could work his controls as if I'd never been away from them—like they always say about riding a bicycle. By squeezing the various bulbs in my hands, I could make him wrinkle his nose or roll his eyes or dimple up charmingly at the sound of their collective "Awww." I'd almost forgotten how this felt—to be there and yet not be there, to be the living heart of something but not the thing itself. "Isn't he cute?" they would coo, over and over again, and that blithely inaccurate pronoun hurt just as much as it ever did.

The main thing, of course, was that Jeff was there, watching everything, learning the ins and outs of the suit. When the time came, I knew he'd be able to assist my escape without too many nasty surprises. Just before I climbed into bondage again, he smiled at me slyly and winked, as if to say: "Don't worry. I'll have you out of there in no time."

As we left the studio, I asked him if the scheme seemed more daunting than he'd imagined.

"Not really."

"Still think it's the right thing to do?"

"Absolutely." He turned and looked at me. "You spoken to Callum lately?"

"Just briefly," I told him. "He called to say he was glad I was doing the tribute. Why?"

"Just wondered."

"I didn't tell him you'd be there, if that's what you mean."

"It doesn't matter."

I asked him what had happened with the GLAAD protest.

He shrugged. "We picketed."

"We?"

"I went. Big deal. I believe in it."

"Did Callum see you?"

"Yeah, I think so."

"Didn't that feel weird?" I asked.

And he said: "Not as weird as hiding in that kitchenette."

My resolve began to weaken on the short ride home, only to be bolstered again by a quick browse through *Variety*, where I learned that *Batman Returns* was using little people in penguin suits to augment a flock of regular penguins. Now, *there* was a job worthy of a serious actor's commitment. Meanwhile, plans were in the works elsewhere for a film called *Leprechaun,* a thriller about a little green serial killer who disrupts the peace of an average American household. So much for humanizing us. They might as well have called it *Fatal Enchantment*. This was all the reminder I needed that drastic measures were in order if I expected to turn my life around.

By the time Renee got home, I'd already made a good start on my sewing. She kicked off her shoes and sat next to me on the floor, then held up the gown to examine the beginnings of sleeves, letting the bugle beads catch the light. "This is so elegant," she exclaimed. "I'm glad we picked it."

I agreed.

"Neil will love it," she said.

"Neil won't see it," I said, "except on TV."

"He's not coming?"

"No."

"Why not?"

"Because I didn't tell him what I'm doing."

"Why not? He loves the way you sing. I betcha he'll think it's a neat idea."

"Yeah ... well, it was just too complicated."

She frowned at me. "Did something happen?"

"No."

"Something did, Cady. What?"

How is it, I wonder, that a woman who uses "betcha" and "neat" in the same sentence can be so adept sometimes at reading my distress? "His ex came by with his kid," I explained.

"Oh."

"The morning I was there."

Renee's fingers flew to her mouth. "You were in bed, you mean?"

"No. Nothing like that."

"Oh."

"It was just weird, that's all. Everyone was so proper and stilted and jolly. Like a really empty episode of *The Cosby Show.* I felt like such an outlaw. Like I didn't belong there at all."

Renee squinted at me in confusion. "Because you're white?"

"No. Because he was embarrassed. He tried hard not to be, but he was."

"Embarrassed?"

"Yes."

"Because you were white?"

"Forget white! Because I'm … me."

"I really don't think—"

"Well, you weren't there, were you?"

"But he took you to Catalina."

"So?"

"Wasn't his wife there then?"

"His ex-wife. Yeah. So?"

"Well, he wasn't embarrassed then."

"Because we weren't fucking yet."

She winced at my naughty word. "What does that have to do with it?"

"Everything," I told her. "Everything. It was fine for us to be friends; it just made him look like a nice guy. It is *not* fine for us to be fucking. People will think he's perverted. Especially his family members …"

"Oh, now …"

"I'm serious, Renee. Think about it. It's of *crucial* importance in this culture where dicks get put."

She blushed like a virgin. "Do you think she knows?"

"I'm not sure."

"Well, then …"

"It doesn't matter. The point is, he'll never cop to it."

"Well, maybe later."

"No. Never. And certainly not to that kid he spends half his life with. Daddy can't have this for a girlfriend."

Renee looked at the floor.

"I knew this was coming," I added gently. "I just didn't know when. This is the way it works, you know. Eventually. You can ignore it or not. I went for not."

Renee looked up at me balefully and started to get quivery-lipped.

"The thing is," I said, "it was stupid of me to think I could pull it off. I knew what the rules were."

"But he's such a nice guy."

"As nice as they get," I said.

She was holding the gown as if she might decide at any moment to use it as Kleenex, so I took it away from her. "If you're gonna blubber, go in the other room."

"Aren't you sad?" she asked.

"I can't afford to be," I said. "I have a show to do."

23

I've just had a weird thought. What if all the noise around my debut flushes out my father? He's out there somewhere, presumably, still in his fifties. What if he's flipping channels one night, or flipping through a magazine, and comes across this multi-talented dwarf with a distinctive name. Will fame be enough to make him seek me out after twenty-seven years? Will he show up here one day soon, filled with remorse, or at least with respect for the life I've made for myself? Will I forgive him if he does?

No, no, and no.

24

Three hours to go.

I should be napping, I guess, but I'm sitting on *shpilkes,* as Mom used to say about twice a day. I also want to get this down while I can, since there'll be lots more to tell you after tonight.

Jeff took me to the tech rehearsal this morning at the Beverly Hilton. Leonard was there for a while and made a big gushy show of hugging me. When I introduced him to Jeff, such a look passed between the two of them you could've hung laundry on it. Part of this has to do with *Gut Reaction* furor and part with the fact that each regards the other as Callum's corrupter—so Leonard obviously saw Jeff as an infiltrator of sorts, a loose cannon with a backstage pass. They were civil to each other, though, at least on the surface.

When I remarked on how skinny Leonard looked, he rattled on so long about his latest diet (a woman brings him Baggies of greens once a week) that I thought he must have thought that I thought he had AIDS. That would be just like Leonard, to think that. For all I know, he does have AIDS; he's not the sort of guy you'd hear it from first. He looked pretty good, at any rate—tanner than ever. His concern over Jeff's presence may have worked for me in some ways, since it allowed me to cast myself in a less dangerous light. I tried to project an air of coolheaded competence, one that said I was just there to do my job and go home, a solid no-nonsense professional.

The ballroom was bigger than I'd imagined. (One of the biggest, according to Leonard, which is why the Hilton does so many of these industry events.) The place was empty except for a few techies, a few stray producers. The stage was fairly small, since the all-star audience was obviously the whole show. To make for good television, the guests would be seated cabaret-style on tiers surrounding the stage—a great big drinkless party full of startlingly familiar faces. Some of the chairs were labeled with masking tape and Magic Marker, so Jeff sprang from tier to tier, reconnoitering on my behalf. When he returned, grinning like a bandit, he took a piece of tape off his arm and stuck it on mine. It said: MRS. FORTENSKY.

"Put that back!" I said.

"Why?"

"Because ..." I took off the tape and gave it back to him. "I want Mrs. Fortensky to have a good seat."

He laughed.

"Is there a 'Mr. Fortensky'?" I asked.

"Of course," he said, "and a 'Mr. Eber' next to them."

"Makes sense. It's a long evening. They could have hair failure."

He smiled.

"What else?"

"Callum's two seats away from 'Miss Foster.'"

"You're kidding."

"No."

"What else?" I asked.

He smiled. "No more. You'll overload."

"I fucking love this!"

"No shit," he said.

Later, the stage manager heard us laughing and came to introduce himself. He led us to a dressing room, where the elf already awaited, dormant in his coffin—a metal crate with a big lock, designed to safeguard all that costly machinery. I remembered it from the old days, with nothing like fondness. As promised, the dressing room was all mine, which had obviously been no big deal, since the other performers will arrive at the hotel in evening clothes and take the stage that way. In fact, as far as I can tell, I'm the only person who even requires a place to change.

The stage manager said the MC for the evening will be Fleet Parker. (The obvious choice, when you think about it, given the number of Blenheim films in which he's flashed those lovely silicone pecs.) I make my entrance at the very end, just after Callum, who'll plug his new movie and talk about what a great dad Philip was to him on the set. Then Fleet will come back and say a few more words, prompting Philip to leave the imperial box he's been occupying all evening and join the actor onstage. They talk a while—yodda, yodda, yodda—which leads to my cue. I toddle on adorably, hand Philip the award (which is hideous), issue my heart-warming prerecorded message, and toddle off again.

"It's fairly straightforward," the stage manager said, summing up. "Just a quick fix for the audience and off again, before it wears off. The element of surprise is what we're going for here."

"Gotcha."

"How long should she be suited?" asked Jeff.

"Before, you mean?"

"Yeah."

"Oh, an hour or so. They want you here at seven, but you won't have to put on the rig until about nine. There'll be somebody here to help with that."

"That's what I'm here for," said Jeff.

"No. I mean somebody to check the wiring, make sure everything's up."

"Oh."

"Will you be with her backstage?"

"Oh, yeah," said Jeff, trying to sound like a voice of authority.

The stage manager's brow creased ever so slightly, so I added: "I need somebody … you know …" I widened my eyes and left the sentence unfinished as if to suggest that the stage manager could easily imagine the sort of personal, unmentionable services a person like me might require.

"Right," he said, nodding, not really wanting to know.

Our first small storm cloud had passed, so I was gladder than ever I'd asked Jeff to remove his WE'RE HERE, WE'RE QUEER button before we entered the ballroom. The way I saw it, the fewer waves we made, the better.

The stage manager was called away about a lighting problem, which enabled us to case out the place on our own. There was a fairly short, straight route from the dressing room to the stage, so the gauntlet I'd have to run as myself wasn't as bad as it might have been. As for mikes, there were several on stands along the edge of the stage, so Jeff agreed to bolt out and leave one on the floor during the brief moment of darkness before my entrance. I should grab it on my way to Philip, Jeff said, and just start singing.

"What if it's dead?" I asked.

"I'll find you a live one."

I told him, if he didn't, *he'd* be dead.

"What about the award?"

"What about it?"

"Can you carry that *and* the microphone?"

"Fuck, no." This fairly crucial logistical point hadn't even occurred to me.

"OK … then leave the award."

I popped my eyes at him. "He has to get the award, Jeff."

"Why?"

"He just does. I'm not trying to ruin his evening."

"Then come back and get it. Or I'll bring it to you."

"That's not very graceful."

He shrugged. "A coup d'état never is."

"If you're trying to make me nervous," I told him, "you're doing a swell job."

He gave me a droopy-eyed smile. "Take the award out with you, then, and put it down when you pick up the mike. And take

your time about it—work it. You know what to do. A spot'll follow you the whole way, so make it into shtick. This isn't *anybody*
walking onto that stage, Cady. You will have their attention. And
you've got some good props to work with."

This made sense, I admit, even as it suggested new horrors.
"What if they turn off the spot?"

"When?"

"When they see that it's me."

"They won't do that."

"Why won't they?"

"Because Blenheim will be onstage, for one thing."

"And?"

"And … this could be some last-minute surprise he planned
himself. Isn't he kind of famous for that?"

"Kind of."

"So if he's up there reacting to you—smiling and everything—
they'll think everything's cool."

"What if he's not smiling?"

"He will be. He thinks he's liberal, remember?" Jeff seemed to
ponder something for a moment, then asked: "Are you just gonna
sing?"

"What do you mean, *just?*"

He chuckled. "I mean … are you gonna say anything to him?"

"I guess I'll have to."

"Like what?"

"Who knows?" I'd thought about this a lot, of course, but still
hadn't decided on anything.

"What's Mr. Woods' big line?" asked Jeff. "The thing the suit
says."

I told him to forget it.

"Why? That might be the logical thing. It would help to connect you with the character."

"Why do I have to be connected?"

"So they'll know why you're out there, Cadence. Besides, you
want credit for the role, don't you?"

"I guess so."

"Makes sense to me."

I told him he was right. Again. We left shortly after that, as soon as I'd checked out the stage from the top of the tiers. My heart did a few somersaults when I imagined the tiny fleck of flotsam I'd make in that sea of celebrity, but I was basically all right about it. Getting out of the suit was obviously the biggest hurdle; the rest would be like working a birthday party—only bigger.

Jeff dropped me off here at the house just after noon, arranging to pick me up again at six. He was bland about his goodbye—largely on my account, I think—but I could tell he was just as wired as I was. He honked a second farewell as he turned the corner out of sight, as if to assure me one more time that we were absolutely doing the right thing.

The house was a mess, since I've been anything but tidy lately in my preoccupation with the tribute. I fluffed a few pillows in the living room, threw out old newspapers, raked my dirty laundry into a single pile in the closet. They say this helps order the mind, but it didn't do shit for me. I decided to confront my demons head-on and rehearse my number one more time, using what I'd learned about the layout of the stage. Enlisting my vibrator, Big Ed, as a substitute microphone, I slinked my way across the backyard, singing at the top of my lungs, stopping when I reached the banana tree that was supposed to be Philip.

I got through the whole song without a hitch. At the end, where the sea roar of applause should have come, I heard only the un-Zenlike sound of two hands clapping. This startled me so that I dropped Big Ed in the grass, then looked up to see Mrs. Bob Stoate grinning at me over the fence.

"That's really pretty," she said.

"Thanks."

"I hope I didn't scare you."

"No."

"Is that a hobby or something?"

"No," I said evenly. "I do it professionally."

"Really? I never knew that. I mean, I know you do movies sometimes, but ... well, I never knew this."

She was so obviously impressed that I lost my head and told her I was singing tonight.

"Really? Where?"

"At the Beverly Hilton. With Bette Midler and Madonna and Meryl Streep."

She gave me a sickly little smile that made it clear she thought I was several sandwiches short of a picnic.

25

My coming-out party, cont.

Jeff returned when he said he would and drove me and Renee back to the hotel. He hadn't expected Renee, of course, so he eye-balled me in a prim, chastising way, but didn't say anything. I knew damn well he thought she was too drifty for the job ahead, but I really didn't care. I'd decided at the last minute that Renee's loyalty and cheery outlook would be good for my morale—the right instinct, clearly, considering what happened later.

When we arrived at the hotel, I stood up in the front seat of the Civic to check out the scene. The entrance was already cor-doned off against fans, and there were klieg lights slashing their way anemically through the pale winter twilight. I saw several early arrivals being disgorged from limos, but they were all gray, anony-mous producer types. Renee gasped histrionically at the sight of a sequin-sheathed blonde on the sidewalk she took to be Meryl Streep. When I broke the sad news to her—that it was actually Sally Kirkland—her face fell like a soufflé in a thunderstorm; she'd never heard of Sally Kirkland.

I could have stood there forever, I think, spying on my audience-to-be, if a cop hadn't flagged us on. Jeff pulled off the street and parked in a side lot the stage manager had told us about. We tumbled out of the car, identified ourselves to a security guard, and made our way through a space that felt more like a tradesmen's entrance than a stage door. Inside, there was such a mob scene around the dressing rooms that Renee and Jeff had to run interference for me—a human shield, front and rear. I looked for stars in that crush of humanity, with no success, though Renee assured me when we finally got inside that I'd spent "at least a whole minute" in communion with the legs of Lucie Arnaz.

There was champagne from Philip awaiting us—an expensive brand, according to Jeff—and several dozen yellow roses from Callum and Leonard. That's what the card said: "Callum and Leonard." In the handwriting of some florist.

I showed it to Jeff. "Are they a couple now?"

He laughed. "I don't think so."

"Why not?"

"Because Leonard and his lover would never break up their Stickley collection."

"He could still be doing it with Callum."

Jeff smiled ruefully. "I hope he likes preppie porn."

Renee was flashing like a caution signal at all this gay talk, so I gave her a reassuring wink. "What do you think of our headquarters?"

"It's nice," she said, then glanced at the elf's metal carrying case. "Is that ... uh...?"

I nodded.

"Gah."

"Is somebody coming to ... put it on you?"

"Eventually," I said.

Renee tried to smile bravely and look prepared, but she reminded me of someone standing on the edge of a bridge, waiting ever so demurely for her turn at bungee jumping.

★ ★ ★

We had lots of time to kill, so Renee and Jeff took turns venturing into the backstage hallways, even into the ballroom itself, returning with accounts of all the famous faces they'd spotted. Renee saw Meredith Baxter Birney, Tori Spelling, and "that guy who plays the retarded man on *L.A. Law.*" Jeff identified Jonathan Demme, Michael Douglas, and Jamie Lee Curtis. I stayed put, sipping champagne and collecting myself, while the chatter of the swelling audience droned in the distance like low-level industrial noise.

Eventually I was joined by two technicians from Icon, who removed the creature from his case and checked his circuitry. They made polite conversation as they worked, and one of them even asked me to autograph a program for his kids. Once they were satisfied with the functioning of my armor, they left, to return fifteen minutes later with one of Philip's underlings, an earnest young woman named Ruth, who said she was just checking to make sure I was comfortable. She loitered there so long that I had to introduce her to Renee and Jeff. I identified them as "friends who came along for moral support," secure in the basic truth of that description. She welcomed them like insiders, I was relieved to see, without a trace of suspicion. I felt that much closer to victory.

Traffic in the dressing room thinned dramatically as soon as the show started. In no time at all it was just the three of us, pricking our ears as Fleet Parker boomed out the names of the great, one by one, and a star-hungry spotlight roamed the risers.

The show was more of a high-class roast—and less of a concert—than I'd imagined (or Leonard had described). Most of it consisted of short, funny, and/or touching testimonials from Philip's famous friends and colleagues. Madonna *did* sing (Jeff saw her bolting out of one of the dressing rooms), but the music was prerecorded. There was no orchestra at all, in fact. All of this came as a relief, since it meant the evening would be more about star power than pure entertainment. My half-assed little entrance wouldn't be that much out of place, after all.

The technicians returned at the appointed hour and helped me into the suit. Renee and Jeff watched this procedure wordlessly, with such huge, haunted eyes that I might have been entering a space capsule. I think their growing awareness of the people in the other room had begun to lend an unexpected weight to the task ahead of us. I snapped them out of it—or rather Mr. Woods did—with an electronic wink and the cutest smile in his arsenal. Renee squealed with such conviction that even Mrs. Fortensky must have heard her.

"I can't believe this!" she said.

"Believe it," I said.

"You sound like you're under about a zillion mattresses."

I told her that's what it felt like too.

"Oh, gah, I'd get so ..."

Jeff found the word for her. "Claustrophobic."

"Excuse me there," said one of the technicians, needing access to the elf's beard.

Renee jumped back. "Oh, excuse me."

"Maybe we'd better give them some space," Jeff suggested.

"No," I said. "You're OK."

"You sure?" asked Renee.

"I think so," I said. "Aren't they, guys?"

"No sweat," said the younger and cuter of the technicians as he wove twigs into the beard.

"My friends have never seen the suit before," I explained.

"Oh, yeah?"

"Well, Jeff has—I think you guys have met—but this is Renee's first time."

I couldn't see Renee, of course, but I could feel her, blushing extravagantly. "I am the biggest fan of ... this," she said, indicating the shell that encased me. "I can't believe I could just reach out and touch it."

"Go ahead," I said.

"Really?"

"Touch away," said the technician.

Renee knelt and probed delicately at the pebbly flesh on the elf's elbow. "It's so amazing."

"Every one of those hairs was hand placed," the technician told her.

"You swear?"

"Every one of 'em."

"How amazing!"

"Isn't it?"

The technician knelt and joined Renee in her examination of the elf's features. They were so close together, Renee and this guy, that I could see both their faces at once through the gauze peephole in the beard. Their heads were tilted at wacky angles, like those shots you get when two people cram into a photo booth. The guy had that *look* too; there was no mistaking it. I wondered how long he'd been hot for Renee, and if Renee had noticed, and what this might mean to us now.

At first I was worried because I thought he'd never leave. Long after his partner had declared Mr. Woods in tip-top shape and retired somewhere for coffee, Cutie-pie remained, hopelessly smitten, chatting up Renee about every fucking wart and nodule on the elf's nobbly little body. It became chillingly apparent that Renee was loving all this and had no idea whatsoever she might be fatally complicating our plans.

Jeff knelt in front of me and gave me a long, loaded look through the gauze.

"I know," I said.

"What now?" he asked through motionless lips.

"Hang on." I toddled over to the side of the room where Renee and the technician were lost in each other. "I hate to be a spoilsport, guys, but I need a little time to myself."

"Oh, sorry." Renee looked mortified. "What time is it?"

"Time for me to meditate."

"Huh?"

"You know," I said pointedly. "My preshow meditation?"

"Oh, yeah."

"Maybe you guys could finish your conversation outside."

"Oh, no," said Renee. "I'll stay here."

By this, of course, she meant that she wanted to help with my transformation, blithely ignoring the fact that, somehow, we had to get the technician out of the room. I gave her the dirtiest look I could muster through the gauze.

Then, mercifully, the stage manager poked his head through the door and called: "Ten minutes, Mr. Woods."

"All set," I said.

"Uh oh," said the technician. "Better let you meditate."

"Thanks."

"No problem."

"It's just a way I ... get myself together."

"That's cool. Nice meeting you all."

"Nice meeting you," Renee said a little wistfully.

As soon as the technician was gone, Jeff knelt before my beard again. "What now?"

"Does that door lock?"

"I think so."

"Lock it."

Within seconds, I heard the reassuring sound of a bolt being slid into place.

Renee rushed to my peephole. "Cady, look, I'm really sorry if I ..."

"Forget it," I said. "Get your kit. We've got nine minutes."

"I've already got it."

"Where's Jeff?"

"Right here," he said, from somewhere behind me.

"Remember where the snaps are?"

"Sure."

"Go for it."

Within seconds, I felt the pressure of his fingers as they worked their way deftly down my back, peeling the rubber away like some horrid cocoon I was about to lose forever. I leaned forward to let the thing fall from me slowly, feeling the sweet coolness of the air against my already sticky T-shirt. In the process a piece of wiring snagged in my hair, but Jeff untangled it with brisk expertise. I was no sooner out of the suit than Renee was all over me with a towel, mopping up the sweat and sighing elaborately at the enormity of the reparation job that lay ahead for her.

"You OK?" asked Jeff.

"Fine," I said. "Turn around."

"I've seen you naked before."

"I know," I said. "Humor me."

Grumbling about my latent bourgeois streak, Jeff faced the wall while Renee shucked off my T-shirt, blotted me again, and enveloped me in a dust storm of baby powder. "Go easy on that stuff," I told her, screwing up my face.

"You don't want to shine," she said.

I told her I didn't want to suffocate, either.

She grabbed the green gown from her bag, stuffed my arms into it, fastened it up the back with Velcro.

I told Jeff he could look.

"Are you sure nobody's coming back?" he asked.

"Hell no," I said.

Renee had moved to my hair now, ratting furiously, activating her spray can in fits and starts like a renegade graffiti artist with the cops in hot pursuit. It was oddly impressive to see her like this, operating in her pageant mode, a study in grace under pressure. She knew this turf thoroughly, I realized, and it lent her an air of strength and dignity I had never seen before.

"Nice dress," said Jeff.

"Merci."

"Do you remember your song?"

"Yes, Mom, I remember my song."

He smiled at me.

Someone rapped on the door.

"Shit," I whispered. "Ask who it is."

"Who is it?" called Jeff.

"Is everything OK in there?" It was the stage manager.

"Just fine," said Jeff.

"Three minutes," said the stage manager.

"She's ready."

"Break a leg."

"Thanks," yelled Renee, answering for me. She knelt and held a hand mirror so I could fix my lips and check my existing eye makeup. The general effect was raucous up close, but it would read well on the risers, I decided.

"What if he's still outside?" Renee murmured, meaning the stage manager.

I shrugged.

"You're just gonna walk right by him?"

"You got it." I started for the door and stopped. "Shit!"

Jeff went pale on the spot, imagining the worst. "What?"

"The award."

"Oh." He retrieved the phallic monstrosity off a shelf and handed it to me. "Good idea."

"Well," I said, taking it, "here goes something."

"Piece o' cake," he said.

I stood at the door and waited for him to open it.

"Wait," said Renee, falling to her knees next to me. "There's just one teeny little …" She fussed for a moment with a heavily varnished curl at my temple. "There. You're perfect now."

Our eyes met in a moment of sisterly bonding. "Thanks," I said.

"You're welcome."

I took a good deep breath, and Jeff opened the door. For the moment, at least, the coast seemed clear, a straight shot to the wings without a watchdog in sight. I celebrated this small miracle with a cavalier wink to Renee and Jeff and set off in the direction of the music—Bette Midler at this point—clutching Philip's trophy in my hot little hands. Soon Fleet Parker would begin the longish speech that would end in my cue: "So here, to present the award, is someone as old as all the rest of us put together."

Within twenty feet of freedom, I saw the stage manager round a corner out of nowhere. "There you are. Holy shit! Where's the suit?"

"We're not doing that," I told him.

"What?"

"This is something new."

"I'll say."

"The producers know about it. They just called."

"Called where?"

"The dressing room."

"There's no phone in there."

"There is now."

"Since when?"

"We had one put in."

"What about Mr. Woods, then?"

"He's toast," I said, and continued walking.

When I reached the wings, I gazed out at the little stage, where Miss Midler was in her stately mode, wringing something heart-breaking and ethereal out of "I Remember You." I set the trophy down and caught my breath, fretting that the stage manager was contacting the director at that very moment to check on the truth of my story. I let Bette's ballad soothe me as much as it could, taking comfort in the darkness and the warming nearness of a mellow and responsive audience. This will work, I told myself, the worst is behind you.

Unless …

The microphone! Jeff was supposed to get it down for me!

Already computing the time it would take to get back to the dressing room and find Jeff, I spun on my heels and ran smack into … Jeff's legs.

"Jesus," I whispered.

"I'm here," he whispered back.

"I completely forgot."

"When does it go black?"

"After Bette finishes."

"Shit, that's her, isn't it?"

"That's her," I said.

"Which mike do you want?"

"The one in the middle."

"The one she's using?"

"Right." I gave him a faint, ironic smile as if to say I deserved it.

"It's yours," he said.

When I was little, Mom used to read to me from a novel called *Memoirs of a Midget,* by Walter de la Mare. It was written in the twenties, I think, though its flowery, slow-going style was strictly Victorian. The narrator, known only as Miss M, was an overwrought little prig whose chief object in life was to disappear completely from the public eye. Given all that, you'd think I'd have detested her, but I didn't. I related completely to the endless abuse she received at the hands of cruel bourgeois patrons and under the wheels of speeding carriages. She was such a deity around our house, such a defining force, that I actually thought she'd cut an album the first time I saw her nickname applied to Bette Midler.

I tell you this because it's what I was thinking as I stood there in the wings, waiting for my turn in the spotlight, just behind that *other* Miss M, feeling a curious, wet heaviness begin to spread in my chest. My first thought, silly as it seems, was that I was somehow in that suit again, enduring its weight and heat and confinement. My second thought was the right one, the one that has circled my consciousness, buzzardlike, ever since Mom bit the big one in the parking lot at Pack 'n Save. I put my hand against Jeff's leg to steady myself.

"What is it?" he asked.

I remember trying not to scare him, trying to say something flip about my fabulous timing as usual, but there wasn't breath for words, or the strength to form them. I was a block of hardening concrete—or a fly caught in the center of that block. The pain, however, was something polished and metallic, something completely new. Before Bette had finished her song, I was on my back and Jeff was on his knees next to me, blowing into my mouth and yelling into the blackness for Renee.

The last thing I remember was the sound of Velcro being torn.

26

OBVIOUSLY I'M NOT DEAD. I WROTE THAT LAST ENTRY YESTERDAY morning—my first morning here—in secret defiance of my doctor, who gave me strict orders to vegetate. According to my nearest neighbor, a grumpy old Greek in the next bed, they always say that to people in the cardiac unit, and almost never enforce it, so I'm having another shot at it, knowing they can't do shit to me if I get caught. I'm writing sheet by sheet on pink three-hole paper Renee found in the hospital gift shop. She didn't want to get it for me at first, putting up a big fight, until I reminded her sweetly that the movie of our lives will never be made if nobody knows how the fuck it turns out.

I've had a "mild heart attack." Nothing to be terribly concerned about, they say, unless I have another one in the next few days or so. Swell. I feel pretty good, except for a sort of shadowy ache in my chest—more like a lingering body memory, I think, than anything else. I was wheezing like a calliope when they brought me in, but I've since had regular hits of oxygen and seem to be pretty much back to normal.

In case you're interested, my untimely collapse never made so much as a ripple at the tribute. Before Fleet Parker had finished his speech, the stage manager delivered a note to him explaining my indisposition, and Fleet ended up presenting the award himself; the audience never even heard that line about "someone as old as all the rest of us put together." Since Philip sent a mammoth pot of hydrangeas to the hospital, along with an unusually sweet note, I harbored the hope that he might have told the press about me, but there was nothing in the paper this morning and zilch on *Entertainment Tonight* last night. The event itself was covered in scrupulous detail, right down to the gowns in the audience, but there was no mention of the minor medical crisis in the wings.

Jeff and Renee rode with me in the ambulance to the hospital, so we've since lost track of the world back there, knowing only what we learn from the media. I'm not even sure if Philip is aware of my heretical change of costume. I'm assuming the stage manager told him, or told someone who told Philip, so it's a little perplexing that he's being so sweet now. Taking a wild guess, I'd say he knows the score but is nervous I'll blab to the tabloids, thereby tarnishing his moment of glory (THE REAL MR. WOODS IN BIZARRE BACK-STAGE MISHAP). Which, come to think of it, wouldn't be the worst idea in the world. The *Star* pays big money, I hear.

There hasn't been a peep out of Callum. Jeff thinks Leonard may have advised him against contacting me, since he, Jeff, is here most of the time, and that could only mean trouble. Who knows? You'd think he would've called, at least—for the news-grabbing symbolism of the act if nothing else.

Renee and Jeff have been here from the beginning, though they spell each other occasionally, dashing off for hot showers and fast food. They're both plagued by varying degrees of guilt, each holding himself personally responsible for the heart attack, since, in their eyes, they abetted the activity that seems to have brought it on. I haven't wasted a lot of energy dispelling this tiresome notion, because there isn't energy to spare, but I told them to lighten up in no uncertain terms.

Renee and Jeff seem to have formed a sort of shaky unofficial partnership, based solely upon this turn of events. In less than three days I've seen them learn to catch each other's eyes and finish each other's sentences like an old married couple. They accommodate one another in ways I wouldn't have believed possible. Jeff doesn't yell anymore when Renee reads to herself from her little white Bible—even though her lips move just as much—and Renee no longer winces at Jeff's Keith Haring throbbing-dick T-shirts. We have a system, the three of us, now that one of us is in the hospital. Jeff and I had a system like that with Ned once, so there are curious echoes all the time, moments of shared déjà vu that pass without acknowledgment, between the two of us.

There are five cardiac patients in this room, each with his own curtained cubicle. I've met only the old Greek guy and a southern-sounding lady on the other side, who seems to think I'm an extremely precocious child, judging by the tone she uses with me. I haven't seen the others, since their curtains are always closed. I hear them, though—sometimes in the middle of the night—and the sounds are not encouraging.

No, I have not called Neil.

Renee and Jeff have both been pushing for that, but I've resisted so far, since I never told Neil about the plan and he would probably think I'm looking for validation after the fact. I have no strength for explanations at the moment. There's also the chance he might try to convince me that what happened at his house that morning wasn't a true measure of his feelings. Or, worse yet, the chance that he might not. I'm sorry, but I can't open that can of wienies right now—not for a while.

I don't blame him for anything, really. The mere fact of my sexuality is tough enough for most people to handle, so there's no reason to think that Neil would be any different, especially when it comes to defending his own role in that uncomfortable reality. Because of who he is and what I'm not, he's made deviate by a culture that claims to regard sex as the union of kindred souls but doesn't really believe that—and never will.

Renee is in a chair by the bed, standing guard while I write. She is reading a back issue of *Highlights for Children* she found in the waiting room. She looks quite lovely today, wondrously soft and peachy, even without her makeup. There's a becoming new light in her eyes I can only attribute to a certain Mike Gunderson, that Icon technician we evicted from the dressing room the night of the tribute. Mike, I've learned, helped Jeff fend off the curious after I dropped, staying close by Renee's side and calmly reassuring her until the ambulance arrived. Renee has remarked more than once about how sweet and kind and absolutely adorable he was, so it doesn't take a genius to see what's happened.

A little while ago I told her she should call Mike at Icon and thank him for his trouble.

"Why?" she asked warily.

"For me," I said.

Her eyes narrowed. "Why don't you call him, then?"

"Because I'm not the one who wants to fuck him."

"Caaady …"

"What's the big deal? If you like him, why don't you say so?"

"Because it's tacky."

"Oh, and those blind dates of yours aren't."

She pouted into her magazine for a moment, then looked up again. "You aren't writing that, are you?"

"Writing what?"

"About me and Mike."

"What's to write? Anyway, it's none of your business."

She looked down again.

"I can tell he likes you," I said. "I could tell it that night. If you let him get away, it's your own fault."

"Same to you," she said.

27

Speak of the devil. Jeff just returned with one of the trashier tabloids, fresh from the checkout counter at Ralph's, the front cover of which is dominated by a stock shot of Jeremy and Mr. Woods and the headline: MR. WOODS KID TARGET OF UGLY GAY SMEAR. Inside, next to a recent picture of Callum, is the news that "fanatical gay activists" have been circulating "vicious rumors" about the homosexuality of the former child star, but that "megabucks superagent Leonard Lord" had "categorically denied" the truth of those rumors. "Callum Duff is all man," Leonard was quoted as saying.

Jeff saw me grin when I got to that part. "Can you fucking believe that?"

"He's too smart to say that," I said.

"I'm sure he didn't."

I asked him if he thought Leonard had called the tabloid or vice versa.

"I don't think they even talked to each other. This was just the safest way to break the story—as an indignant denial. It lets 'em reaffirm the awfulness of being queer and dish the dirt at the same time. And Leonard can't do shit about it."

"Why not?"

"What's he gonna do? Deny that he denied it?"

I asked him what he thought would happen now.

"Oh … the so-called *responsible* press will feel sorry for Callum and run lots of items about the special girl in his life, whoever the lucky dyke starlet happens to be, and it'll all be fine, because there are no queers in Hollywood." He collapsed into the chair with a sigh and peered into the paper sack he'd brought with him. "Can you be arrested for smuggling jelly doughnuts into a cardiac ward?"

I must admit, I hadn't thought he'd actually bring them. "Be still, my heart."

"Yeah, exactly," he said.

"How many?"

"One," he said, handing it to me. "And take it slow."

I nibbled away at what I thought to be a reasonable rate. "What else is in there?"

"Well … Big Ed, for one."

I laughed. "You're lying."

He smiled at me. "No."

"You nasty thing. What else?"

"Just some magazines. How's the diary going?"

"OK." Since this seemed as good a time as any, I added: "I need to ask a favor, Jeff."

"What?"

"Would you deliver it for me? To Philip Blenheim?"

"The diary?"

"Yeah."

"When?"

"When I'm finished," I told him pointedly.

Jeff blinked at me for a moment, absorbing the implications of that. "OK," he said finally.

"You'll have to transcribe it first. I don't want him having the only copy."

He nodded.

"And don't edit."

"Yes, Your Majesty."
I smiled at him, and he smiled back.
"Is that it?" he asked.
"That's it."
"You aren't planning to … finish it anytime soon, are you?"
I told him I didn't know.

28

I've become Exhibit A around here. There are more and more doctors all the time, a Great Wall of clipboards surrounding the bed. Whether this was provoked by my present condition or my lifelong one, I couldn't begin to tell you. They smile a lot and take notes and leave, often returning with eager reinforcements in a matter of minutes. Everyone has remarked on this, even Mrs. Haywood, the tight-lipped southern lady in the next cubicle, who can barely contain her resentment over all the attention I've received. I've been gracious about this so far, but I'm on the verge of telling her to fuck herself.

Renee arrived this morning with Mike Gunderson in tow. She finally worked up the nerve to call him, and they had their first quasi date last night—dinner in the hospital cafeteria. She was so pleased with herself. She looked the way a cat looks when it drops an impressive corpse on its owner's doorstep. Which is not to say our Mike is even slightly inert. He exudes a vigorous midwestern earnestness that Renee interprets as "a great personality." I'm keeping my fingers crossed.

Last night, while Renee and Mike were at dinner, Jeff came by and dropped a small bomb on me.

"Don't get mad," he began.

"What is it?"

"I know what you told me, but ..."

"*What*, Jeff?"

"Neil is outside."

"Oh, fuck."

"He left a note on the door. I had to tell him."

"Left it where? Here?"

"At the house."

"What did it say?"

"He just wondered where you were. He's a great guy, Cadence."

"You've talked to him?"

"Some. Yeah."

Don't ask me why, but I immediately got paranoid. The very thought of those two guys getting together to discuss me was supremely unnerving. I had no choice but to bully Jeff with sarcasm. "Have you two been bonding or something?"

"Cadence ..."

"You have, haven't you? That's cute."

"Piss off."

"You've been reading to each other from *Iron John*."

"Do you want your purse?"

He held it in front of me without waiting for an answer, so I took it from him and began fixing my face.

"You know," he said, sulking, "that shows how little you know about me."

"How's that?"

"*Iron John* is the last thing I'd read. Fags don't need that Hairy Man shit. We've always been tribal."

"Who cares? How do I look?"

"Even."

"*Even?*"

"The lipstick is on the lips, Cadence. What do you want me to say?"

I stuck out my tongue at him.

"I'll send him in," he said.

Neil was in his nice gabardine slacks, looking ominously well shaven and dressed. "Hi."

"Hi."

"You look good," he said.

"Better than you expected?"

He shrugged, smiling.

"You heard about … the caper?"

He nodded.

"Pretty nuts, huh?"

Another nod, another smile.

"That's why I didn't tell you," I said.

"I figured."

"You're such a pussy."

"I know."

"Well, stop it, then," I said. "It's not healthy to be that scared."

Unfinished business hung in the air like ozone after a thunderstorm.

"I plan to tell them about us," he said.

"Forget it."

"No. I want to."

"It doesn't matter."

"It does to me."

"Why?"

"I don't know … but it does." He sat on the edge of the bed and looked around. "I should've brought you flowers. These are nice."

"I've got flowers out the ass," I told him. "Or somebody does. I left a bunch back at my dressing room."

"I'll bet you did." He reached over tentatively and stroked the side of my face. "I brought you something else, though."

"What?"

"Is this a good time?"

"Well, no," I said, "now that you mention it, but a week from Thursday might work out."

"I just wondered about disturbing your roommates."

"What is it, for God's sake?"

He smiled and stood up. "I'll get it."

He left the room and returned sheepishly a moment later with a bulky wooden four-wheeled object that had to be turned on its side before it would fit through the door. I didn't realize what it was until he rolled it across the floor and I saw two sturdy little steps jutting out from one side.

"My stage," I said.

"Or pedestal ... whichever you prefer."

"My stage-pedestal."

"See ..." He knelt next to the thing and fiddled with something at the bottom. "I put a little brake down here that stabilizes it once it's in place...."

"So I don't slalom into the audience during the big finale."

He laughed. "Exactly."

"Good thinking."

Curiosity, I noticed, had gotten the best of Mrs. Haywood, who was leaning so far out of her bed she looked as if she'd hit the floor any second. "It's a pedestal," I yelled.

"For what?" she called back.

"For me."

"Oh."

"She hates me," I told Neil under my breath. "She was the star here until I arrived."

29

Neil stayed as long as they'd let him, then took my pedestal home with him, since the nurses kept tripping over it. I dreamed about it last night, though, dreamed that it was still here, next to the bed, keeping me company while I slept. I woke to the sound of it—or dreamed that I woke—just before dawn, recognizing the whir of those tiny wheels across the linoleum. I opened an eye and waited, perfectly still. The dark plywood mass was next to me, moving slowly toward the foot of the bed like a giant tortoise. Nobody was visible from here, so whoever—or whatever—propelled it was most certainly under the bed.

I sat up. The pedestal stopped in its tracks, playing dead. I almost giggled, since it reminded me of one of those movies where an intruder poses as a statue to keep from being seen. *Nobody here but us pedestals.* I cocked my head and listened, hearing only a distant, tinny siren and a blubbery snore from another bed, probably Mrs. Haywood's. It was still dark in the room, but the big windows had begun to turn a pale and pearly blue. I lay still for a while, mimicking sleep, and soon enough the pedestal began to move again. After a moment or two, some part of it (those steps, I presume) struck the leg of the bed with a rude bonk, provoking its hijacker to emit a small, exasperated groan.

I knew who it was before he came out. I caught a whiff of wet loam and wood smoke and stale sweat, with something sharply herbal at the core. It was odd to recognize him from the smell alone, because I'd never used that sense on him before. Like everyone else who claims to know him well, I've always been limited to what I could see and hear. The smell was right for him, I realized, and it somehow put me at ease. I stayed calm even when he abandoned his efforts at stealth and climbed onto the pedestal to grin at me.

"What do you think you're doing?" I asked in a stern whisper.

He pointed to the pedestal, then to the door.

"No way," I said. "It stays."

He shook his head.

"I'm calling the nurse."

This only made him cackle ecstatically. I gazed around to see if he'd woken any of the other patients, but the place was quiet. He climbed down from the pedestal, using those funny little steps of Neil's, then sprang up onto the bed with enviable agility. I pulled the covers up under my chin and tried to stare him down, getting an eyeful in the process.

He seemed several centuries older in real life. What made him so authentic was not so much those familiar Earth-blue eyes as the specks of crud encrusted in their corners. I could see liver spots at this distance, and the genuine crepiness of the skin on his neck. When he smiled, I saw a broken tooth, yellow as antique scrimshaw; when he turned his head for a moment, I glimpsed a blackhead in the folds of his pointy ear. Every new imperfection just made him more like the real thing.

I remember thinking: *This is incredible. What will Philip come up with next?*

He just sat there for a moment, legs crossed, hands folded in his lap, letting me take him in.

"You're early," I said.

He widened his eyes and shrugged, then dug into the pocket of his tattered tweed trousers and produced a tarnished gold watch—obviously broken—which he consulted with grave ceremony, tapping its face and nodding, as if it explained everything.

THE DIRECTOR'S LETTER

Dear Di,

Gee, it was terrific to see you at the tribute last week. You and Roger both looked great, and it was good to hear the new screenplay is coming along so well. Tell Marty he's a fool if he doesn't shoot the third act as written.

The enclosed notebooks are sent to you in strictest confidence for reasons you'll understand as soon as you read them. They're the diaries of Cady Roth, the dwarf we hired for the additional movement sequences in Mr. Woods. Remember? They were delivered to me, at her instruction, by one Jeff Kassabian, who turned up here several days ago in a T-shirt that depicted Clark Kent and Dick Tracy kissing each other. (All will be explained in the manuscript.) Cady's very ill—in a coma at a hospital in the Valley—if she hasn't already passed away.

Bear with me. I'm sending you this because I value your opinion more than any other and because your own brilliant mythology looms large in the story that (I hope) you're about to read. I could be way off the deep end here, but I think this material could be the basis for an important film. That may surprise you when you read it, since I'm cast as kind of a heavy, but I'm sure you'll understand my excitement over the chance to reflect ironically on the ramifications of my own work—of our work. This could be a "small film" that would stand as a wise and elegant companion piece to a mainstream classic without detracting from it in any way. No director in my memory has ever done this, so I'd like to be the first to try. Of course, certain elements of the story would have to be altered for legal and dramatic purposes, but the central idea is extremely appealing to me. See what you think, anyway. Look at this as raw material and go from there. You're obviously the only one to write the movie.

Lucy would want me to send you her love.

Philip

THE SCREENWRITER'S REPLY

Dear Philip,

  I actually woke this morning thinking about those diaries, so I guess it's time I told you I think you're onto something big. The idea of this tiny, ambitious, infuriating, lovable woman who is both enslaved and ennobled by an icon of popular culture is one that seems completely fresh to me. At the same time, it's old-fashioned and highly moral in the best sort of Dickensian way. There is, as well, a liberal feminist subtext that suits me to a T, as you no doubt recognized when you sent it to me.

  I presume you'll want to fictionalize the story, so we're dealing more in terms of a modern parable than a docudrama. This would give us the freedom to play and explore our themes more fully without the attendant legal hassles. (It's fascinating to consider what Mr. Woods might become in this new version. An interplanetary creature? A troll who lives under a bridge?) In any event, the fact that you're holding a mirror to your own life's work, much as Fellini did in 8½, won't be lost on anyone in the critical establishment.

  The trick will be to keep our heroine fully human, to position the audience at her level, on her side through it all, without resorting heavily to low-level camera angles. (Not that you would, my love.) I hardly need tell you that such an off-the-wall character, particularly a central one, has to be set amid familiar and reassuring points of reference, so that the audience will accept her into their hearts with the same matter-of-factness with which Jeremy accepted Mr. Woods. To this end, here are a few thoughts:

  How wed are we to Cady's romantic life? The sex scenes made me extremely uncomfortable, and I can assure you I won't be the only woman who'll feel that way, however priggish that makes me sound. It seems to me the real relationship in the diaries is between Cady and Renee, two women held hostage by their own bodies for entirely different reasons. That's where the crux of the drama lies, that's what we should build on. If I were God here, the central romantic relationship would be between Renee and Neil. I felt there was potential for that all along, and I would find it far more intriguing (and moving, ultimately) if Cady were acting as a sort of witty mediator between the full-sized lovers. We don't want to know who she fucks. We really don't.

The interracial component is interesting but risky, only because it could make the film issue-heavy and dissipate its ultimate effectiveness. There's a fine line, I believe, between breaking ground and digging a pit. We have enough obstacles as it is. Besides, if Renee is to be our love interest, I doubt seriously she'd end up with a black boyfriend; it just doesn't fit the character, airhead Valley Girl that she is. We already know that she sees herself as Melanie Griffith, so why not go with that and find her a Don Johnson? Or a Richard Gere? Or a Jeff Bridges? He could still be Cady's accompanist, and we'd avoid the potentially offensive stereotype of the black piano player. Or maybe the boyfriend could be that technician. What do you think?

As to Callum's private life (the reason I'm not faxing this), it's obvious we have to abandon that strand completely. I can hear the lawyers right now, and that business in the park just lends a sordid air to a story that's fundamentally innocent. I'm sure you feel the same, given your affection for Callum. There's hardly room for it, anyway, if we intend to beef up the relationship between Cady and Renee. We could still see her in one scene with a gay friend (perhaps one a little less strident) as a way of adding color and showing Cady's tolerance. I think that would be nice, as long as it doesn't overwhelm us. Balance is everything.

Incidentally, I don't agree at all that you come off as a heavy. In my reading of it you're just the natural scapegoat of Cady's self-delusion, her need to believe at all costs. Maybe she was really as talented as she thinks she was—I can't begin to tell from the diaries—but I doubt it seriously. What that fact will offer to the right actress in terms of tragic nuance is thrilling to think about.

Casting will be a challenge, to put it mildly, though it will certainly offer a rich publicity angle. Our actress will obviously have to be taller than Cady, unless we decide to make her Yugoslavian. (Small joke.) Taller would be fine, really, maybe even easier to sell in the long run. Also, I know I'm jumping the gun, but I'd think seriously about using a midget instead of a dwarf, someone perfectly proportioned but small, which is less off-putting, I think.

This is all off the top of my head, of course. I wanted to get things rolling as soon as possible. I can't remember when I've been so excited about a project.

Love,

Di

P.S. How does Maybe the Moon *sound as a title? I found it in the diaries and I think it strikes just the right note of striving for the impossible.*

P.P.S. The enclosed clipping is from today's Variety—*in case you missed it.*

Cadence Roth

Cadence Roth, the 31-inch actress who played the title role in the Philip Blenheim film "Mr. Woods," died Tuesday at age 30.

Roth died at Medical Center of North Hollywood of respiratory problems and heart failure, said a longtime friend.

Roth was discovered by Blenheim at the Farmers Market in Los Angeles and hired on the spot to play the elf in the now-classic film.

Although the director had urged silence about whether the special effects of Mr. Woods were inhabited, Roth publicly stated that she had played the character in scenes that required movement, while a mechanical Mr. Woods was used in close-ups.

There are no survivors.

Services are scheduled for tomorrow at Forest Lawn Memorial Park in North Hollywood.